W9-AKD-344

ANCIENT FORCES
collection

FORBIDDEN DOORS

ANCIENT FORCES
collection

The Ancients

The Wiccan

The Cards

The Ancients written by JAMES RIORDAN

*The Wiccan and The Cards
written by* BOB DEMOSS

*Based on the Forbidden Doors series
created by* BILL MYERS

ZONDERVAN.com/
AUTHORTRACKER
follow your favorite authors

ZONDERVAN®

Ancient Forces Collection
Copyright © 2008 by Bill Myers

The Ancients
Copyright © 1998 by Bill Myers

The Wiccan
Copyright © 2003 by Bill Myers

The Cards
Copyright © 2003 by Bill Myers

Requests for information should be addressed to:

Zondervan, Grand Rapids, Michigan 49530

ISBN 978-0-310-71537-5

Interior design by Christine Orejuela-Winkelman

Printed in the United States of America

08 09 10 11 12 13 • 22 21 20 19 18 17 16 15 14 13 12 11 10 9 8 7 6 5 4 3 2 1

The Ancients

The Spirit clearly says that in later times some will abandon the faith and follow deceiving spirits and things taught by demons.

1 Timothy 4:1

1

The eagle soared through the clear blue sky. Sleek and beautiful, it rose higher and higher. Suddenly it dipped and dived, screaming through the air like a jet fighter.

Rebecca Williams watched in delight as the wonderful creature swooped low toward the ground. Then, at the last second, it pulled up and sailed high into the sky in a graceful arc.

And what a sky. Becka's delight changed to wonder as she saw that the sky had taken on a dark, purplish hue. But what really mesmerized her was the weird geometric pattern covering the sky: lines, triangles, and squares swirled in a concentric pattern that made them impossible to distinguish from one another. And yet the pattern was strong and focused, making an instant imprint on her mind.

The eagle's harsh cry rang out across the horizon, distracting Becka from the pattern in the sky.

"Becka! Be careful!"

She turned to see Ryan Riordan shouting and running toward her. She looked back at the eagle. Now it was diving toward her. She threw her hands in front of her face and darted to the left. But the eagle did not follow. It swooshed past her, heading directly for Ryan.

She turned and saw Ryan's mouth open. He lifted his hand to protect his face. He began to scream, but it was too late. The sharp, leathery talons slashed at his neck and—

"Noooo!" Becka woke up with a start. Sweat dampened her face, and her breath came in gasps.

Before she could get her bearings she heard, "Will you stop all that whimpering?"

She spun around to see Scott, her younger brother. She was about to yell at him for being in her room when she realized that she wasn't in her room at all. In fact, she wasn't even in her house. She had been napping on a plane.

A plane heading for New Mexico.

"Honey, are you all right?" Mom looked at her from the seat next to Scott's, her face showing concern.

"I'm okay," Becka said, wiping the perspiration from her forehead. "I just had ... It was only a dream."

"Must have been pretty weird," Scott said. "You were making all kinds of noise."

"It was an eagle," Becka explained. "A huge one. It flew right at me and then wound up attacking Ryan."

Scott held her gaze a moment. There was no missing the trace of concern in his eyes. This had happened before. Her dreams. Usually they had something to do with an upcoming adventure. Finally, he shrugged. "You're just worried about the trip."

She could tell he was trying to reassure her. "Yeah. It's just ..."

He glanced back at her. "Just what?"

"This whole assignment." She hesitated, then continued, "Doesn't it seem a little stranger than the others?"

Scott gave a half smirk. "Stranger than fighting voodoo in Louisiana?"

Becka said nothing.

"Or tracking down make-believe vampires in Transylvania? Or facing down demons in Los Angeles?"

Becka took a deep breath. Okay, so he had a point. Life had become pretty incredible. Still . . .

"What are you guys talking about?" It was Ryan, Becka's sort-of boyfriend. He had turned around from the seat ahead of them and was grinning.

Becka felt a wave of relief. She knew she'd been dreaming, but it was still good to see him and know he was all right. Come to think of it, it was always good to see Ryan Riordan. If not because of their special friendship, then because of the gentle warmth she always felt inside when they were together.

"We were talking about this trip," Scott said. "Becka's afraid this one is stranger than the others."

Ryan's smile faded. "What makes you say that?"

"I don't know." She shrugged. "Just a feeling, I guess."

"At least we get to stay in a fancy hotel again," Scott said. "What's it called? The Western Ground on the Cliff?" He leaned back, folding his hands behind his head. "Sounds pretty hoity-toity to me. Like one of those expensive, something-on-the-something hotels in Beverly Hills."

"I'm just glad to be going this time," Ryan said. "I went crazy when you guys were in L.A."

Becka was glad he was with them too.

"Well, Becka's right about one thing," Scott admitted. "Something's definitely up. Z never sends us out on boring assignments, that's for sure."

Becka and Ryan both nodded in agreement. Z was their friend from the Internet. He'd sent them to help people all over the world. And yet, to this day, Scott and Becka had no idea who Z really was. Not that they hadn't tried to find out . . . but somehow, someway, their attempts had always met with failure. Z's identity remained a mystery.

"Actually," Ryan said with a grin, "I'm pretty excited to be visiting an Indian tribe. I mean, I've always liked reading about Native American culture. I think they're a noble people who got a raw deal."

Rebecca nodded. "Taking their land was a wrong that we'll never fully repay. Kinda like slavery. And you're right about their culture. They've got a real respect for nature."

"I suppose," Scott said. "But aren't some tribes really involved in weird spiritual stuff? You know, like shamanism and séances and visions?"

Ryan nodded slowly. "But some of that is in the Bible."

"So?" Scott asked.

"So they must have some truth to them."

"There's some truth in everything," Scott countered. "That's the devil's favorite trick ... a little truth, a lotta lie."

Before Ryan could answer, Becka called out, "Wow! Look down at that canyon!"

Mom and Scott crowded in close to her so they could see out the window. There below them lay a beautiful canyon, its cliff walls shimmering red, yellow, and purple in the sunset.

The captain's voice sounded over the loudspeaker. "Well, folks, we're beginning our descent into Albuquerque. Please fasten your seat belts. We should be on the ground in just a few minutes."

👁 👁

On the ground far below the plane, an Indian brave ran through the desert. Above him, the huge canyon walls towered and rose toward the sky. Beside him, a river flowed, its power thundering and cutting into the rock and sandstone.

Swift Arrow ran because he wanted to crest the hill at the far end of the canyon in time to see the sunset. As he neared the top, he could see the bright yellow sun dipping behind the mountain ahead. When he arrived, he raised his hands to the sky and called, "Father, you are the master creator. I praise you for the beauty you have made."

Far in the distance, a rumble caught his attention. He turned and looked behind him. Dark clouds were beginning to gather. A storm was brewing. Suddenly a great lightning bolt cut through the sky and then another and another. Jagged lines seemed to fill the sky, forming triangles and squares, all arranged in a swirling, concentric pattern ...

Swift Arrow stared as the light from the bolts faded, his heart beginning to pound in fear. He'd seen that sign in the sky before. He lowered his head and began to pray. "Lord, deliver my people from their bondage. Free them from the snares of a thousand years. Help them to see beyond the old legends, the old fears, the ancient beliefs. Help them see your truth."

Another burst of light startled him, and he raised his head just in time to see the remainder of its jagged tail slice through the sky.

Swift Arrow grimaced as a mixture of fear and concern swept over him.

Becka lurched forward in her seat as the Jeep roared across the bumpy desert road. It had been nearly three hours since they'd boarded the vehicle at the Albuquerque airport. And judging by the bruises she was accumulating and the perpetual look of discomfort on Mom's face in the front seat, it was about two hours and fifty-nine minutes too long.

Of course, Scott and Ryan enjoyed every bone-jarring bounce and buck. They were busy having a great time. Red rock formations rose all around, high into the bright blue sky. To the left of the vehicle, three colossal boulders, each about three stories high, balanced on top of each other. To their right, a five-hundred-foot butte jutted upward, its smooth, flat top a stark contrast to its jagged sides. In the distance rose a vast range of peaks. Their driver pointed to those peaks, saying, "The village is in the middle of that mountain range. I can drive you most of the way up, but you'll have to go the last few miles on foot. No one can reach Starved Rock by car or truck."

"You want us to climb those peaks?" Scott asked in alarm. "Are you kidding?"

The driver laughed. "It's not that hard, boy. And it won't take you too long. Come Saturday, I'll be waiting at the drop-off point to pick you up. Noon sound all right?"

Mom nodded. "That should give us enough time to make our flight, Mr. Doakey."

The driver grinned. "Just call me Oakie. Everyone else does."

"Oakie?" Scott asked.

"Sure, when your last name is Doakey, what else would you expect?"

"Oakie Doakey?" Scott laughed. "That's good." He threw Ryan a look, but Ryan didn't seem to notice.

Becka frowned. Ryan had spent most of the ride in silence, his attention focused on the scenery. When he had spoken, it was in a soft and reverent voice — almost as though he were inside a huge church. Granted, he seemed peaceful and relaxed. But he also seemed preoccupied — as if he wasn't entirely there. Becka wasn't sure why this made her uncomfortable. Maybe it was just jealousy. After all, she was used to being the focus of much of Ryan's attention. But deep inside, she knew that wasn't it. Something else was bothering her . . .

She couldn't put her finger on it, but she could swear something was happening. Something . . . unnatural. Try as she might, she couldn't stop the feeling from rising up inside her. Something was wrong.

They'd been in New Mexico for only a few hours, but already she knew something was very wrong.

2

An hour later, Oakie Doakey pulled the Jeep to a stop near the base of a steep hill. For some time now the road had grown steeper, and now it dead-ended into a wall of sheer rock.

"This is as far as I can take you," he said. "A footbridge just over that hill connects you to the next cliff. Once you cross to the other side, you just keep heading up the same direction through the hills and you'll hit the village of Starved Rock before you know it. But I'd hurry. Looks like a storm brewing."

All four of them turned in the direction Oakie was looking. An awesome thunderhead was building in the west.

"We'd better get going," Mom said as she hoisted a small suitcase out of the back of the Jeep.

"I'm glad we packed light," Becka said as she grabbed her makeup kit and another small bag.

Ryan lifted his backpack out of the Jeep, while Scott grabbed the laptop computer, his backpack, and a few other odds and ends.

Mom paused and turned back to Oakie. "Excuse me, but did you say something about a footbridge?"

Oakie nodded. "That's right. It's a rope bridge. You'll find them once in a while in these back areas. The Indians use them to get around the cliffs."

Becka and Mom glanced at each other. The words *rope bridge* and *cliff* did not sound encouraging. Finally, Mom cleared her throat, but Becka noted that her voice sounded a little thinner and just a little higher than before when she said, "I presume they are safe?"

Oakie flashed her a grin. "Just take one step at a time and you'll be fine."

"I see." Mom nodded, though it was obvious she was anything but reassured. "Well, thank you for your help, Mr. Doakey ... and for the advice."

Oakie dropped the Jeep into gear and turned it around. "See you all on Saturday!" he shouted. "And good luck."

Becka wasn't sure, but it almost sounded like he was laughing as he started back down the steep road. Suddenly she felt a sense of abandonment. Here they were, out in the wilderness, completely on their own. Well, not completely. She knew God was with them. He always was. Still ...

She took a deep breath to calm herself. It wouldn't have been so bad if the sky weren't growing darker and far more ominous with each passing minute.

"We'd better get moving," Mom said, and they were off. The climb was steep but not impossible. As the storm cloud continued to build in front of them, it eventually cast its shadow over them. The coolness brought welcome relief from the heat ... Becka figured it had dropped from 105 to 95 degrees. Not exactly a cold snap, but it did feel better. Then there was the darkness. Becka felt grateful for the shade and its coolness, but there was something eerie about that darkness. She didn't like it ... not one bit.

After climbing for nearly half an hour they finally saw it. The hanging bridge. From a distance it looked like a slender thread suspended between two mountains.

"Think that will hold us?" Ryan asked.

"I don't know," Scott said. "From here it looks like a piece of dental floss."

"At least dental floss is hard to break," Becka said. "That bridge looks more like it's made from cobwebs."

"Now, kids," Mom said. It was obvious she was as nervous as they were. "I'm sure when we get there we'll see that it will hold us just fine."

Becka wished Mom had sounded more convincing … but that was hard to do when you weren't convinced. And she knew Mom wasn't.

They continued to approach the bridge. Fortunately, the closer they got, the better it looked. The rope was heavy and well constructed. There were, however, two small problems …

First of all, the rope was heavily knotted and formed squares that were eighteen inches on each side. But while it was easy enough to walk on, it was also easy enough to see through. All the way to the ground. Five hundred feet below.

"Just don't look down," Scott suggested.

"We've *got* to look down," Becka complained. "We have to make sure we step on a piece of rope and not a piece of sky."

Ryan nodded but added, "As long as we hold on to the sides, we'll be okay."

Becka studied the bridge. He was right. A thick rope on each side provided grips to hold on to. The only problem was that the ropes moved right along with the bridge, which brought them to the second problem … *everything* moved. Constantly. Even a slight breeze caused the entire bridge to swing and sway.

For a long moment, everyone stood and stared. Finally, Ryan cleared his throat. "I'll, uh, I'll go first." He adjusted his backpack in preparation. Then he turned to Mom. "You want me to take your suitcase? I've got a free hand."

Mom hesitated, but Becka knew she was aware that hanging on to the suitcase and hanging on to the rope could be a problem. "Well, I — " She looked at Ryan, a concerned expression crossing her face. "Are you sure you'll be all right?"

"No problem." Ryan took the bag from her and started out onto the bridge. Immediately it began to sway.

"Be careful," Becka called, although she was sure he would be. Who wouldn't be careful with a five-hundred-foot drop staring you in the face?

The bridge was only a hundred feet across, but by the time Ryan got to the middle, it was swaying pretty hard. Still, after another minute or two, he had managed to cross it safely.

"I'll go next," Scott said as he grabbed the computer and other gear.

The bridge seemed to sway even more as Scott eased his way across, but, like Ryan, he arrived on the other side without much of a problem.

Mom went next. A little more slowly, a little more carefully, but finally, she also made it to the other side.

Now it was Rebecca's turn.

"Hurry, Beck!" Scott called. "That thundercloud is getting a lot closer."

Becka glanced up. It was true. The cloud hovered directly overhead, and it seemed to draw lower and closer. She took a deep breath, wrapped the handle of the makeup bag around her wrist, and stepped out.

Instantly, the bridge swayed under her weight. It was scary, but nothing she couldn't handle. She gripped the side ropes fiercely and took two more steps. Then another, another, and another. Except for the slight dizziness she felt when she glanced down (a five-hundred-foot drop will do that to a person), she was doing just fine.

Until the wind came.

Although they had all been watching the thundercloud approach, no one had expected the wind to kick up so fast. Or so hard.

Almost instantly the bridge began to sway. Violently.

Becka screamed and froze. She didn't dare move her feet. It was all she could do to keep her balance when she stood still, let alone when she walked.

"Come on, Beck!" Scott shouted. "Keep coming!"

But Becka could not. She would not. She could barely move at all.

The wind grew stronger, and the bridge swayed harder. It arced out a full ten feet to the left and then swung back a full twelve feet to the right. The arc grew with each swing, and Becka found it more and more difficult to hang on.

"Hold on!" Mom screamed. Then, turning to the boys, she shouted, "She's losing her grip!"

Despite the heat of the day, cold terror filled Becka. She swung to the left fifteen feet, then to the right almost twenty. Things were getting worse as she kept swinging back and forth, farther and farther.

Then on the fourth or fifth swing she lost her footing. Her left foot shot through the gap in the ropes, and she went down.

She screamed as she fell — until her right leg snagged in the rope.

The bridge swayed back to the left. Becka's weight pushed hard against the ropes, and they spread farther apart. As they spread, Becka slipped farther through the gap.

Now the bridge swayed to the right. As it did, Becka's body slipped the rest of the way through the gap. Fortunately her leg was still caught in the ropes, but that meant she was hanging, dangling over the gorge by a single leg.

"Becka!" Ryan shouted. "Beck, hang on!"

She lunged for the nearest rope rail but failed, unable to grab it. The bridge swayed back to the left — and her leg slipped.

Mom screamed. Becka saw her mom start toward the bridge, but Ryan and Scott grabbed her arm.

"No!" Ryan shouted. "You can't go out there. The extra weight on the bridge will only make things worse."

Scott turned to Becka and yelled, "Grab the rail! You can do it!"

There were only seconds to spare. Becka's leg was loosening, and she would fall. She lunged for the rope again.

And missed again.

Her leg slipped a bit more. She tried again, but the farther she reached, the more her leg slipped. Realizing that her makeup bag hampered her reach, she let it go, watching for a brief, dizzying second as it tumbled toward the desert floor.

She had time for one more try. If she missed, she would follow the makeup bag's descent.

The bridge started back to the right.

"Please, Jesus!" she gasped. "Help me ... Help me ..." Becka stretched for all she was worth — but her leg pulled free, and she began to fall. She screamed, her arms waving and flaying ... until she caught hold of something. One last strand of rope.

But would it hold? More important, could she pull herself back up onto the bridge? But as the bridge reached the arc of its swing and began falling in the other direction, the force helped lift her. She took advantage of the movement and with one hard tug found herself lying back on the bridge, gripping its sides with both hands as it swayed back and forth, back and forth.

She was safe.

"Thank you, Jesus. Thank you ..."

She heard commotion at the end of the bridge. Scott was shouting about going out and saving her.

"Just stay there!" she yelled. "I'm all right! Just stay there till the wind dies down!"

Slowly the wind began to ease. The swaying grew less and less. When Becka was finally sure it was safe to stand again, she rose to her feet. And then, with the encouragement of the others, she slowly finished crossing the bridge.

When she arrived, she fell into Ryan's arms, trying to hold back her tears, to catch her breath. As Ryan held her, and as Mom and Scott asked again and again if she was okay, Becka slowly raised her eyes from the bridge—up toward the nearest peak. She wasn't sure why she looked up, but she immediately wished she hadn't.

It appeared for only an instant. Then it was gone. But she knew she'd seen it. The outline of a man, silhouetted against the setting sun ...

A man with two great horns rising from his skull.

3

Once they crossed the bridge, they faced less danger, but things weren't any easier. The heat grew more and more oppressive until it was nearly unbearable, which only made their climb over rocks and rugged terrain that much more difficult. Rain would have brought welcome, cooling relief. But though the storm continued to flash its lightning and boom with thunder, not a drop fell.

Within half an hour the ground had leveled off. The straggling group had reached the top of the plateau. Now all they had to do was cross to the village, which Oakie Doakey had said was nestled in the hills up ahead.

Although no rain fell, the wind kicked up again. It whipped and howled through the surrounding hills, making a mournful, wailing cry. Becka thought it sounded almost human.

Awwooo ...

Becka and Scott glanced at each other uncomfortably.

"Was that my imagination, or did the wind just say, 'Yoouuu'?" Scott asked.

Becka tried to shrug it off. "It's just the wind."

Awwooo ...

"See?" she said, doing her best to sound cheerful. "Same as before. It's just the wind."

Scaaah...

"Did you hear that?" Scott exclaimed. "It called my name!"

"No, it didn't. It said, 'Scaaah.'"

"So I should feel better because it can't spell?" he quipped.

Becka laughed in spite of herself.

"Hey, guys," Ryan called from up ahead. "I think I see the village."

Scott, Becka, and Mom hurried to catch up with him. Now they could see it too. Rows and rows of crude shacks and small sod huts peeked out from behind a distant hill.

"That must be it," Mom said.

"Yeah," Scott agreed. "Only where's our hotel?"

"It's probably at the other end of the village," Ryan suggested. "That looks like the older part of the village. All the new stuff must be at the other end, behind that ridge."

They walked for nearly an hour. As they came closer and closer to the village, Becka noticed that Ryan's gaze seldom left the huts. "This is so cool," he said. "It's just like I imagined. Just like the history books. It's like we've been dropped back in time."

"Yeah, great," Scott replied. "Only where's our hotel? We should be able to see it by now."

At last they reached the edge of the village and entered. A young Indian woman carrying a baby came out of a nearby hut and watched them. They waved self-consciously, and she nodded—but she said nothing.

Farther on, an old man, his long white hair divided into two braids, approached them. When he came within ten feet of them, he simply stopped and continued to stare.

"Hello, there," Ryan ventured. He gave a slight wave to the old man. But the man barely acknowledged his presence.

Ryan shrugged and looked around. Becka followed his

gaze and spotted a younger man—she guessed he was around twenty—lugging a large bag of grain over his shoulder.

"Excuse me," Ryan called. "Would you help us out?"

The man turned and stopped. He studied Ryan suspiciously.

"Do you speak English?" Ryan asked.

"Of course. Everyone speaks English."

"Great," Ryan said. "We're looking for a man named Swift Arrow. We have something to—"

The Indian cut him off. "He's not here. He's gone on a walkabout."

"A what?" Ryan asked.

"A walkabout."

"I don't understand ..."

"It's like a meditation. A man goes into the desert to think and pray."

"Ah."

"He should be back tomorrow."

"Okay," Ryan answered politely. "A walkabout, eh? That's an Indian term I wasn't familiar with."

"It's not Indian," the man replied. "It's Australian. Didn't you see *Crocodile Dundee*?"

"What?"

"It's a movie."

"Oh ... well, yes, of course."

"You can rent it down at my video store if you're interested."

"You have a video store?" Scott asked in surprise.

"Fully stocked, from the classics to all the latest movies."

"Do you guys have computers?"

The young man gave him a puzzled look and then broke into a grin. Suddenly he raised his arm and, in a stiff, melodramatic fashion, answered, "Yes ... we sell 'um many buffalo hides to buy magic screen that glow in dark."

"Pardon me?"

"Glowing screen, heap big magic. Help me speak to spirits on Internet. Impress many squaws."

Becka bit her lip to keep from laughing. Ryan's expression showed he felt foolish enough without her adding to his humiliation. "Oh, I get it," he said with a slow, self-deprecating grin. "Just because the village looks like it's out of the history books doesn't mean the people are."

The young man shrugged good-naturedly. "I know it's hard to believe, but we're as up-to-date in the twenty-first century as anyone." He returned Ryan's smile and turned to leave. "See you around."

"Wait! Excuse me," Becka called.

The man turned back again.

"Would you tell us where our hotel is ... the, uh ..." She turned to Mom. "What is it called?"

"The Western Ground on the Cliff," Mom said.

The young man look puzzled, then broke into another grin. "The Western Ground on the Cliff is over there. Just past that row of homes to your left. You can't miss it."

"Thanks!" Becka said.

"Don't mention it," the man said with a chuckle and then moved off.

The group headed in the direction the Indian had indicated. And sure enough, as soon as they had passed the row of huts, they came to a sign that read The Western Ground on the Cliff. But there was no hotel in sight. Only the sign, which was made up of white paint scrawled on some faded, wooden planks.

"I don't get it," Scott said. "Where's the hotel?"

"You must be the Williams party."

They turned to see a boy of eleven or twelve approaching them from a nearby hut.

"That's—that's not the hotel, is it?" Becka pointed toward the hut with a worried look.

The boy laughed. "Nah, that's just where my family and I live."

"So could you tell us exactly where the hotel is?" Mom asked.

The boy smiled again. "There is no hotel, ma'am. This is a campground."

Becka and Scott looked at each other. Then at Ryan. Then at Mom. No one looked terribly happy.

The boy continued, "Your friend has reserved two of our best campsites for you. He also purchased two tents, four sleeping bags, and a week's worth of supplies."

For a long moment there was nothing but silence. Finally, Scott began shaking his head and mumbling, "Good ol' Z . . ."

"Well, at least we have sleeping bags," Mom said with what was clearly forced cheerfulness. "Let's make the most of it, shall we? You boys can have one tent, and we girls will take the other."

"Wonderful," Scott continued to mutter. "Just wonderful."

Becka echoed her brother's lack of enthusiasm.

But not Ryan. He actually seemed excited. "I think it's great," he said. "I wouldn't feel right staying in a fancy hotel here anyway. This is like an adventure."

"We'll see how adventurous you feel after a night on this hard ground," Scott grumbled as he kicked the rocky soil.

Ryan didn't seem to even hear him.

"You'd better start setting up your tents," the Indian boy said. "It's going to be dark soon."

👁 👁

A few hours later, Becka leaned against Ryan's shoulder. The group sat around the fire, cooking hot dogs and baked beans. It wasn't as elegant as room service in some fancy hotel, but it was definitely more romantic, and Becka loved it. She would have loved it even more if Ryan had paid some attention to her.

It wasn't that he ignored her, but she definitely got the feeling she came in second when compared to the sights and sounds around them: the mountains, the desert night sky, and all of the Indian culture. Well—Becka glanced around them—who could blame him? How could anyone compete with such majestic beauty?

When they finally crawled into their tents, Becka was surprised at how much the ordeal at the bridge had taken out of her. Despite the hard ground, when she slid into her sleeping bag, she was asleep within seconds.

The next morning she woke up to the sound of a hawk screeching overhead. For the briefest second she remembered her dream on the airplane. But the memory quickly faded in the peace and tranquillity of early morning at Starved Rock. Though she heard Scott and Ryan shuffling about making breakfast—most likely cold cereal and milk—she gave a long stretch and decided to stay with Mom a bit longer in the tent. Something about the chilly morning, the warm tent, and the complete and utter peace Becka felt made it more than a little difficult to rise and get moving.

After breakfast, Scott and Ryan decided they'd explore the village a bit. Last night when they had arrived, it was nearly dark and they really hadn't seen much. So now they were ready to go.

They spotted the Indian boy who ran the campground, and Scott asked him what there was to see.

"Not much, I'll tell you that. But if you want the grand tour, I'll take you."

"Great," Scott said. "But don't you have to check in people coming to the camp?"

The boy smiled sadly. "Nobody comes to this camp. Not anymore."

Scott and Ryan exchanged glances.

"My name is Little Creek," the boy said, extending his hand.

"Hi, Little Creek." Ryan reached out and shook his hand. "My name is Ryan."

"And I'm Scott Williams," Scott added, also shaking Little Creek's hand.

"I'm very glad you have come to visit," Little Creek said. "We used to get tourists but not for several months now ... not since the drought. Come on, I'll show you the sights." With that, he turned and started down the road. Scott and Ryan fell in step beside him.

"How long has the drought been going on?" Scott asked.

"It started during the last growing season, killing most of last year's crop."

Ryan scowled. "I'm sorry to hear that."

Little Creek nodded. "And it's continued into this year. Many people didn't even plant this spring because the soil is so dry."

"Can't you irrigate or something?" Scott asked. "I mean, isn't that what modern farmers do?"

"*Wealthy* modern farmers, sure. But it costs too much to run irrigation pipes all the way up into these mountains."

"That's not a great situation," Ryan said.

"Our people have always depended on the rain," Little Creek answered. "The crops we grow don't need much, but there has been no rain for so long that many people are thinking of leaving the village and moving."

Scott glanced about as they moved past the small shacks and sod huts. "Why don't you just pack up the whole village?" he asked. "Doesn't seem like it would be too hard. There's not that much stuff."

Little Creek smiled. "Things are easy to pack, but people

aren't. Our traditions weigh much more than our material goods."

"What's that supposed to mean?" Ryan asked.

"It means the old people are too stubborn to move."

Soon the three came to the end of the village. Just beyond it was a huge rock, bigger than any boulder Scott had ever seen. "Check it out," he said, pointing to the colossal rock. It jutted up against the sky like a gnarled, clenched fist.

"That's Starved Rock," Little Creek explained. "That's where the village gets its name."

"Why do they call it that?" Ryan asked as they moved closer to examine the big boulder.

"Back in the 1880s, a hundred braves made their last stand in this place. They were surrounded by cavalry, but instead of the soldiers coming up the mountain and fighting like men, they merely stopped the braves from escaping ... until each and every one had died of starvation."

"That's awful," Ryan said.

"Yes," Little Creek replied. "It is said that their spirits still cry out from these rocks at night."

"No kidding?" Scott asked.

"It's all very sad," Ryan said, shaking his head.

Little Creek hesitated a moment, then shrugged. "All Indian stories are sad. I learned early not to ask my grandfather the meanings of the names and locations of things. There were always sad stories behind them."

"If you didn't ask your grandfather, then how did you learn them?" Ryan asked.

Little Creek laughed. "Grandfather told me, whether I asked or not. We Indians are very big on oral history, you know. It's another one of our traditions."

"So what about these spirits that are supposed to cry out at night?" Scott asked. "Have you ever heard them?"

Again Little Creek shrugged. "Yes and no. It could just be the wind. No one is certain. Dark Bear claims that they are spirit voices. He also claims that he is the only one who knows what they are saying."

Scott and Ryan exchanged looks. Scott knew they both were remembering the eerie sounds they had heard in the wind on their way up to the village.

"Who's Dark Bear?" Scott asked.

For a moment Little Creek said nothing; then he took a deep breath and answered, "He's the tribal shaman, a very powerful medicine man. I don't know if you guys believe in that kind of thing, but ... Dark Bear is the one person you should avoid contact with in our village."

"Why?" Scott asked.

Little Creek cleared his throat nervously. "Because he has the kind of magic that can kill."

"You're not serious?" Ryan asked.

"Oh yes, I am very serious. Not only does he have the kind of magic that can kill ... but he does not hesitate to use it."

4

Swift Arrow walked quickly through the heat of the day. He prayed quietly, thinking and meditating as he crossed the canyon floor. He passed a dried-up riverbed and saw the skeleton of a long-dead coyote. He wondered if the animal had died of thirst. Perhaps it had crawled for miles to reach the river, only to discover that it was bone-dry.

Swift Arrow stopped and looked down at the skeleton. His body grew tense. Carefully, he stooped down onto one knee for a closer look. There was something about the pattern of the bones on the sand ... It was the same jagged pattern that he had seen in the lightning.

Suddenly anxiety filled him. He couldn't explain it, but the need to return to his village seized him. He needed to return at once. Swift Arrow stood and started for home.

❦ ❦

As they moved along the ridge, Little Creek entertained Scott and Ryan by telling them various legends and stories. One of his favorites was the legend of Buffalo Cry, a very strong brave who lived over a hundred summers ago. His tribe sent him to bring the peace pipe to his enemies, but on the way a rattlesnake bit him. As he lay dying, he chanted to the eagle god. After he died, his spirit entered an eagle, which came and took the peace pipe from his hand and flew with it to the enemy tribe. When the rival chief saw the eagle carrying the Apache peace pipe, he declared peace between the two tribes. The peace lasted many years.

"So you really think Buffalo Cry's spirit entered the eagle?" Scott asked.

Little Creek shrugged. "The eagle did exactly as Buffalo Cry wished. Man cannot order a wild eagle."

"I suppose not," Scott agreed. "But maybe God just used the eagle to answer Buffalo Cry's prayer for peace."

"What's the difference?" Little Creek asked. "Whether God commanded the eagle or the spirit of the brave entered the eagle, it's all the same. Buffalo Cry's eagle brought peace between the tribes."

"I don't know," Scott said, shaking his head. "I just can't buy the idea of a person's spirit entering some animal. The Bible says when we die we go to face God, not hang out inside some eagle."

"I think it's kinda cool," Ryan said. "Just because it's different from the way we grew up doesn't mean it's wrong."

Before Scott could disagree, Little Creek continued, "It's the heart of shamanism. Shamans believe that by chanting and using certain herbs they can become one with the souls of animals, particularly the eagle, the wolf, and the lizard."

Again Scott shook his head. "Sorry, it's too weird for me."

Ryan didn't respond, but to Scott his silence said tons.

A moment later Ryan shouted, "Hey, check it out!" Scott and Little Creek turned, but Ryan was already hurrying down the hill.

Scott looked to the bottom and saw a bunch of stones carefully laid out in some sort of pattern, almost as if they were spelling out words or forming crude stick figures. Intrigued, Scott also started down the hill.

"Wait," Little Creek called to them as he followed after Scott. "Be careful not to upset the stones. This is one of Dark Bear's holy places."

But Scott had already reached the bottom and began hopping on the stones, jumping from one to the other. "I'm not hurting them," he said. "I won't mess them up."

"Scott," Ryan said, "you should really show more respect. I mean, what if somebody saw you?"

"Oh, all right," Scott sighed. "If it's that big of a deal, I'll get off."

He'd barely hopped off when they heard a loud cracking sound toward the top of the mountain. All three spun around to see a huge cloud of dust and debris billowing down the slope—directly toward them.

"It's an avalanche!" Little Creek cried. "Run!"

No one had to be told twice, but it was too close and coming too fast. In a matter of seconds the first of the boulders descended upon them.

Ryan was the first to be hit. A boulder the size of a basketball grazed his thigh. He let out a cry but continued running.

Scott was luckier. He dodged an even bigger rock that crashed into the ground immediately beside him. Soon rock and sand and dust surrounded the three. Through the thick, hazy cloud, Scott saw another boulder, several times larger than any other that had fallen. He leaped out of the way just as the two-ton rock bounced past, missing him by inches.

It ended almost as quickly as it had begun. Except for their coughing and gasping for breath, everything grew quiet.

"Everyone all right?" Little Creek called.

"Yeah," Scott answered, choking.

"We're okay," Ryan coughed.

The guys climbed out of the gravel and rocks, then looked

back at where they had been standing. It was covered in rock. Coincidence? Maybe.

After a few moments, Ryan said, "Well, I guess we should probably be heading back."

"Yes." Little Creek's agreement was quick. "I'm afraid we've offended the spirits. It would not be safe to continue."

"'Offended the spirits,'" Scott scoffed. "You don't really believe that."

But Little Creek said nothing. Nor did Ryan. Instead, they turned and started climbing back up to the path. As they walked, Ryan turned around several times and looked back down at the pile of rocks. Scott couldn't be certain, but Ryan seemed strangely drawn to the place. Over the months the two of them had become good friends. And, like most good friends, each could often tell what the other was thinking. It was becoming more and more obvious to Scott that Ryan was getting caught up in the Indian myths and legends. And, while Scott knew this wasn't wrong, something about Ryan's fascination caused him concern.

"Hey—" Ryan stopped abruptly and pointed toward the top of the hill—"look."

Scott stopped and turned but saw nothing. "What?" he asked.

"He's gone now."

"There was somebody out here?"

Ryan nodded.

"Who?"

"I don't know ... but he had something coming out of his head."

"Horns?" Little Creek asked. "Did they look like horns?"

"Well, yeah."

"Then we'd better hurry." Little Creek suddenly broke into a trot.

"Why?" Ryan asked, jogging beside him. "What's going on?"

"If what you saw were horns, then we'd better get out of here. Fast."

"But *why?*"

Little Creek didn't answer. "Come on," he insisted, continuing to run. "Come *on.*"

Scott didn't press the issue and neither did Ryan. Whatever it was that Ryan had seen had made Little Creek pretty nervous. And whatever it was, neither Scott nor Ryan felt inclined to stick around and find out why.

An hour later as they approached camp, Little Creek said a hasty good-bye. He still would not tell them the reason for his concern, but it was obvious he was anxious to get away from them. Scott and Ryan wished him farewell and headed toward their tent.

As they walked up, a tantalizing aroma filled the air. "What's that smell?" Scott called. "I'm starved."

"You're *always* starved," Becka said as she stooped over the grill to check on the thick, sizzling hamburgers.

"You boys are just in time for lunch," Mom called.

"Great," Ryan said.

"But look at you—you're filthy. What happened?"

"Oh, we just had a little run-in with a falling mountain," Scott quipped.

"You what?"

"We just had a little—"

"Never mind," Mom interrupted. "Go wash up. When you get back you can tell us all about it."

❧   ❧

Becka watched the burgers carefully, making sure they didn't burn. When Scott and Ryan returned from washing up, she grinned. "It's about time! These things are ready to serve up."

"What do you boys want on them?" Mom asked.

"Oh ... anything's fine," Ryan said.

"Yeah," Scott agreed. "Whatever you got."

"Whatever we've got?" Becka repeated, laughing. "That sounds pretty suspicious coming from someone who complains about everything."

"Who? Me?" Scott asked, pretending to sound indignant.

"Yeah, you."

The guys each grabbed a plate, bun, burger, and some chips before settling down at the picnic table near their tent.

"Still no sign of Swift Arrow," Becka sighed. "We checked, and he hasn't come back yet. Nothing to do but just keep waiting, I guess."

"That's okay with me," Scott said. "I've had enough excitement for one day."

"It's okay with me too," Ryan agreed. "I'd say the longer we can stay here, the better."

Becka glanced at Ryan. The guy was practically beaming. As the sun reflected off his jet-black hair, she couldn't help thinking how gorgeous he looked ... and how lucky she was. For the past year their friendship had been growing stronger. Oh, sure, they'd had their disagreements, but something was growing between them. Something deep. When Ryan looked at her a certain way, Becka felt herself become weak and trembly inside.

Now she crossed over and sat beside him as she had so many times before. But instead of turning to smile at her, he barely seemed to notice her.

"I'm really starting to enjoy this trip too," she said. "It's different from the others. So quiet, so peaceful ..."

Ryan nodded, but when she glanced into his eyes, hoping for that special connection they always shared, she saw that he wasn't even looking at her. Once again he was off somewhere. And once again she felt a twinge of jealousy. Was it her imagination, or was he purposely ignoring her? She tried to push the thought from her mind, but it kept returning. Finally, she asked softly, "Ryan, is everything okay?"

As if coming back from a dream, Ryan turned to her and smiled. "Okay?" he asked. "Sure, everything's fine. You're right—this place is incredible. There's nothing the matter at all."

"Unless you count the avalanche that almost killed us," Scott said with a chuckle. "Other than that, Ryan's right, nothing's the matter."

Becka looked at him, startled.

"Avalanche?" Mom asked. She seemed equally startled—and concerned.

"Yep," Scott replied. And then, obviously enjoying his role as storyteller, he began to explain all that had happened to them ... from Little Creek's warnings about Dark Bear to Scott's playing on the holy stones to the avalanche and finally to the horned figure Ryan claimed to have seen on the top of the ridge.

"You saw a guy ... with horns?" Becka asked, feeling a sense of cold dread fill her.

"Yeah," Ryan answered. "I mean, it was pretty fast. One second he was there; the next he was gone. But I'm sure he had horns."

"I'm not sure what all this means," Mom said slowly, "but I think you kids had better be a lot more careful in the future."

The guys nodded, but Becka didn't respond. Ryan's last phrase had sent a chill shooting up her back and through her shoulders. It was part of her built-in warning system. One that she'd grown to trust through their many encounters with evil. She shifted her weight, trying to shake off the feeling, but it would not go away.

"What's wrong?" Ryan asked. "Are you all right?"

Becka swallowed hard and looked out at the rocks. "Yesterday ... when I almost fell off that rope bridge ..."

"Yeah?"

"When it was all over, I looked up. And, well, I thought it was my imagination, but now ..." She looked down. "When I looked up, I saw somebody standing on the ridge above us."

"Really?"

Becka tried to swallow again, but this time her mouth was bone-dry. "It was like you said—he was there only for a second and then he was gone."

As if sensing there was more, Ryan asked, "And ...?"

"And—" Becka finally raised her eyes to meet Ryan's—"on top of his head were two large horns."

5

It was early in the morning when Ryan awoke—around four o'clock, according to his watch. He listened carefully, sure he'd heard something. Of course, camping out in the New Mexico mountains meant you were bound to hear lots of strange noises during the night—the howl of a coyote, the hoot of an owl, the rhythmic buzz of countless, unknown insects. But this was slightly different.

Karahhh . . . Karahhh . . .

There it was again. Very nearby. Almost animal, but strangely human.

Karahhh . . . Karahhh . . .

Now Ryan was wide-awake. He decided against waking Scott. After all, the sound wasn't particularly threatening—and he didn't want to seem foolish or afraid.

Karahhh . . . Karahhh . . .

Quietly, Ryan unzipped his sleeping bag and crawled out. He slipped on his jeans and grabbed a long-sleeved shirt for a jacket. Ever so silently, he unzipped the tent flaps and stepped out into the shadows.

The air was cool and slightly sticky. And the smells. Sage and dust and a hundred others he couldn't recognize. The moon was nearly full, filling the desert and mountains with its light. Everything was so peaceful, so silent, so—

Karahhh ... Karahhh ...

Ryan felt his heart beat a little harder. It was definitely no animal he'd ever heard. And although he couldn't explain why, he felt it calling.

Calling to him.

He crossed the dozen or so yards to the entrance of the campground.

Karahhh ... Karahhh ...

It sounded like it came from the side of the road. Slowing to a stop, he paused to peer into the moonlight.

Nothing. It sounded so close, and yet there was nothing.

He took in a breath to steady himself, then kept going. Maybe it was a raccoon. Or maybe it was some kind of weird bird.

Karahhh ... Karahhh ...

No, that was no bird. And he was nearly on top of it.

He had reached the side of the road when he saw it. Something in the shadows. Something big. And it was moving!

"I knew you'd come."

Ryan let out a gasp as Little Creek stepped into the moonlight.

"You scared me half to death!" Ryan exclaimed.

Little Creek smiled, his white teeth gleaming in the light. "I summoned you the Indian way, and you came. You have the heart of an initiate."

"A what?"

"A potential brave. I have seen that you are someone who may truly understand and appreciate the ways of my people. I want to show you someplace special. Will you come with me?"

Something told Ryan to refuse. It was like someone tugging at his mind—a kind of warning. But Little Creek seemed so excited ... Before he knew it, Ryan was nodding. "Yeah. Sure."

Again Little Creek smiled. Without another word, he turned and started down the path. Ryan joined him.

An hour later they were walking past Dark Bear's holy place, the location of the avalanche. Ryan felt a slight chill as he looked down at the pile of rock and stone. Instinctively, he glanced up to the peak where he had seen the man with the horns, but no one was there. Maybe no one ever had been.

"This way," Little Creek called as he disappeared into some tall weeds.

Ryan turned off the road and followed.

"Be careful—the ground drops off here."

Ryan was grateful for the warning as the ground began such a sudden slope that he had to struggle to keep his balance.

At last Little Creek called out, "Over here."

Ryan looked up to see the boy standing at the entrance to a small cave.

"It looks small now," Little Creek said, "but after a few feet inside you can stand up."

Once again Ryan felt that small tug, that sense of caution, of warning. And once again, he brushed it aside. What was wrong with checking out a cave?

"Come on." Little Creek motioned for Ryan to follow him inside. Ryan obeyed. He had to stoop to enter. Immediately, he felt a coolness—a good fifteen to twenty degrees cooler than outside. What's more, it was pitch-black. Fortunately Little Creek had a small flashlight, and its light reflected off the walls and ceiling. The walls rose rapidly, and after half a dozen steps Ryan was able to stand.

"How far does this thing go?" he asked.

"A very long way," Little Creek replied. "This, too, is a holy place, so I must ask you not to show it to anyone. I'm showing it to you because I believe you have the mind to understand."

Ryan felt himself swell a little with pride. This was quite an honor Little Creek was bestowing on him. What other secrets did he have to share?

After several more feet, Little Creek finally came to a stop. "Over there," he said, motioning with his flashlight. "Look at that wall."

Ryan caught his breath. On the near wall was a crude painting of an Indian brandishing a long spear and stalking a buffalo. The painting could have been a thousand years old.

"This was painted by my ancestors," Little Creek said in almost a whisper. "We don't know when, but legend says the brave in the painting is Dark Bear's great-great-grandfather."

Ryan whistled softly. "It looks even older than that," he said quietly.

Little Creek chuckled. "Not if you believe the other legend."

"Other legend?"

"That, like Dark Bear, his grandfathers before him each lived to be a thousand years old."

Ryan looked at Little Creek. "They ... what?"

Little Creek shrugged. "It's not impossible. Doesn't the Bible talk about people living that long?"

"Well ... yes, but—"

"So if it's in the Bible, it's possible, isn't it?"

Ryan nodded slowly. He wasn't sure he believed Little Creek, but he didn't want to argue. After all, he was in a cave in the middle of the New Mexico desert, looking at a painting that was made thousands of years ago, listening to its legends—things just didn't get any cooler than this!

If only that small voice inside would stop nudging him, making him feel guilty, saying he should be careful ...

He shook his head. It was a stupid feeling. There was nothing dangerous here. He was doing nothing wrong.

"Come with me," Little Creek said, breaking into Ryan's thoughts.

Ryan followed the boy as he turned and a few steps later

rounded a small bend. The cave grew larger and larger. Now it was several times Ryan's height, and the ceiling grew higher with every step. Soon they'd entered a huge, magnificent cavern.

"This painting has even more color," Little Creek said as he flashed the light across the cavern to the far wall.

The light revealed the portrait of a medicine man calling down lightning. All around him other Indians cowered in fear as the thunderbolt struck the ground.

"Is this a battle scene?" Ryan asked.

"No," Little Creek replied. "We call it *The Wrath of Shaman*. It's supposed to be an angry medicine man calling down fire on members of the tribe who disobeyed his council."

"Could he really do that?"

"It depends on the power of the shaman. Sometimes he also fasts and takes herbs to help him see."

"What do you mean, 'see'?"

"To see into the netherworld, the spirit world."

Ryan felt a sudden chill. But this time it had nothing to do with the temperature inside the cave.

Little Creek continued, "Sometimes the shaman can see the cause of a sickness or the path to solve another person's problem."

"The herbs can help him do that?" Ryan asked.

Little Creek nodded. "The herbs clear his mind of the things of this world so he can focus on the supernatural. They help him get in touch with the Great Spirit."

Ryan said nothing as they made their way out of the cave, but during the trip back to the camp, he asked Little Creek if he would teach him more about the ways of his tribe.

"Sure." Little Creek grinned. "It's like I said—I think you have the potential of a brave."

Once again Ryan felt pride swelling inside his chest.

Little Creek continued, "You should try some of the

tea we drink at ceremony. I bet you could also see into the supernatural."

There was that nervous feeling again, but this time it was easy to shove it aside. There were far too many questions, too many new things to explore, to let his nerves stop him now. "Can't you see into the supernatural without the tea?"

"Some can," Little Creek answered. "But Dark Bear is the only one I know who can communicate with the Great Spirit without it."

Ryan nodded. After a while he turned to his little friend with a question—a question that had been forming in his mind most of the morning. "Little Creek?"

"Yes?"

"Do you think this Great Spirit you're always talking about ... do you think that's just another name for God?"

Little Creek smiled. "Sure. What else could it be?"

👁 👁

As the boys returned to the camp, the sun was just cresting over the eastern ridge. It was a beautiful, golden dawn. And there in the distance a dark speck was walking toward them.

"Is that ...?" Ryan asked. "Is that Dark Bear?"

Little Creek slowed and peered into the distance. "No," he said, shaking his head. "It's Swift Arrow. He has finally returned from his time of seeking."

"Great," Ryan exclaimed, "that's the guy we're supposed to talk to. Now we'll finally find out why we were sent here."

"I'm sure he's been fasting," Little Creek said. "Why don't you invite him to join your group for breakfast?"

"Good idea."

👁 👁

An hour later Mom was dishing up bacon and eggs for the group and their newest acquaintance, Swift Arrow.

As they sat eating around the picnic table, Becka couldn't help noticing how lean and muscular Swift Arrow was. As far as she could tell, the brave didn't have an ounce of fat on him.

"So," Scott asked as Becka passed around seconds, "are you a friend of Z's?"

Swift Arrow frowned. "I'm sorry. I don't recognize the name."

"Z," Scott repeated.

Swift Arrow shook his head.

"Do you surf much?"

Again Swift Arrow looked confused. "There are no large bodies of water near here ... Even the river is dried up, so it would be difficult to — "

"No, no," Ryan chuckled. "He doesn't mean surf, like ride a board. He means, do you surf the Net? You know, visit the Internet with your computer?"

Swift Arrow grinned at the mistake. "I'm afraid I don't have a computer. Why do you ask?"

"That's where we met Z," Scott explained. "On the Net."

"At least that's where we think we met him," Becka corrected. "But he seems to know so much personal stuff about us that we suspect we might have run into him before."

"He's never told you who he is?"

"That's right." Becka nodded. "Which is one of the things that makes him so mysterious."

"That and the fact that he sends us all around the world to help folks out," Scott added.

"Well, I don't know why this Z has sent you," Swift Arrow said. "But I'm glad you came. For the past three days, I have been walking and praying, seeking for just such guidance. You are the answer to my prayers."

"How can we help?" Becka asked, pleased but confused by the young man's obvious relief.

"Two years ago I left the reservation and went to the university. During that time I became a Christian—"

"No kidding?" Scott interrupted. "We're all Christians too."

"That's great." Swift Arrow grinned.

"Go on," Becka said. "You were walking and praying because ..."

Swift Arrow nodded. "When I returned to my village after college, I was very anxious to share the things I'd learned about Jesus. Like many Native Americans, I had grown up thinking that Jesus was a white man's God, opposed to everything we believed. But that's not true. Many of Christ's teachings fit in with what I have learned from nature, from *his* creation. In fact, the gospel actually completes our teachings ... helping us make sense out of them. It also helped me understand what parts of the old teachings were true and what parts were not."

"I'll bet you found a lot that was true," Ryan said.

Becka glanced at him. She knew Ryan had developed a real interest in and appreciation for these people, and that was good. But it seemed he was going beyond that—as though he was trying to rationalize that all Native American beliefs were the same as those of Christianity.

"Yes, some things are the same," Swift Arrow answered. Then he hesitated, as though unsure if he should go on.

"Please," Mom urged him quietly, "tell us what happened."

He continued, "When I arrived home, I was not able to share these new truths with my people. Worries about the drought consumed their every thought. I tried praying with some of them, but the rain did not come, and soon they lost interest in my prayers. And my faith."

"I'm sorry to hear that," Becka said.

"But there's more. Last week the tribal shaman, Dark Bear, began saying that my return to the village had actually prolonged the drought. That I had brought a plague onto the village because of my belief in the white man's religion."

"That's terrible," Scott protested.

Becka glanced at Scott, nodding in agreement. That's when she saw it—another storm cloud starting to form off in the distance, toward the southwest. It was similar to the huge thunderhead that had brought the wind the day they'd come to the village—the wind that had nearly knocked her off the bridge. She felt a little knot of uneasiness grow inside.

"The drought has greatly tested my faith," Swift Arrow continued. "I went on the walkabout to fast and pray for God to show me what to do. I want to share my faith with the people, but it is hard for minds to be open when bellies are empty."

Becka glanced back at the cloud. It continued its slow approach.

"We are running out of the grain we've stored, and there are no new crops. Unless it rains, we will have to abandon this, the home of our forefathers."

"That would be awful," Ryan protested.

Swift Arrow nodded. "It is either that or starve."

"There must be something you can do," Mom said.

"Dark Bear claims I have rejected the faith of my people. I want to challenge him, to prove that he is wrong and that God has far greater power than he does. But until now I have been afraid."

"Until now?" Becka asked.

Swift Arrow smiled. "Now four strangers come—strangers who share my faith. It is the sign I was hoping for."

"I still don't understand," Becka said. "What exactly do you think we can do about a drought?"

"Hold that thought," Mom said as she crossed to the fire to scoop up more eggs. She passed around the food and everyone, including Becka, dug in. It was surprising how the fresh air and exercise increased their appetites.

"This is very good," Swift Arrow said.

"Yeah, Mom," Scott agreed. "Good job."

Becka noticed that the thunderhead was much closer. She was surprised at how quickly clouds formed and moved through these parts.

"Go ahead," Ryan urged Swift Arrow. "You were telling us about the drought."

"To me your arrival is a sign that I must take a stand against Dark Bear. I must tell the truth about the Christian God, and then the drought will end. Because once I have—"

But Swift Arrow never finished. Suddenly there was an explosion, a thunderclap so loud that it shook the table. All five of them jumped and looked up at the sky.

Becka was the first to spot him. It was the same man she had seen from the bridge. The same one Ryan had said he'd seen at the avalanche. He stood high above them, on the very top of Starved Rock. He was wearing a buffalo headdress, complete with horns. And even from that distance it was possible to see his piercing stare, glaring down at them.

"Dark Bear," Swift Arrow whispered.

Several seconds passed, with only the echoing roll of thunder in the background. And then, ever so slowly, Dark Bear began to chant and dance in a small circle atop the rock.

Becka turned to Swift Arrow. She wanted to ask what Dark Bear was doing, but the expression on the young man's face stopped her cold. Fear. No, worse than fear . . . terror.

Swift Arrow glanced back up at the sky; then he leaped up from the table and shouted, "Get away from the table! Everybody get away!"

The panic in his voice spurred the others to move.

"Jump back!" he shouted. "Get away from the table! Do it now!

"Hurry!" Swift Arrow shouted, grabbing Mom and Becka by the arms, pulling them away. *"Get back! Get back!"*

Ryan and Scott followed suit, although not without the usual questions: "What's going on? What's wrong?"

Before Swift Arrow could answer, a tremendous, blinding flash filled the sky. Becka and Mom screamed. Air crackled and burned all around them. Suddenly a powerful blast — an explosion of thunder so intense — knocked all five of them to the ground.

And then it ended as quickly as it had begun. Only the echo of thunder against the hills — and the ringing in their ears — remained.

"What ... what happened?" Scott stammered as he struggled to his feet.

"I think we were almost hit by lightning!" Mom answered, her voice shaking.

"Look at that!" Ryan exclaimed. He was pointing to the table and benches. Or to what was left of them. The table had split in two. The benches had tipped over and cracked, and all of the wood had been charred and now lay smoldering on the ground.

A shaken Becka looked over at Swift Arrow, who rose to his feet, trembling. He did not say a word. He only tilted his head and looked back up at the top of Starved Rock.

Becka followed his gaze. Dark Bear stood there with his arms folded across his chest, glowering down at them. Her eyes darted back to Swift Arrow. "Did he do that?" she asked incredulously. "He couldn't have done that, could he?"

Swift Arrow tried to answer, but no words came. Becka watched him swallow and try again. Still nothing. He just stared.

And then Becka heard another voice — distant but heavy and full of ominous authority.

"Let this be a warning!" It was Dark Bear, calling down from the rock. "A warning to you all. It is *I* who commune with the gods of nature. It is *I* who will make the rain. And all who oppose me or my magic ... will surely die."

6

It was huge. In fact, it seemed to Becka that it was as tall as the mountains themselves, though she knew that was impossible. Still, the eagle's wings covered most of the sky as it cast its shadow on the desert floor. Becka stared, trying to grasp its size, when the giant bird spotted them.

Instantly, it began to dive. Already Becka suspected she was dreaming ... but it seemed so real. And the bird was so big. She tried to wake herself, but it was no use. The bird continued its dive.

"Run!" she shouted to Ryan. *"Run!"*

"But it's only a dream," Ryan protested.

"It doesn't matter. Run!"

She started off, but Ryan refused to move. Reluctantly, she doubled back and grabbed his arm. She tugged, but he wouldn't move. The eagle was still some way off, but it was coming in fast. And it was screaming. Under its cry she could hear the wind whizzing past the giant wings as they cut through the air.

Becka tugged again until Ryan finally started to move. Now they were holding hands, racing across the desert floor, heading for a clump of trees. She glanced over her shoulder. The bird was gaining on them. She knew they would never make it. Even if they did, she doubted the trees would offer much protection against such a creature.

All at once her legs grew heavy. Deadweight. But she had to keep going, even if it was only a dream. She knew that if she slowed down the bird would attack and rip them to pieces.

Then everything went black. She and Ryan were still running—she could feel her legs moving, hear Ryan gasping beside her—but they were running in darkness!

Again she tried to force herself awake, and again she failed.

They continued running. Her lungs burned for air; her cheeks were streaked with tears of hopelessness. And then she saw it. Sensed it, really. The great claw of the beast dropping down, reaching out for Ryan.

"Don't worry," he shouted, "it's only a dream!"

The talons reached out and closed around his neck. Rebecca screamed and watched in horror as the talons tore into him, lifting him high into the air.

She screamed again, but it did no good. Then, suddenly, the eagle disappeared, and Becka was all alone. In the dark. Gasping for breath . . .

She heard the sound of insects buzzing outside her tent and, off in the distance, the lone call of an eagle.

She was awake. Or was she? Becka lay there, unsure. She looked around her tent. The dream was over. At least, she thought it had been a dream. But if she'd been dreaming, then what about the eagle call she'd just heard?

With more than a little anxiety, Becka climbed out of her sleeping bag and pulled on her jeans. She unzipped the tent. It was still dark outside, but as far as she could tell, no giant eagles hovered in the sky. She stepped outside and crept over to Scott and Ryan's tent. Already she could hear Scott snoring away. It was a sound she was all too familiar with, but one that, at least for now, she found very comforting.

Carefully she listened outside their tent. Only one person's snoring—definitely Scott's—greeted her ears. Becka peeked inside the tent. Where was Ryan? Only a ripped sleeping bag and his torn and shredded clothing... and feathers, lots and lots of giant eagle feathers.

Becka covered her mouth to stifle a scream. And then she saw it, high overhead: a giant eagle swooping down out of the darkness, coming directly at her. She tried to run but was paralyzed. She opened her mouth to scream, but no sound would come. And then...

She forced herself awake.

This time it was real. But just to be sure, she reached out to pinch her arm. Hard. The shock of pain was a comforting confirmation. Yes, she was awake. She was in her tent, inside her sleeping bag, trying to catch her breath.

"Beck?" She heard a whisper. "Becka, are you all right?" It was Ryan. He was just outside her tent. A wave of relief washed over her.

"Becka?"

"Yeah," she whispered. "Hang on, I'll be right there."

Quickly she slipped out of her sleeping bag and into her jeans and shirt, threw open the tent, and raced into his arms. "Oh, Ryan!" She was practically sobbing.

"Are you all right?" he asked again with surprise.

"I thought you were eaten ... or got snatched up by the eagle or ... or ..." She knew she wasn't making much sense, but it didn't matter. The important thing was that Ryan was all right.

"What eagle?" he asked. "What are you talking about?"

"Nothing," she said, taking a deep breath and forcing the last of the sleep from her mind. "It was a dream ... a dream inside of a dream. And I knew it was a dream, but still—everything seemed so real." Once again she hugged him, grateful to feel his arms around her.

"It's all right, Beck," he said, almost chuckling. "I'm okay. Really."

At last she pulled back to look at him, to gaze into those deep blue eyes. "What are you doing outside at this time of night?"

He shrugged. "I was just enjoying the view ... until I heard you calling. Look—" he motioned toward the sky—"take a look at those stars, will you? Have you ever seen anything more beautiful?"

Becka tilted her head back to look up into the night. The sky glowed with stars. They looked so close it was as if the surrounding peaks nearly touched them.

"I thought I'd take a walk up to the ridge again. You want to come along?" he asked.

"Sure. I'm so wound up about that dream, I don't think I'd be able to get back to sleep anyway."

Ryan looked at her and smiled. It was the smile that always melted her. The one that made her legs just a little bit weak. She could never figure out if he knew when he was using it or not.

She coughed slightly and tried to change the subject. "Scott's still asleep."

"Yeah, he was up most of the night, down at the general store, trying to get a hold of Z."

Becka looked at him, a quick hope stirring inside her. "Did he?"

Ryan shook his head. "He got the modem all set up, but Z never came online."

"Oh," Becka said, disappointed.

"But there was a message waiting."

"What did it say?"

"Not much. Just a Bible verse and a note to write back tomorrow."

"A Bible verse?"

"Uh-huh."

"Which one?"

"Here, I wrote it down."

Becka waited as he reached into his shirt pocket and unfolded a piece of paper.

"It's from Timothy. Here ... 'The Spirit clearly says that in later times some will abandon the faith and follow deceiving spirits and things taught by demons.'"

They both stared at the paper for a moment.

"Have any idea what it means?" Ryan looked at her curiously.

Becka frowned. "No. Do you?"

He shook his head, and they stared at the verse again. Finally, Ryan sighed and folded it back up. "Well, Z will probably fill us in on it tomorrow."

Becka nodded. "I hope so."

Becka laced her arm through Ryan's, and they started their walk toward the ridge. The gorgeous New Mexico mountains, the full moon, an incredible-looking and super-caring boyfriend on her arm ... these were the types of moments she dreamed of. Unfortunately another dream still clung to the back of her mind. This had been the second dream of an eagle attack. What did it mean? And what did that Bible verse mean?

As if that weren't enough to worry about, there was Ryan. He was different. Ever since they'd arrived here, he seemed to be growing more distant. The fact that he rarely looked at her was one thing. The fact that they'd barely had a conversation in two days was another. It was as though everything about this place—the mountains, the village, the people, their beliefs—fascinated him so much that he barely acknowledged she was there.

All right, maybe she was just being overly sensitive. It wouldn't be the first time. Or worse yet, maybe she was jealous—but ... of what?

They walked together in silence for several minutes as she debated whether or not to talk to him about her worries—but she had never been one to keep her feelings too tightly wrapped. "Ryan, are you all right?"

He nodded slightly but did not look at her.

"Ryan?"

"Hmm? Oh—yeah?" He gave her a sheepish smile. "Sorry, Beck. What did you say?"

She softly repeated the question. "Is everything okay?"

"It's just this place ... I mean, it's so ... mysterious and wonderful. It can get a guy thinking, that's all."

"About what?" she asked quietly. "Thinking about what?"

"Nothing." He shrugged. "Nothing, really ... and everything."

Not exactly the kinds of answers that made her quit worrying. What *was* he thinking about? Her? Them? Or was it something else? Something even deeper? She'd noticed that he hadn't cracked open his Bible once since they'd arrived. Back in the beginning, when he'd first become a Christian, he practically devoured the thing. Back then, he was full of so many questions and he was always studying the Bible to find answers. But now ...

She wanted to ask him about a whole lot more—including their relationship—but Becka knew better than to throw herself at Ryan. It was important to give him his space, to let him work things out.

Still ...

A shooting star that blazed through the eastern sky interrupted her thoughts. It looked like a Fourth of July sparkler lighting the entire sky before burning out. Too soon, it faded from sight.

"There's something ..." Ryan cleared his throat and started again. "There's something about this place, these people ..."

Becka listened intently.

"The way they live off the land—no cars, no factories. It's so honest that it makes our money-grubbing way of life look pretty sick by comparison. I mean, they're such a noble people."

Becka agreed. She had to give him that. She also wanted

to mention that these very same people were starving because they'd based their entire economy on rainfall in the desert, but when someone is waxing emotional, logic is usually an unwelcome guest.

"And when I hear Little Creek talk about the Great Spirit and nature and Mother Earth ... I'm not so sure they're all that wrong. I mean, there's certainly nothing evil about respecting the earth and treating her correctly."

"Respecting the earth is a very good thing. It's worshiping it that gets to be the problem," Becka responded.

Ryan looked at her strangely, then smiled. "I think you're just afraid because this is all so new to you."

Becka started to answer, then thought better of it. She was afraid, all right, but not because things were new. After all, she and her brother had spent most of their lives in the South American rain forests, living around people who worshiped nature and believed in animal spirits. Shamanism was nothing new to her. The vocabulary and details might be a little different, but for Becka many of the things she'd been seeing and hearing were all too familiar.

She wasn't afraid for herself. She threw another look at Ryan. She wasn't afraid for herself at all.

Scott heard the commotion before he was really awake. Several of the people from the village were nearby, talking in loud voices. He rolled over to see that Ryan had already gone. He roused himself enough to hear what the people were saying. A few spoke English, but most spoke a language he couldn't understand. He did, however, make out occasional English phrases like *big meeting, time something was done,* and *full moon.*

Whatever they were discussing, it sounded important. So Scott quickly rose, dressed, and stepped into the morning light. The group was a few dozen feet away, walking past the campground toward the village. Little Creek was trailing along behind them. "Hey, Scott! What's up?" he asked when he caught sight of Scott.

Scott shrugged. "You tell me."

"Dark Bear has called a council meeting on the first night of the full moon. That's two days from now. He wants to have Swift Arrow expelled from the village."

"What?" Scott said.

"And there's more. He wants to throw you guys out with him."

"You're kidding me."

Little Creek shook his head. "Nope, that's what it says."

Feeling his face start to burn with anger and unsure what to do, Scott turned back to his tent and pulled out his sleeping bag and started rolling it up. "I'd like to see him try," he snorted. "Just 'cause ol' Antler Head can do special effects with lightning doesn't mean he has any power over us."

"You're in his village," Little Creek replied simply. "He has the power. Besides, I would think that after yesterday, you would have stopped mocking his power."

Scott paused and looked back up at Little Creek. "I'm not mocking his power. I'm just not quaking in fear over it." He turned back to his sleeping bag and continued rolling it up. "Besides, if you ask me—"

Suddenly he stopped mid-sentence. There, inches from his hand, a rattlesnake slithered out of the folds of his sleeping bag.

"Careful ... Don't move," Little Creek whispered. "That one is deadly."

Scott froze, holding his breath as the snake's tongue darted in and out and the creature glided even closer to his outstretched fingers. Any second it would strike. Any second it would—

Shuuuushing!

A steel-tipped arrow hit its mark, flying directly between

Scott's fingers and straight into the snake's head. The darting tongue ceased its movement.

Scott stared in astonishment, his usually witty brain numb, his usually smart mouth dumb.

"Didn't get you, did it?" Swift Arrow asked.

Scott slowly turned to see Swift Arrow standing on a slight ridge, about twenty feet away. True to his name, the young man had fired the arrow and killed the snake just as it was about to strike.

"No ...," Scott half spoke, half wheezed. "I'm fine." He swallowed hard. "Just fine ..."

"That was close," Little Creek said, marveling. "Nice shot."

Swift Arrow nodded a thank-you and approached. "I suppose you saw these notices," he said to Scott while pointing to the yellow sheet in Little Creek's hand.

Scott still wasn't sure if he had a voice, but he gave it a try. "What ... what are you going to do?"

Swift Arrow seemed to wilt slightly. "I'm not sure. Perhaps I heard the Lord wrong. Perhaps I am causing more trouble here than good."

"When things start going nuts around you, sometimes that means you're on the right track."

"But sometimes it can mean you are not in God's will."

Scott paused before responding. "Maybe. All I'm saying is, don't be so quick to give up. Haven't you been doing what you know is right?"

"Yes. I've followed what I believe is true, but ..."

"But what?"

"But Dark Bear has very strong medicine."

"It may be strong, but it's not right."

Swift Arrow shook his head. "I don't know. I mean ... much of the way he believes is how I grew up."

Scott carefully searched the young man's face before

he continued. "Do you believe the spirit of a human can go into an eagle? Do you believe that the earth is something to worship?"

"No," Swift Arrow replied. "But I know that my grandfather, like most of the tribe, based his life on such beliefs. And my father, he believes some of the legends still. Besides, it's not just a question of what I believe. Little by little my people are adopting the white man's ways. We are a disappearing people."

"Things aren't like that," Scott argued. "If something is true, then it's true, and if it's not, then it's not. It doesn't matter whose grandfather believed what."

Swift Arrow shook his head. "Only a white man would say something like that."

"But you can't believe something just because your grandfather believed it. That doesn't make sense. Don't let that trick you into running away."

Swift Arrow nodded slowly. "Much of what you say is true. Maybe ... maybe I'm just afraid."

"Well now, being afraid is something I can relate to." Scott grinned. He couldn't help throwing a look over to the charred remains of the picnic table. "And there's nothing wrong with being afraid, especially when it comes to this kind of stuff. But God can handle even our fear. If we let him."

Swift Arrow stared at Scott for a long moment. Finally, he spoke. "I don't know how you people came to me. I don't know who this Z is—though I have a friend who is into computers with whom I have spoken about these problems. Perhaps he knows your Z. Then again, maybe you are simply angels who have come to help me."

"Whoa!" Scott protested. "I'm no angel."

"That's for sure!"

Scott turned to see Becka and Ryan approaching from the road.

Swift Arrow laughed. "Maybe not, but you bring messages from on high, and they help keep me to the path."

"We call that being a friend," Scott said with a grin.

Swift Arrow returned the smile, but it slowly faded, and he let out a long sigh. "Well then, my friends, I must tell you. This friend of yours is afraid. He is afraid to face Dark Bear, and he is afraid not to."

👁 👁

Later that evening, Mom, Becka, and Scott stood around the telephone, which rested on the worn wooden counter of the general store. Scott had his laptop up and running, trying to contact Z.

"After all," he said, punching up the number, "Z's the one who got us into this mess. Hopefully he'll have an idea how to get us out."

Becka glanced out the window. The sun had already set, and it was getting steadily darker. "I just wish Ryan were here," she said quietly. "This could be really important."

"He's out with Little Creek looking at more Indian stuff," Scott said as he typed away.

"Again?" Becka sighed.

"I know," Scott agreed. "It's like the guy can never get enough. He loves everything about Indians. What they eat, where they live, what they believe …"

"That's what I mean," Becka said. "It's like he's completely carried away with it. I just wish he were here to talk to Z."

"I do too. But if Swift Arrow's going to do anything before Dark Bear's council, it should be soon. We'll just have to fill Ryan in later."

Becka nodded. She knew Scott was right. She just wished he wasn't.

Moments later the familiar Internet logo came up on the laptop screen.

"Got him!" Scott exclaimed. "We're both online."

Mom and Becka moved in closer to watch. They'd talked to Z dozens of times and had received dozens of pieces of advice. But contacting the mysterious stranger was always an important event for them. One they never seemed to tire of.

After Scott filled Z in on all that had happened, there was a long pause. Finally, the words of Z's answer began to form:

There is a spiritual battle raging. Much is at stake. Swift Arrow has been called to bring his people the gospel. Dark Bear will never allow it.

Scott reached for the keyboard and typed:

Then what should we do?

As they waited for a reply, there was a rumble of thunder in the distance. Becka glanced out the window. "Looks like the wind's picking up."

As if in answer, lightning flashed again, followed seconds later by a much louder clap of thunder.

Scott sighed impatiently. "What's taking him so long to respond?" For the briefest second the lights in the store dimmed and the computer screen flickered. "Oh no," Scott groaned.

"What's wrong?" Mom asked.

"The phone line may be going." But the screen stabilized, and Scott said, "It's coming back." And then a moment later, "Ah, here we go."

Once again Becka leaned forward to read the words as they came on:

You have encountered situations similar to this. You know your authority. Swift Arrow need not be afraid. However, be careful not to underestimate Dark Bear's power.

Scott and Becka exchanged glances. But Z wasn't finished.

Did you receive the Bible verse?

Scott typed:

Yes, but we didn't understand. Who's it for? What does it mean?

Once again the lights and the screen flickered, and once again power returned. Mom, Becka, and Scott watched as Z's answer formed.

You are waging two battles. One is offense, the other defense. I am very concerned that one of you is about to fall. And if one falls, you all will fall.

Quickly Scott typed:

Who are you concerned about?

No answer. Scott tried again.

Z? Z, who are you concerned about?

And then once again the verse formed.

"The Spirit clearly says that in later times some will abandon the faith and follow deceiving spirits and things taught by demons." 1 Timothy 4:1

Scott let out a sigh of frustration and typed:

Yes, yes, we have that verse, but what are we supposed to

Scott never finished. There was another flash of lightning, and the telephone line went dead. The computer was disconnected.

7

The next morning Swift Arrow came to their camp at daybreak. "I have decided to call a council of my own a day before Dark Bear's. I will speak to the people about my beliefs."

"Hey, that's great," Scott said.

Swift Arrow nodded. "But I need your help to get the word out."

"We can do that," Becka said. "When will it be?"

"It must be tonight. For it is tomorrow that Dark Bear will try to incite the people to drive us out."

Scott and Becka agreed to spend the morning going through the village and telling everyone about the meeting. At least that was their plan. Unfortunately they ended up spending most of that time looking for Ryan. Apparently he'd taken off before sunrise with Little Creek, and no one knew where they had gone. And now Becka wasn't just kind of worried. She was really worried.

"This is a waste of time," Scott complained. "We need to tell the village about Swift Arrow's council. We'd better forget about Ryan until later."

Becka sighed. Forgetting about Ryan was the last thing she

wanted to do, but she knew her little brother had a point. "I suppose you're right. I just feel like he should be with us, that's all."

Scott nodded. "I know. But we'll look for him later. I promise."

It didn't take long for the two to visit the people of the village. In less than an hour they had nearly finished going up and down the rows of small homes, speaking to the people they met. Whenever they encountered a villager who wasn't quite as fluent in English, they showed a message Swift Arrow had written out for them in the tribal language. In fact, they were showing this very note to an old woman when Dark Bear himself stepped out from behind the door of the house.

When Becka saw the shaman, she went cold. He looked even more menacing close-up than when he was perched high atop the rock. He approached them, his eyes steely and full of rage. Instinctively, Scott and Becka stepped back.

"Depart from here," he growled. "This is not your battle. It's about the ways of my people."

After a moment Becka finally found her voice. When she did, she was surprised at how even and controlled it sounded. "No. That's not all that this is about."

"Beck ...," Scott warned.

But she had already started, and there was no backing down. "It's about truth. Spiritual truth. And that is the same for everyone."

Dark Bear glared at her. "You risk much, girl ... This is not your fight."

Becka was breathing harder now, but she forced herself to continue, trying to stay collected and calm. "Listen, Mr ... Dark Bear. Why don't you come to Swift Arrow's council tonight? Not to fight, but just to listen to what he says. Later, after you've heard Swift Arrow's side, maybe you can decide what's really right for your people to believe."

She waited for an answer as Dark Bear's eyes shifted from her to Scott. She wasn't sure what he was looking at ... until she heard the choking sounds.

She turned to see Scott holding his throat with both hands. He was gasping for breath.

"Scott!" she cried. "Scotty, what's wrong?"

But Scott couldn't answer. All he could do was gasp, pointing to his throat, trying to catch his breath.

Becka spun back to Dark Bear. She'd seen this before in past encounters. And she knew the solution. The shaman's gaze was fierce, intimidating, but she knew who had the real authority. "Release him!" she ordered.

Dark Bear glared at her, but she would not back down. "In the name and power of the Lord Jesus Christ, I command you to release him."

At first Dark Bear smiled, but then, as Becka stood her ground, he realized she meant business. Slowly his smile faded.

Scott coughed loudly and started breathing, dragging in deep gulps of air. Becka glanced at him. She knew the choking was a tactic to try to scare them. But she also knew that, because they were committed believers in Christ, Dark Bear had no real power over them. These were just more "special effects" in an attempt to frighten them. And they weren't going to work.

Becka smiled at Scott, and he nodded. They turned to face Dark Bear, to continue the encounter ... but the medicine man had disappeared.

👁 👁

Ryan and Little Creek sat cross-legged in the coolness of the cave. Little Creek had lit a small lantern, and the light hit the wall. Immediately, the painting of the great warrior hunting the buffalo appeared in the light. Ryan stared intently at the warrior's face. Was Dark Bear really a direct descendant of this brave as he'd claimed?

Ryan's thoughts were interrupted as Little Creek took a small flask from his shirt pocket. "It's the tea I told you about," Little Creek said, smiling.

"Tea?" Ryan repeated.

"Yes, remember? I said it will help you better hear the call of the Great Spirit." He leaned toward Ryan and held the flask out.

Ryan hesitated.

"Don't worry. There is only a small amount of the red berries in this mixture."

"Red berries?" Ryan asked, staring at the flask.

"Yes. It is berries that give the tea its hallucinogenic powers. I just put a little bit in because this is your first time. It won't hurt you, honest."

Again Little Creek held it out to him, and again Ryan hesitated.

"It's okay. I promise. You're a spiritual person, Ryan. It will be easy for you to contact the Great Spirit, but you must do so with the tea."

The little tug hit Ryan again, telling him it was wrong, to be careful ... But weren't they all talking about the same God, the one and only Great Spirit? And if this were really a way to connect with God, if he could combine the best of both worlds—his Christian faith and this spiritual ritual with the tea—then what was the harm?

Little Creek continued holding the flask out to him. "If you really want to understand our ways, this is the fastest and easiest method. Please, it is okay. I promise."

Ryan watched as his hand reached out to take the flask. It was almost like watching someone else. Then he raised it to his lips. He hesitated and looked at Little Creek one last time. The boy smiled, and Ryan opened his mouth to drink the tea.

For a while nothing happened. As before, they discussed the history of Little Creek's tribe, his beliefs, and his heritage. Then Ryan felt a wave of dizziness. At first he shrugged it off. They had left camp before breakfast, and he was getting pretty hungry. It was only natural that he would feel a little light-headed.

Then he noticed something else. On the cave painting. He hadn't seen it before, but in the right-hand corner perched on a cliff was an eagle. It was so small, it was no wonder he hadn't noticed it before. But as he watched, the bird started to grow.

Ryan turned to Little Creek and tried to tell him, but the words wouldn't come. "Thhhhe paintttting . . ." was all he managed to slur.

Little Creek smiled. "Relax, my friend. The tea is taking effect. Focus inward, and see what the Great Spirit will show you."

Ryan couldn't focus on anything. He felt like he was going to throw up. His head began to spin, and his stomach started to churn. When he looked back at the painting, the eagle appeared as large as the hunter. What was worse, its wings moved in a steady rhythm!

Ryan closed his eyes, hoping to force himself back into reality. It was as if he were looking over the edge of a very high cliff or stumbling through a dark tunnel knowing that there was a great hole somewhere in front of him . . . a huge chasm that went on forever. If he wasn't careful, he would stumble and fall to certain death.

When he reopened his eyes, the eagle loomed so large that one of its wings pushed out of the painting, extending across the cave wall.

Ryan's heart began to pound. He started breathing rapidly. What if the drug didn't wear off? What if it damaged him? What if he had to live like this, with his brain scrambled, for the rest of his life?

Or, worse yet, what if the images he was seeing were real?

All of these thoughts froze when the eagle turned its lifeless eye directly toward him. It had seen him. Ryan was sure of it.

Just as he was sure that it wanted him. Slowly, with great effort, it detached itself from the wall and started flying toward him.

With open beak, it drew closer and closer. Ryan covered his face. And still, somehow, he could see it coming—its jet-black, lifeless eyes growing larger and larger as it flew closer. Suddenly Ryan realized it wasn't the creature's beak but its eye that was going to devour him. That eye was going to absorb him, swallow him ...

The eye ... the eye ... the eye ... the eye ...

👁 👁

Two hours later, Ryan woke up. He lay outside the cave, vaguely aware that Little Creek was wiping his forehead with a damp handkerchief.

"How are you feeling?" Little Creek asked.

Ryan bobbed his head. "I don't know. Woozy, I guess. How did I get out here?"

"You got up and started to run. We were just sitting there looking at the painting when you jumped up and tried to run. You managed a few steps before you crashed into the wall. It knocked you out cold."

Ryan winced as he touched the lump on his forehead. "That would explain this headache."

"I carried you out here hoping the fresh air and sunlight would help. You've been sleeping for a long time."

Already memories of the vision were returning. "I—I saw an eagle," Ryan stammered.

"An eagle?" Little Creek's mouth dropped open. "Really?"

Ryan nodded. "It flew out of the painting right at me."

"There is no eagle in that painting," Little Creek said, unable to hold back his excitement.

"But I'm sure—"

"No, no, but this is a wondrous sign. The Great Spirit is sending the eagle to you. This means he has much to teach you!"

"Really?"

Little Creek smiled broadly. "I was right! You *are* an initiate. The Great Spirit will use you in many ways. Congratulations!" Little Creek extended his hand toward Ryan.

Ryan looked at it for a moment and then shook it warmly. "Thanks," he murmured. It was hard not to catch Little Creek's excitement. So he had been chosen. Chosen by the Great Spirit himself. And the eagle, the eagle was coming . . . coming just for him!

As evening approached, most of the village turned out for Swift Arrow's council. Scott and Becka stayed in the background since they didn't want their friendship with him to cause a problem. He had already been accused of following the ways of the white man, and having two white kids by his side probably wouldn't help him much. Still, from their vantage point they could see most of the tribe and enjoy looking at all the ceremonial clothing.

"I wish Ryan were here," Becka sighed for the hundredth time. "He would love this."

"Yeah," Scott said, apparently barely listening. "Check out that fellow over there. He must have a thousand feathers."

Becka turned to see a tall brave wearing a full headdress made of bright red feathers from head to toe. "Wow!" she exclaimed. "He looks awesome."

Scott nodded. "But he must have wiped out the entire cardinal population from here to the Arizona state line."

"Those aren't cardinal feathers." Becka almost laughed. "They dye the feathers to get them that color."

"Oh yeah," Scott said, obviously trying to cover his ignorance, "I knew that."

Becka smiled.

"But the thing that really gets me is—"

"Shh," she said, "Swift Arrow is talking again. Listen."

They directed their attention back to the clearing where Swift Arrow stood on a tree stump, trying to explain Christianity to his people. "You need not be afraid of angry gods," he was saying. "There is only one God, and he is a loving God. The Father of us all."

There was a quiet buzz among the people. Swift Arrow continued, "The evil in the world comes from the devil. But he is not all-powerful. He is only a fallen angel. You do not have to make sacrifices to him for protection. All you have to do is believe in God's Son, Jesus Christ. He came down from heaven to die for what we have done wrong. He came to suffer and take the punishment for our sins. We need only believe in him and ask him to be our chief, our Lord. We need only obey him and accept his free gift of salvation in order that we might have everlasting peace with our Father."

"What of the teachings of our ancestors?" a tall brave with three feathers in his hair demanded.

"It is as you've always suspected," Swift Arrow answered. "Some of it is true, and some of it is false. Dark Bear has twisted the teachings to suit himself. He is keeping you from the real truth."

Scott leaned over to Becka and whispered, "He preaches a pretty good sermon."

Becka nodded as she searched the crowd.

"Who are you looking for?" Scott asked.

"Dark Bear. I was hoping he'd at least drop by for a listen."

"Or a major showdown," Scott added.

"Well, even that might have been okay. But if he's not here, where is he? What is he up to?"

          👁 👁

Not far away, at the site of the avalanche and Dark Bear's holy place, a small fire burned. And Dark Bear danced around that fire furiously. He paused only for a moment, just long enough to throw an angry look back toward Swift Arrow's council. And then, ever so slowly, he reached into the satchel hanging around his neck. He pulled out a handful of fine, blue powder, then tossed it into the fire.

There was a loud whoosh as flames shot high into the sky, then immediately died down. Once again, Dark Bear lowered his head and began dancing ... and chanting ...

"Jesus Christ is not the white man's God." Swift Arrow continued speaking to the crowd, and some were beginning to listen. "He is everyone's God. He was born a Jew and lived and died in Palestine two thousand years ago — nearly fifteen hundred years before the white man came and drove us from our land. The white man has embraced his truth, yes, but so have millions of Chinese, Africans, Latin Americans, and people all over the world. The God of the Bible is not the God of the white man. He is the God of *all* people."

A loud crack of thunder jolted the group. Instinctively, Swift Arrow turned toward Dark Bear's holy place. In the distance, he could see the reflection of a fire as it burned. Against the cliffs, he could make out the flickering of a shadow ... the shadow of a man dancing.

Swift Arrow forced himself to continue. "It is not my fault that the rain has not come. It is not a punishment from the gods. Dark Bear has misled you."

A handful of people nodded their heads in agreement. A few coughed lightly. Soft at first, the coughing grew until it was obvious someone was starting to choke.

Becka tensed. It was the same choking Scott had experienced earlier. Now others were starting to cough and gasp for breath.

Becka threw a look to Scott. This was not good. Not good

at all. One, two, a handful of people dropped to their knees, coughing, choking, and struggling to breathe. And to make matters worse, they were the very ones who had been nodding their heads in agreement. "Dark Bear," Becka whispered.

"We'd better do something fast."

"Like what? What can we do?"

"Satan," Scott spoke softly, "in the name of Jesus Christ, we command you to stop this coughing."

"That's right," Becka whispered in agreement. "In the name of Christ, we demand that you stop this attack."

Scott nodded. "Whatever evil is at work here, we remind you that the name of Jesus is stronger than any other name, and it is by his name that we order you to leave and command that peace and health be restored back to these people. Now. We command you to leave now!"

Immediately, the coughing subsided. While a few people remained on the ground, trying to recover their wits, others rose and began to breathe normally. Most, however, were simply anxious to leave. They knew what had happened, and they wanted no more of it. They started moving, shoving, and trying to get as far away from Swift Arrow's council as possible.

Swift Arrow watched helplessly as his people left the clearing and headed for their homes. He looked broken and defeated. His council was over. And if anything had been proven, it was that Dark Bear's strength and influence were more powerful than his own.

8

Before going to bed that night, Becka and Scott offered to pray with Swift Arrow. He clearly felt defeated, and they wanted to encourage him.

"Listen," Becka told him, "when things get the toughest, that's when God works his greatest miracles."

"That's right," Scott agreed. "When we're our weakest, that's when he's the strongest."

Swift Arrow nodded, but it was obvious his heart was anything but encouraged. He had finally worked up the courage to face Dark Bear, and all he had been met with was defeat.

"Dear Lord," Becka prayed as they bowed their heads together, "we know you shine brightest in the darkest places. And right now, at least on the surface, everything looks bad. We ask—we pray in Jesus' name—that you step in now. That you take what our enemy has chosen for evil and turn it around for good. We ask this because of your great love for us and for this whole village. We ask this in your Son's precious and holy name. Amen."

Scott and Swift Arrow joined in saying amen. Then, before they headed off to bed, all three agreed to pray again first thing in the morning. Becka could see that that gave Swift Arrow some assurance, but she was still concerned. About Ryan.

She hadn't seen him all day, and her worries had only increased. She chose to wait up for him. It was nearly ten o'clock when he finally lumbered into camp. He looked very tired, and there was a strangely distant look in his eyes.

"We missed you tonight," Becka said as he approached, heading for his tent.

He slowed to a stop but said nothing.

She tried again. "You would have really loved the council. Swift Arrow made a great speech, and you should have seen all the people dressed in their outfits."

"Ceremonial clothes," Ryan corrected her.

"Right, ceremonial clothes. It was great." She waited for him to say something else, but when he didn't, she finally asked, "Where were you?"

"Off with Little Creek. He's teaching me a lot of stuff."

It was Becka's turn to remain quiet. The silence grew.

"Listen," Ryan finally said, "I'm sorry I haven't been around very much lately, but I'm really trying to make the most of this trip."

"Sure," Becka answered hesitantly, not really understanding. By "making the most of this trip," did he mean staying away from her? Was he saying he wanted to cool off their relationship? Or was it something else? Was it more about God than about her? There was so much she wanted to ask Ryan. Maybe another moonlight stroll on the ridge would help. Maybe there he could finally open up and share what he was feeling. She was just about to suggest it when he turned abruptly and started for his tent.

"Ryan ..."

He turned back toward her. "What?"

But the words would not come. She shrugged. "Nothing."

He started to turn, but she had to say something.

"Just ... we could sure use your support tomorrow. Dark Bear did a real number at Swift Arrow's council tonight. People were choking and gasping for air and everything. And tomorrow night is Dark Bear's council. So we're going to get together first thing in the morning and pray with Swift Arrow."

Ryan nodded absently. "I'll try to be there. Listen, it's getting pretty late ..."

Becka shrugged again. "Of course, back home we'd consider this too early to go to bed."

"Yeah," Ryan answered, "but things are a lot different here than back home."

They certainly were, Becka thought.

"Well ... good night." And then, without another word, he stooped down and disappeared into his tent.

Becka sat there trying to swallow back the tightness growing in her throat. Maybe it really was over between them. Maybe he really did want to call it quits. She closed her eyes. Actually, that would be good news compared to her other fear. The fear that something was coming between Ryan and God.

"'In later times some will abandon the faith,'" Z had quoted. "'They will follow deceiving spirits and things taught by demons.'"

She took a deep breath and let it out. She knew whom Z was talking about. Something was happening to Ryan. Something spiritual. And something very, very evil ...

❧ ❧

Aaaooowlll ...

The wind blew strongly that night. It howled through the canyon, making it impossible for Ryan to sleep. He lay awake, his mind running in a thousand directions at once. What he'd experienced in the cave ... was that really the Great Spirit choosing him? And was the Great Spirit really God, the same God he had learned to follow and love as a Christian? But if it was the same God, why did he feel so uneasy? And yet why was he so attracted to it, so anxious to go deeper, to connect more fully with it, with this ... spirit?

Aaaooowlll ...

Scott bolted up in his sleeping bag, even though he looked like he was still half asleep. "What was that?" he mumbled.

"I think it's the wind," Ryan said.

"I don't know," Scott muttered. "I was dreaming about a wolf. Maybe it's a wolf."

Aaaooowlll ...

"Whatever it is, it's down in the canyon," Ryan said. "Maybe it's Dark Bear. Little Creek says some of the old shamans could change themselves into animals—usually wolves or bears. They call it ... shape-shifting."

Scott didn't answer, and Ryan realized he had already drifted back to sleep.

Aaaooowlll ...

Ryan knew it was no wolf. But he also knew it was more than the wind. There was something inside it, something calling. Something connected to the eagle. Something calling him ...

Unable to sleep and growing more and more attracted to the sound, Ryan quietly crawled from his sleeping bag, slipped on his clothes, and stepped out into the night.

It was exhilarating. The stars. The full moon. The wind. He'd barely stepped out of the tent, drinking it all in, when the cry came again.

Aaaooowlll ...

For the briefest second, he thought it was Little Creek signaling him. But this was something far deeper and more important. He sensed that it was somehow connected to the Great Spirit. Feeling the pull more strongly, he finally gave in to the impulse. He began walking toward Dark Bear's holy place.

Ever since the avalanche, he had wanted to go back to the place of stones. And since the encounter with the eagle in the cave, the desire had become irresistible.

As he walked, Ryan reached into his jacket pocket. The flask Little Creek had given him was still there. Ryan knew he had another choice awaiting him. He could continue being what he now thought was a coward—he could continue going only halfway, being caught between the two worlds and never finding out the truth. Or he could have the courage to go all the way, to see what was really out there, to totally give in and see what the Great Spirit really had in store.

With a deep breath, he chose the latter. He shook the flask, making sure there was still plenty of tea left. He unscrewed the lid. The warning bells went off again, but this time they were faint, barely discernible. Still, just to be certain, he lifted the flask to his lips and quickly drank down the tea before he could change his mind.

There … now he'd done it. In just a few minutes, it would begin.

It wasn't long before the canyon began to shift and move, almost like it was a living organism. The wind continued its howling, but now he could hear the voices clearly. Human voices. By the time he arrived at the place of stones, the tea's effect was incredible. Ryan looked up. There, just as he had expected, perched on the highest rock, was the magnificent eagle.

It sat there majestically, looking at him, waiting for him. And then, a moment later, it spread out its giant wings.

Instinctively, Ryan extended his own arms as if he, too, had wings.

Then they were flying. Together. Soaring over the great peaks and canyons, taking turns diving into the valley. Circling higher and higher and higher.

And then Ryan slept.

◈ ◈

Becka was up at dawn. She dressed and headed for the boys' tent. This was the morning of prayer, when they would join together and intercede for Swift Arrow, against Dark Bear. This was when the job would really be done. But when Becka got to the tent and saw the open flap door, she knew Ryan was gone.

"Scott!" she called. She reached in and shook him. "Scotty, wake up!"

"Wha-what?"

"Where's Ryan?" she demanded. "Where did Ryan go?"

Scott roused himself a bit and looked over at Ryan's sleeping bag. "He's ... Where'd he go?" Scott frowned, trying to remember. "The wolf."

"What are you talking about?"

"He left last night." Scott reached for his shirt. "Give me a sec, and I'll help you look for him."

A minute later the two were off looking for Ryan.

"What were you saying about wolves?" Becka asked.

"I don't remember. I mean, it sounded like a wolf."

"There was a wolf out here?" Becka cried in alarm. "You let him go out and see if there was a wolf?"

Scott rubbed his head. "No ... that was the dream part. At least, I think it was a dream. But I do remember the wind howling and him getting up in the middle of the night."

"We've got to find him," Becka said. "Something's wrong. I know it."

But they didn't find him. The two looked everywhere in the village but with no success. And since they didn't see Little Creek, they assumed he and Ryan were together.

"I think we need to talk to Z again," Becka finally said. "That Bible verse he gave us—I'm pretty sure I understand it now."

"You do?"

"I think part of it is a warning for Ryan."

"Let me head back to the tent and get my laptop," Scott said. "I'll meet you at the general store in five minutes."

Becka agreed, and in less than half that time, they were again connecting the computer to the store's phone outlet.

When Scott logged on, Z was not there, but his answer was already waiting:

Remember, you are fighting two battles ... one offense, the other defense. Regardless of the fight, your weapons are the same: prayer and the Word of God. Activate these weapons through faith. If you do, you will be victorious. If you do not, you will perish.

Z

Ryan woke up in the cave. He wasn't sure how he'd gotten there until he saw Little Creek by the dim light of the lantern.

"Hello," Little Creek said. "I found you asleep on top of the stones in Dark Bear's holy place. I couldn't rouse you, and I was afraid you'd be blistered by the sun, so I dragged you in here."

"I'm in the cave *again?*" Ryan groaned.

Little Creek chuckled. "Yeah. If I'm to be your personal taxi and haul you from place to place, I'll have to start charging a fare."

Ryan smiled, and Little Creek asked, "You took the tea again, didn't you?"

Ryan slowly sat up, then looked deep into his friend's eyes. "I flew with the eagle."

"No!" Little Creek cried in astonishment. "Really?"

Ryan nodded.

"You flew with the eagle? I only know one other who has done such a thing. What was it like?"

"It was ..." Ryan paused, remembering. And then he grinned. "Incredible."

When Becka and Scott returned to their tent, they found Swift Arrow already waiting with their mom.

"Before we start our prayer," Swift Arrow said quietly, "I must say I'm not even certain I have heard correctly from the Lord."

"What do you mean?" Mom asked gently.

Swift Arrow frowned. "How do I even know this is what the Lord wants?"

"Swift Arrow," Becka began, "we just got off the Internet with Z. He says we have two tools—the Bible and prayer. You know the Word; you know God wants to reach your village with his love. He wants to reach everybody."

Swift Arrow looked down. "I know God wants the people of Starved Rock to be saved. But perhaps ... I'm not the man to do it. I am too timid, too weak."

"No way," Scott protested. "David was just a punk kid when God used him against Goliath. He was weak, but he was strong because his strength depended upon God."

Swift Arrow nodded. "But David was a man of great faith."

"What about Moses?" Mom added. "He had so little faith he didn't want the job God asked him to do. Or Jonah. He tried to get out of what God had called him for. The Bible couldn't be clearer, Swift Arrow. God uses whom he chooses. It doesn't have to make sense to us, just to God. All you have to do is be willing to obey."

Swift Arrow looked at the three of them. "I guess I'd better start agreeing with you or you will never stop preaching at me. Am I correct?"

Scott and Becka both broke out laughing. Mom grinned along with them.

"You got that right," Scott agreed.

"Just tell us you'll obey God's Word and not give up," Becka said.

Swift Arrow almost smiled. "All right, all right. I will obey. I will not give up."

"That's all it takes," Mom said.

"But what should I do?"

"Follow Z's advice," Becka said. "We know what the Word of God says about this situation. Now all that is left is to pray."

"May we begin?" Swift Arrow asked.

"Let's do it," Scott said.

And so the four began to pray … At first they started off with quiet worshiping, thanking God for his past faithfulness. Then they sang a couple of worship songs that they all knew. And finally, they began thanking the Lord in advance for what he was about to do. They weren't sure what the details would be, but they were sure of one thing: It would be awesome. It always was when God did something.

But even as they prayed, even as they prepared for whatever that night would bring, Becka could not shake the nagging feeling in the back of her mind.

Ryan was in danger.

9

It was nearly lunchtime when Ryan returned to camp. Becka was lighting the grill to cook hot dogs. When she saw Ryan and Little Creek, she leaped to her feet and raced to Ryan.

"Where have you been? I've been worried about you ... Where did you go?"

Ryan threw her a glance. For the first time she could remember, he looked angry at her. "I just went out, okay? Your brother thought he heard a noise, and I went out to investigate."

"What did you find?"

He looked at her strangely. "Where?"

"When you went out to investigate. What did you find?"

Ryan shrugged. "Nothing."

"Then why didn't you come back? Why weren't you here for prayer with Swift Arrow, like you said you would be?"

Finally, Ryan exploded. "Will you stop trying to own me?"

A moment of silence followed. Part of Becka wanted to turn and run away, but there was something wrong here, and she had to get to the bottom of it. When she answered, she was surprised at how calm and controlled her voice sounded. "I just asked where you were."

"I was busy," he snapped.

Becka stood, unsure what to do. She was grateful when Mom, always the peacekeeper, called out from her place near the grill, "Ryan ... are you guys hungry? We've got plenty of hot dogs here. What about you, Little Creek? You must be starved."

"Thanks," Ryan said softly. "I'm famished."

"Me too," Little Creek added.

After lunch Mom headed back to the store for some groceries, and Scott and Little Creek decided to gather up firewood for the evening. That left Becka sitting by herself, staring off into the mountains.

"Beautiful, aren't they?" Ryan said softly from behind her.

Becka sighed. "Yeah, I suppose."

"You suppose?" he asked as he crossed to the log and joined her.

She gave no answer.

"Look," Ryan began, "I know I let you down this morning."

Becka said nothing.

"But the reason we're out here is for spiritual stuff, isn't it? I'm just trying to learn all these cool things God is showing me."

Becka looked at him, meeting his eyes for the first time. "How do you know that?"

"How do I know it's cool? Because Little Creek has been—"

"No," Becka interrupted. "How do you know *God* is showing you these things?"

Ryan shook his head. "Don't be afraid of stuff just because it's different, Beck."

"I'm not afraid, but I'm not taking dangerous chances either."

"Who's taking chances?" There was no missing the edge in Ryan's voice. "I'm just learning about another culture."

"By trying out all its rituals?" Becka asked. "After all we've been through, that sounds pretty risky to me."

Ryan looked away. She'd hit a nerve, and she knew it.

Suddenly he was on his feet. "I knew you'd take it this way," he muttered angrily. "I was hoping to be able to share with you some of the wonderful experiences I've been having, but of course you're judging me before I can get a word out."

He started walking away, but now Becka was on her feet. "Then why don't you tell me?" He stopped, and she continued, "You're right, Ryan. I am being judgmental, but it's because I don't know anything you've been doing. I mean, what do you and Little Creek do out there all day? Where do you go?"

Before Ryan could answer, Scott and Little Creek appeared, each carrying an armload of firewood.

"Hey, guys," Scott said. "What's up?"

"Your sister," Ryan grumbled. "As usual, she's up in her ivory tower trying to tell the rest of us what to do."

Becka bit her lip. She felt hot tears spring to her eyes, but she would not let Ryan see her cry. Not now. Not here.

Ryan spun around and headed back out, away from camp. Little Creek dumped his load of firewood and started after him. "Hey, Ryan! Ryan, wait up."

A long moment of silence followed. Now the tears were spilling onto Becka's cheeks. But that was okay because now there was nobody to see them.

"Hey, Beck . . ." Nobody but Scott. "Becka, you all right?"

She nodded without looking at him. "Yeah." Her voice was hoarse with emotion. "Yeah, I'm okay."

"Did you find out what's eating him?"

Becka shook her head.

He sighed loudly. "That's too bad." Then he turned and walked away.

Becka was grateful that Scott was leaving because she had

made up her mind. If Ryan wouldn't tell her what he was up to, she would find out for herself.

It wasn't difficult to follow Ryan and Little Creek out of the village and into the mountains. Knowing Little Creek's keen senses, Becka gave the boys plenty of leeway so they wouldn't see or hear her. Soon they arrived at what she took to be Dark Bear's holy place. It fit what they'd described ... and it gave her the creeps. The ground was still covered from the avalanche. She looked at the stones and frowned. There was a pattern in the way they lay on the ground.

Dark Bear had been hard at work.

Just then Little Creek and Ryan veered off the path and headed into the weeds. Becka followed. The brush and grass were up to her chest, and it was hard not to lose track of the guys while trying to walk as quietly as possible.

They were approaching a tall, looming cliff. The ground sloped steeply, and she struggled to keep her footing as she followed them. Eventually they came to the base of the cliff. At the bottom was a round, dark shadow ... a cave.

Crouching low in the weeds, Becka watched Ryan and Little Creek enter the cave. She wondered how far it went, if she could follow them in without being spotted—or getting lost. It was worth the risk. She silently crossed to the cave, took a look inside, and then entered.

It was entirely dark inside, except for the reflection of Little Creek's light up ahead. Carefully, Becka inched her way along the cave floor, trying to keep quiet and yet trying to keep the light in view. But she could not do both. The light was moving too quickly. For one brief moment she wanted to run back to the entrance before she was plunged into total darkness, but she fought off the impulse. She'd come this far, and she wasn't about to back down now.

She glanced back toward the dim light. To her relief, it no longer seemed to be moving. The guys must have stopped. She scurried along, trying to be as quiet as possible. She eased forward little by little until, finally, she saw them.

Ryan and Little Creek were building a fire in the middle of a large, open cavern. The flames came to life, lighting the cavern and creating dancing shadows on the walls. Becka watched as Little Creek took a small flask out of his bag and handed it to Ryan. "Are you sure you want to take it again so close to the last time?"

Ryan nodded and silently reached for the flask. He unscrewed the lid, tilted his head back, and drank. When he finished, he handed the flask to Little Creek and asked, "Will you stay?"

The Indian shook his head. "It is your time," he said almost reverently. "I will go, but I will leave the light."

Ryan gave a single nod. "Thank you, my brother."

Little Creek turned and headed back out of the cavern, toward Becka. She pressed herself flat against the opposite wall as the boy approached. Without a light, she knew it would be difficult for him to see her. As long as she remained low and quiet, he would pass and she would remain unnoticed. She held her breath as he moved past her.

It seemed like minutes before she could no longer hear his steps. Then, ever so carefully, she eased back around the corner. Ryan now stood in the center of the large cavern. He was looking intently at a wall about ten feet away. From what she could see of his expression, she had the terrible feeling that whatever he'd drunk was some sort of drug ... and that it had already started to take effect. He was staring at the wall as if he were seeing something, but there was nothing there.

Or was there?

For the briefest second she thought she saw movement. It was up above, more toward the center of the cavern. She caught the flicker of something ... a shadow. It disappeared as quickly as it had appeared, but there was no mistaking its form. It appeared to be a giant eagle.

She saw it again, longer this time. It was a misty apparition, half-solid, half-transparent. Becka gasped, and a chill of dread swept over her. It was the eagle from her dreams. Her heart began to pound as she watched it circle above the cavern.

Then she noticed something even more frightening: the crevices and cracks of the cavern's ceiling formed a pattern — the same pattern she had seen covering the sky in her dreams! The lines, triangles, and squares were arranged in the same swirling, concentric design.

Then, just as in her dream, the eagle's harsh cry rang out. She watched in terror as the ghost bird hovered one last moment before beginning its dive.

It was headed directly for Ryan!

"Ryan!" Her cry echoed through the cavern. "Ryan, look out!" He turned toward her — not much, but enough to save him from the bird's talons, which flew past, missing his face by inches.

Becka was on her feet, running toward him. "Ryan! Run, Ryan! Get out of here!"

He stared at her, his face full of confusion, as though he didn't know who she was, why she was there.

The eagle rose toward the ceiling, preparing for another assault. Once again Becka noted how translucent it was — there and yet *not* there. But she had little time to ponder this as it turned and began another dive.

She wouldn't reach Ryan, not in time. All she could do was pray. "Be gone, dark spirit!" she shouted. "You have no power over a servant of Christ!"

At the mention of Christ's name, the eagle shrieked.

Becka watched in astonishment as the bird suddenly changed shape. The eagle's sleek and elegant form mutated before her eyes. Its wings remained, but the colorful feathers turned to crusty, black leather. At the same time, the creature's legs grew to thick, stubby knobs and its talons grew longer—sharper and more deadly.

But the greatest change was the bird's head. The smooth crown rippled into craggy bone and flesh, taking on a hideous appearance that was part toad, part gargoyle.

Instantly Becka recognized it. She'd seen its kind before, on more than one occasion. And although she felt a cold shiver ripple down her spine, she knew what to do.

She planted her feet firmly and shouted, "Demon of hell, in the name of Jesus Christ, I command you to leave this place!"

👁 👁

Ryan stood watching, unable to move. He felt as if he were in a dream. He knew what was happening, but he couldn't react. All he could do was stare at Becka as she took her stand. But then, behind her, he saw something else. Another movement.

Dark Bear had entered the cavern.

Ryan wanted to yell, to warn her, but the drug wouldn't allow him to speak. He watched in terror as Dark Bear crept up behind Becka and raised his staff. Desperately Ryan tried to move his mouth, his lips, anything to make a noise, to warn her. But no sound would come.

He watched helplessly as Dark Bear brought the staff down hard onto Becka's head. She slumped to the floor, unconscious. Ryan continued to stare as the shaman picked up Becka and carried her back toward an area of the cavern he had never explored. Again Ryan tried to cry out, to move, but again he could make no sound. He could make no movement. Now the cave was starting to spin, to twirl. It began to rotate, starting to fly. Hit by a wave of nausea, Ryan dropped to his knees. He convulsed once, twice, before throwing up. He looked up and caught one final glimpse of Becka. Still in Dark Bear's arms, still being carried off to her death.

And still he could not move. A moment later, he passed out.

10

When Ryan awoke, the effects of the drug had not entirely worn off. His head was still spinning, and the first time he tried to stand, he fell back to the ground. He got up again more slowly—much more slowly—as memories flooded in.

Becka! I have to find Rebecca.

With great difficulty, he staggered to the wall where he'd seen Dark Bear carry her. It was solid rock. Had it been another hallucination? He wasn't sure. Carefully, he felt for an opening, a crack. There was nothing.

Without warning his stomach contracted as nausea again overwhelmed him. He felt awful. But even though his body was weak, his mind continued to race with both fear and regret. If he hadn't taken the tea, he could have saved Becka.

Why did he do it? He knew it was stupid to take drugs. And wrong. He'd even studied this kind of thing. The Bible referred to it as *pharmakeia* ... It was a sin similar to witchcraft. And wasn't that exactly why he had taken it—to get in touch with the mystical? To experience the supernatural? Ryan let out a painful groan. Why hadn't he seen it earlier? That's exactly what he was doing ... practicing a form of witchcraft.

"Dear God," he whispered hoarsely, "I'm sorry. I'm so sorry ... Please forgive me. I'll never do that again, I promise. I'm so sorry. Please, help me find Becka ... Help me to help her. Please ..."

A strong sense of calm came over him, as though someone had put an arm around his shoulders. Well, he reasoned, Someone had. He didn't feel any better, but he knew he was forgiven. Gratitude filled him for God's readiness to forgive. No matter how badly he messed up, all it took was asking forgiveness and being serious about not doing it again. It was as simple as that.

Of course, there were still the consequences of his actions. They had to be faced. Once again he searched for an opening, for some crevice, for anything. And once again nausea overtook him and he fell.

But this time as he struggled to his feet, Ryan reached out to the wall and felt something. A lever. Embedded in the wall. He pulled it. Nothing happened. Then he pushed it.

Suddenly the wall began to move. Ryan staggered back and watched as the large stone rolled to the side. Behind it was a small room, a chamber. And lying on the ground directly in the middle of that chamber, tied and gagged, was Becka.

"Becka?" His voice was raspy and dry. "Rebecca?" There was no answer. He stumbled toward her. As he approached, he noticed that the ground was moving again. At first he thought it was the drug, but as he forced his eyes to focus, he saw that it wasn't the cave floor that was moving ... it was something on the floor. Hundreds of somethings. Brown and orange. And they were huge. Insects? No. His blood ran cold. Not insects.

Scorpions.

＜◈＞　＜◈＞

Back at camp, Mom, Scott, and Swift Arrow shared their growing worry about Becka and Ryan. Dark Bear's council would take place in just a few hours, and the two were nowhere to be found. In fact, nobody had seen them since lunch.

"That's not like Rebecca," Mom said. "She always lets us know where she's going."

"Let's walk through the village," Swift Arrow suggested. "Perhaps she is trying to talk to the people about tonight."

Scott agreed to accompany him, and the two began their search. A few minutes later, Swift Arrow asked, "Do you see how the people avert their eyes from me?"

"After last night, they're all afraid of Dark Bear."

"It looks as though they have already made their choice. Perhaps I was not the man to bring the gospel here."

Scott shook his head. "Don't be discouraged, Swift Arrow. You still have tonight."

"I know, and yet ..."

"And yet what?"

"I can only take the news that your sister and Ryan are missing as another sign favoring Dark Bear."

Scott nodded. "Maybe. But there's a saying in baseball that applies to exactly the type of warfare we're involved in."

"What's that?" Swift Arrow asked.

"It ain't over till it's over."

Ryan had pulled a big stick from the fire and was doing his best to keep the scorpions away from Becka. But no matter how many he swiped away, more continued to come.

It wasn't long before Becka began to stir. When she opened her eyes, she blinked, as though trying to focus. She looked at Ryan, then at what he was doing, and then she rubbed her face against a rock until she was able to finally push the gag from her mouth.

"Ryan!" she said with a cough. "Listen to me ... We've—we've got to pray."

"I *am* praying!" Ryan shouted back, smashing the stick down on the head of another scorpion.

Becka went on as though he hadn't spoken. "I know you didn't mean to, but you've formed some kind of allegiance to Dark Bear ... through all these rituals you've been doing. You've got to renounce it, Ryan. You've got to break his magic's power over you."

Ryan's head still swam from the effects of the drug as he swatted at the scorpions. "What about these—"

"These what?"

"These scorpions!"

Becka lifted her head and narrowed her eyes, as though straining to see. "Ryan, there are no scorpions here."

"What are you talking about?" Was she nuts? They were everywhere!

"There's nothing here," she repeated firmly. "It's more of Dark Bear's magic."

"But ..." He hesitated. Was it possible? Could she be right?

"Pray," Becka urged. "You've got to pray and break your allegiance to Dark Bear."

Ryan watched a particularly nasty scorpion turn and head directly for Becka, directly for her face.

"Pray, Ryan. Pray!"

It was nearly there, approaching her cheek.

"Pray!"

He cried out desperately, "Lord! Lord, forgive me. In the name of Jesus, I break any allegiances I've formed with demonic powers. I break the power of Dark Bear's magic."

Just like that, the scorpion was gone. They were all gone.

Ryan blinked his eyes, trying to take it in. "You're right!" he shouted. "They were an illusion! They're gone. They're all gone."

"Hurry and untie me!" Becka cried. "Dark Bear's council is coming up. Swift Arrow needs our help. Hurry, Ryan. Hurry!"

Back at the village, Dark Bear's council had already begun. He stood next to the crackling fire, addressing the crowd. His eyes were wild with intensity. "There is one here who is a thorn among the flowers, a sharp-edged rock among the smooth. One who speaks against the laws of the ancient ones. One who dares grumble against the god of thunder and lightning. One who has offended the rain god."

Scott stood beside Mom at the back of the crowd. He glanced over at Swift Arrow, who seemed to grow tenser with Dark Bear's every word. In fact, even from this distance, Scott could see him starting to tremble. Not that Scott blamed him. Dark Bear was more than a little menacing. With his warrior clothes, his bright feathers and buffalo-horn headdress, the shaman looked invincible. It was clear that the people feared him. But more terrifying than his appearance was the confidence with which he spoke: "Swift Arrow is the reason there has been no rain!"

Some of the people began to grumble in agreement.

"Swift Arrow has angered the rain god with his white man's lies! There will be no rain until he has been driven from the tribe!"

Scott glanced over at Swift Arrow, and their eyes met. It was now or never. Swift Arrow stepped forward. "That's not true! My tribesmen, the drought began long before I returned to the village. You know that. And I have spoken the truth to you. Jesus is not the white man's God. He is the Son of the one true God. Of everybody's God. And if you will but—"

"Silence!" Dark Bear bellowed. "If we let him speak these lies, rain will never fall upon our ground! Even his white friends have deserted him because they know he lies."

More people started to mumble in agreement. By now everyone in the village knew of Ryan and Becka's disappearance.

It was obvious that this threw Swift Arrow, but he did not back down. "My friends have not deserted me!"

"Then where have they gone?" Dark Bear demanded.

"Look!" He pointed toward Scott and Mom. "Here is the girl's mother. Here is her brother. They have not deserted me. They fear something has happened to the girl and the boy to keep them from being here as well."

Dark Bear took a menacing step closer to Swift Arrow. His voice grew low and vehement. "If something has happened to them, then it is the gods themselves who have taken vengeance."

The declaration almost sent Swift Arrow staggering, but Dark Bear wasn't done. He raised his voice so all could hear. "I warned them not to ally with you, but they would not listen. Instead, they followed your lies, and now they have paid the price."

Suddenly a strong voice shot through the clearing. "It is *you* who lie, Dark Bear."

Becka!

Scott spun around to see her and Ryan approaching.

"Thank you, Lord," he heard Mom pray quietly beside him.

Becka continued, "You lied to your own tribe, Dark Bear. Just now, I heard you. I did not leave Swift Arrow's side. You kidnapped me!"

The tribe murmured.

Becka shouted over them, "You kidnapped me and left me tied up in your cave. You are a *liar*. Like your father, the devil, you are the author of—"

Scott was the first to see it. "Look out!"

The eagle came in so fast that Becka barely had time to duck. It was huge, bigger than any eagle Scott had ever seen. But it was more than an eagle. As it soared back into the sky, preparing for another attack, Scott could actually see stars through its semitransparent wings. No, this was no eagle. It was something far more dangerous. Something he had run into on more than one occasion.

Other people saw it too. They began to race for cover, scrambling for protection. But Becka stood her ground. "Be gone, you spirit of hell!"

The creature continued its course. When it reached the height of its circle, it turned and began to dive ... directly for her.

It was a test. A challenge of Becka's faith, to see if she would back down. For a moment she hesitated, as if unsure if she could continue. Scott saw her fear and broke toward her. But Ryan was already there, stepping up beside her. Now the creature was bearing down toward them both.

"You fooled me once," Ryan shouted, "but not again!"

It continued to dive, but Ryan and Becka remained firm, unflinching.

"You have no authority!" Ryan yelled. "Your power has already been defeated."

It was nearly on top of them, its talons extended, its beak open wide.

Now it was Becka's turn. "By the power and blood of Jesus Christ, we command you to show your true self!"

The talons were within feet of their faces.

"Now!" Ryan added. "Reveal yourself *now!*"

Suddenly the bird veered off, coming so close that wind from its wings blew their hair. But Becka and Ryan didn't budge as the creature swooped upward. Now its movements were sharp, jerky—as though it was struggling with some unseen force. Then there was a flash of light ... and in place of the eagle was the hideous form of a demon.

The villagers shouted and screamed as the reptilian creature was exposed for all to see.

It circled one last time, preparing for the final assault, but by now three other people had joined Becka and Ryan: Scott, Mom, and Swift Arrow.

It started toward them, its wings drawn together as it began screaming through the air. Now it was Swift Arrow who shouted. His voice rang with clear and absolute authority. "Spirit of hell,

I order you to be gone! You have no power here. In the name of Jesus Christ, we cast you into the pit of hell!"

There was another burst of light, much brighter than the first. With the flash came a pounding clap of thunder. And when everyone's eyes readjusted to the darkness, there was no creature to be found. It was gone. Completely.

Some of the crowd emerged from their places of safety, staring up at the sky—then looking at Swift Arrow and marveling at his authority.

But the confrontation wasn't completely over. Not yet.

Dark Bear raised his staff high into the air and shouted, "Swift Arrow, you must die! You and your friends, you all must die!" He spread his arms to the sky and called, "God of the lightning, god of thunder, I beseech you, show these people. Show them once and for all who has the power. Show them who has the authority!"

Suddenly, a great bolt of lightning flashed out of the darkness. It forked through the sky directly toward the gathering. Before anyone had a chance to run or duck, it struck. But it did not strike the crowd. Nor did it strike Swift Arrow and his friends. Instead, it forked sharply to the side and hit Dark Bear, knocking him to the ground.

Everyone stared in astonishment. The man was still breathing, but no one dared approach. No one but Swift Arrow. He started toward him, and as he knelt by Dark Bear's side, Scott heard him speak clearly and with compassion. "The Lord will no longer allow you to use your power for evil, Dark Bear."

Dark Bear opened his eyes but remained motionless.

Swift Arrow continued, "He has spared your life, but God has proven his power. Your strength has been broken, and now our people can see the truth."

He gently reached down to the shaman, helping him sit up—and a most remarkable thing began to happen. Scott was the first to feel it. Something wet and cold on his arm. A drop. And then another ... and another.

"It's starting to rain!" he shouted.

Becka and Mom looked up. It was true. This time the thunder and lightning had finally brought the rain. And it came down faster and harder with each passing minute.

None of the villagers ran for cover this time. Instead, they tilted back their heads. Some opened their mouths. Others were shouting and starting to laugh. Scott laughed too, with relief. With gratitude. Dark Bear's curse had been broken. Swift Arrow's God had shown his power ... and his compassion. Now the villagers knew the truth. It would be up to each of them to decide whether or not to follow it.

But at least they knew the truth.

It was still raining as the group packed to leave the following morning.

"Where is Dark Bear?" Scott asked as he adjusted his backpack and prepared to begin the descent into the valley.

"Dark Bear fled earlier this morning," Swift Arrow explained. "The tribe will soon appoint his replacement."

"I have a sneaking suspicion who that person will be." Becka grinned.

Swift Arrow shrugged and smiled. "That will be up to the Lord. But this time the leader's medicine and his words—" he produced a small pocket Bible—"will be the truth."

The group nodded in agreement. As they prepared to leave, they promised Swift Arrow that they would continue to pray for him and for his village. Hugs were given all around, and promises were made to stay in touch.

"Good-bye, my friends," Swift Arrow said. There was no missing the emotion in his voice. "You have taught me much."

"And you, Swift Arrow," Scott said. "You have taught us a lot too."

And then, after another round of hugs, they were off.

"There's just one other person I wanted to say good-bye to," Ryan said as they made their way through the village.

"Who's that?" Becka asked.

"Ryan! Ryan, wait up."

The group turned to see Little Creek running to catch up with them.

"There you are." Ryan grinned. "I was just saying I was sorry we missed you."

Little Creek smiled and extended his hand. "Good-bye, my friends," he said as he shook each hand. "Good-bye, good-bye, good-bye—" he saved Ryan's hand for last—"and good-bye. I have learned an interesting lesson from you, Ryan."

"What's that?"

"That the teacher should sometimes be the student. I was so anxious to teach you the ways of my tribe that I missed what you had to teach me."

Ryan nodded. "I understand. But Swift Arrow can teach you those things now."

"I believe he can," Little Creek agreed.

Once again Little Creek insisted on shaking each hand as final good-byes were said. And then, at last, they were heading out of the village.

Thanks to the rain, the day was cooler, and the walk across the plateau proved to be refreshing and uneventful. Even the rope bridge was almost enjoyable.

When they finally arrived at the bottom of the range at their designated pick-up point, Oakie Doakey was there waiting for them in his Jeep, just as he had promised.

"Did you folks have an interesting time?" he asked.

"*Interesting* isn't the word!" Mom exclaimed.

"You got that right," Ryan agreed. "I tell you, I sure learned some valuable lessons."

"I think we all did," Becka said softly.

Ryan gave her a hug. And, although he didn't see it, she practically beamed in response.

"Hey, what's this?" Scott asked as he climbed into the back.

"What's what?" Mom asked.

"It's a package with our names on it."

"It arrived at my house the day before yesterday," Oakie Doakey said. "I thought I'd bring it up with me. I was particularly intrigued by the return address."

"Where's it from?" Becka asked.

"It really doesn't have an address, just a name."

"A name?"

"Well, not even that," Oakie said. "Just a single letter."

Becka and Ryan exchanged looks.

"Kind of curious, really. But does the letter *Z* mean anything to anybody?"

The entire group traded glances with one another. There was no need to speak. Everyone knew exactly what the others had on their minds.

Oh, boy, here we go again . . .

The Wiccan

For the time will come when men will not put up with sound doctrine. Instead, to suit their own desires, they will gather around them a great number of teachers to say what their itching ears want to hear. They will turn their ears away from the truth and turn aside to myths.

2 Timothy 4:3–4

1

Becka Williams paced the kitchen floor like a panther trapped in a cage. She gripped the cordless telephone against the side of her head until her ear throbbed. Her face, flushed with anger, burned as if exposed too long to the afternoon sun. She shook her head in disbelief.

"Julie, I thought we were going to a movie for your birthday," Becka said. She plopped down on a chair. "I really don't want to be around her; it's pretty hard to forget what she did to me last year. Remember? That little episode with the knife? In the park? Can't you see why I don't want to hang out with her?"

Julie Mitchell, Becka's best friend and co-captain of the track team, cut her off. "But, Becka, Laura really isn't that bad."

"Yeah? What makes you say that?"

"Well, for one thing, she admits that she followed Brooke too much."

"You can say that again," Becka said under her breath.

Brooke headed up The Society, a group of kids from school who were deep into the occult. They held séances in the back room of the Ascension Bookshop, a New Age bookstore. Becka and Scott had been the target of their wrath on more than one occasion. As their leader, Brooke had a personality about as commanding as a freight train. In a way, Becka knew Laura was just acting on orders from Brooke. Still, it wasn't easy to just ignore that bit of history for the sake of Julie's party.

Julie added, "And don't forget what Susan Murdoch said about reaching out to her."

"You've got a point there," Becka conceded, reflecting on what Susan, one of their youth pastors, had said. According to Susan, Laura was a good kid from a somewhat troubled home.

"Trust me," Julie said. "It'll be all right. She'll be with us just for a little while at the bookstore."

That was news to Becka. "You mean she's not sleeping over at your house with the rest of us?"

"Nope. And, Becka, think about it—it's a chance to meet Sarina Fox! Laura's dad knows Sarina's agent, and Laura said we can all meet Sarina after the book signing, where she'll be signing copies of her new book."

"Whatever." Becka batted a strand of hair away from her face with the grace of swatting at a gnat. Becka didn't spend a lot of time watching television. While meeting someone famous was cool, it wasn't that much of a thrill. At least not to Becka.

"So," Julie said, softening her tone, "what's the deal? Are you coming to my birthday party tonight?"

Becka's stomach churned as if she had eaten something off the bottom of her shoe. She wasn't exactly in the mood to be around Laura Henderson. "I don't know, Julie. I mean, I want to be there because it's your party. Let's just say it's a definite maybe."

Neither spoke for a long moment.

Becka checked her watch and then started pacing again.

"Look, I gotta run," Julie said. "I hope you can make it. Let me know so we don't wait up for you, okay?"

Becka hooked her thin, mousy brown hair over her right

ear. "Sure thing. See ya." She clicked off the phone and, with a whack, set it down on the kitchen table a little too forcefully.

"What was that about?" Becka's mom asked as she walked into the kitchen.

Becka spun around. "Mom, sometimes Julie makes me so—" she started to say, then froze. "Wow, Mom, what happened?" Becka couldn't take her eyes off the woman staring back at her. She sure sounded like Becka's mother, but that's where the similarity ended.

Claire Williams crossed the room to Becka's side. With a turn, she said, "So, do you like it?"

Becka blinked. "What happened to your hair?" she blurted. As far back as she could remember, her mother's hair had been getting more and more gray. Now it was a rich chestnut brown with auburn highlights.

Mrs. Williams' eyes narrowed. "You don't like it, do you?"

"I—I never said that . . . ," Becka stammered. She sat down. "I mean, it looks . . . um . . . great. Really."

"You think so?" Mrs. Williams said. A playful smile danced across her face. She sat down, placing her new purse on the table.

"Gee, like, you look so much younger," Becka said, then thought that sounded rude. "What I mean—"

Her mom waved her off. "I know exactly what you mean. Premature gray hair will do that. Guess you could say I was tired of looking like a grandma. I am, after all, only forty-one."

Becka's brother, Scott, breezed into the kitchen and headed straight for the refrigerator. "Hey, Becka," Scott said as he pulled open the fridge door. Even though he had just finished lunch, he rummaged around for something to eat. He frequently raided the refrigerator, perhaps in an effort to continue his growth spurt, having recently passed Becka in height. He fetched a Mountain Dew from the bottom shelf. As he twisted off the top, he asked, "So, who's your friend?"

Becka laughed and then gave her mom, whose back was to Scott, a wink.

Before she could answer, Scott approached the table and said, "You guys see Mom around? I thought she'd be home by now." He started to guzzle the soda.

Mrs. Williams looked at her son. "Hi, sweetie."

Scott snorted a stream of soda bubbles through his nose. He wiped his face with the back of his hand. "Mom?"

Mrs. Williams primped her hair. "You like?"

"Somebody pinch me," Scott said, smiling so wide it looked to Becka like he had pulled a muscle in his face. "Mom, you look ... well, you look ... unreal ... as in great!"

She blushed. "I'll take that as a compliment."

"What gives?" Scott said, touching her hair in disbelief.

"It's the new me," she said. "Dad may be in heaven now, but I've come to see that God's got me *here* for a reason. I figured I had better start discovering what that special purpose is."

At the mention of their dad, Becka and Scott fell silent. It had been over a year since their father had disappeared and was presumed dead on the mission field in South America, where their family had been stationed. They had moved to Crescent Bay, California, for a fresh start. And while Becka and Scott were distracted with new friends at school, their mom seemed to have aged with each passing day.

Mrs. Williams broke the silence. She opened her purse and pulled out a pocket date book. "Actually, this is just the beginning of my personal transformation," she said with a smile. She consulted her calendar. "This weekend I've decided to go to that Free to Be women's retreat. The speaker is supposed to help us develop our mind, body, and spirit. The kickoff is tonight. I'll be home sometime on Sunday afternoon."

Becka nodded. "I read about that in the church bulletin. Sounds very cool."

"I figured what better way to get started with the new me than with a new do," Mrs. Williams said.

"A what?" Scott said.

"As in hairdo, you harebrain," Becka said.

"Well, excu-u-use me for not being up on the latest hairstyle lingo."

Mrs. Williams pointed to the calendar in front of her. "I hope you guys are ready for the start of school next week."

They nodded in unison.

"Good deal. Now, since I'll be gone all weekend," Mrs. Williams said, "I've made arrangements for you to stay with friends. Becka, I talked to Julie's mom, and she said it's fine for you to stay over tomorrow night too since you'll already be there tonight for Julie's party."

"Actually, Mom, I wasn't totally sure I was going—"

"Then this makes your decision easier," Mrs. Williams said with a wink. She turned to Scott. "Darryl's mom gave her okay for you to stay there. So if that sounds good with both of you, it's all set."

Becka groaned. "Mom, I'm seventeen. I don't need a babysitter."

"Ditto for me," Scott said. "In case you forgot, I'm fifteen. What could go wrong? Can't we just stay here? I'll even be in charge of meals. I'll just order pizza—"

Mrs. Williams shook her head. "Out of the question. I don't want to be worrying about you guys home alone without a car while I'm out of town. Besides," she said, looking at Becka, "it's only for one extra night. I'm sure you and Julie will find something fun to do after the others leave, right?"

Becka's face flushed. "Yeah, but still ... maybe I don't want to go."

"Maybe you don't have a choice this time," her mom said.

Becka looked away. Three seconds later, she felt her mother

squeezing her forearm. "She *is* your best friend, Becka. Is there something going on between you two?"

Becka shifted in her chair, avoiding the question. "Couldn't I stay with Susan?" she asked. Susan Murdock always made Becka feel welcome.

"Actually, she was my first choice," Mrs. Williams said. "But she's going to the retreat too. I just need you to make it work with Julie, okay?"

She studied her mother's face. For the first time in months Becka saw a sparkle in her eyes. And she couldn't miss the touch of hopefulness in her voice. Becka knew her mom had been struggling with her self-confidence, especially since she had difficulty finding a job. Becka figured this conference might be a turning point and didn't want to say anything that might put a damper on things.

"We're cool," Becka said, knowing full well that there were a few major issues she and Julie would have to work out.

"Good," Mrs. Williams said. "Now, I've got a surprise for you."

"Me?" Scott said between guzzles.

"Actually, no," Mrs. Williams said. She pulled something from her purse and then handed it to Becka.

"A cell phone?" Becka's eyes widened. "Wow."

Her mom nodded. "Yup. I figured it was about time you left the Stone Age and joined the human race."

"H-e-l-l-oooo," Scott said. "That's *so* not fair. What am I, chopped liver over here?"

Becka powered up the phone. "Relax, Scott. Since when were you appointed the Fairness Police?"

"It's just that—," Scott began, but was cut off by his mom.

"Maybe there's something in here for you, Scott," she said. She opened a cabinet door behind her, withdrew an oversized padded package, and handed it to Scott. "It's from Z."

Becka put the cell phone down. She watched with interest as

Scott tore into the package from Z, their Internet friend whom they'd never met in person or been able to find out anything about. Sure, they tried to discover his true identity, but Z always managed to stay three steps ahead of them. Not to mention that Z kept coming up with important missions for them to undertake—like last week's trip to New Mexico, which they took with their mother.

There were two things they knew for sure about Z: he was a definite expert when it came to the supernatural. And he knew the Bible inside and out.

"I completely forgot about this," Scott said. The package had arrived several days ago, right after Becka, Scott, and their mother had returned from New Mexico. There, they had a supernatural battle with an Indian shaman named Dark Bear, who had the ability to call down lightning whenever he wanted to torch something—or someone. In their case, *they* had been the target of Dark Bear's fireworks.

Becka shuddered as she remembered the showdown. It had been a case of all-out spiritual warfare battling Dark Bear's black magic, which had held an entire Indian tribe hostage for years. But through their faith in Jesus, their courage, and tons of prayer—along with the help of a new friend, Swift Arrow—they overcame the power of Dark Bear.

"Whatcha got?" Becka said, leaning forward.

Scott pulled out a set of earplugs from what looked like a plastic bag with Becka's name printed on it. A note card was stapled to the bag. "Looks like these are for you," he said. He handed Becka the items.

"Earplugs?" Becka's forehead wrinkled. "What's Z up to?"

"Read the note, pea brain," Scott said.

"Scott—," his mother started to say with that tone of voice that parents use when they're about to ground you for life.

He offered a cheesy smile. "Sorry."

Becka opened the card and read: "'For Becka. Be careful,

little ears, what you hear.'" She looked at Scott and then her mom. "Okay, so call me clueless."

Scott noticed another envelope with Becka's name on it in the package. "Hey, maybe this will help."

She opened the envelope and withdrew a picture. "I don't even know who this is ... do you?"

"No, but she's cute," Scott said, peering over her shoulder. "Maybe she snores, huh?"

Becka ignored the comment as she continued to study the photo. "Actually, there's something familiar about her, but I can't seem to place her face." The girl in the photo was about seventeen or eighteen—at least that was Becka's guess. She stood on a mountain, with an expansive valley in the background. She wore a backpack and hiking clothes. Her safari hat covered the top of her long, dark blonde hair. A gentle smile lit her simple but attractive face.

Scott looked at the image more closely too. "Yeah, I know what you mean. She does look like someone I've met or seen before. I just can't say for sure."

Becka turned the photograph over. "And look. On the back it says, 'Iron sharpens iron. Stay sharp ... and keep a sharp eye on this misguided spirit.'" Becka glanced up at Scott and then back at the photo. "What does Z mean by that?"

Scott shrugged. "I can't figure out how he knows half the stuff he knows. Hey, check this out. I got three free Domino's Pizza coupons. Now you're talking my language, Z."

"That's it?" Becka asked. "I get earplugs ... and you get pizza?"

"Now who's acting like the Fairness Police?" Scott said, elbowing his sister in the ribs.

"Hold on," Mrs. Williams said. "Isn't that a note on the back of one of your coupons?"

Scott flipped it over. "Um, it says 'Remember to pray for

Becka. Z.'" He looked up. "Too bad. Nothing in there about sharing my pizza with you, sis."

Becka's eyes met Scott's. Since moving to Crescent Bay, both Becka and Scott had learned to expect the unexpected, especially when it came to spiritual warfare. And when it came to Z, there was always some deeper significance to the things he sent their way. Only this time, neither could make out where Z was headed.

Mrs. Williams stood to leave. "I'm sure this will all make sense in due time. It always does, doesn't it?"

Becka nodded, but for some reason she felt a growing uneasiness about spending the weekend with Julie. It was the same sensation she seemed to get in her stomach whenever she was about to face some form of spiritual counterfeit.

"So, Mom," Becka said, clearing her throat, "how can I get in touch with you ... you know, like if I needed you for something?"

Mrs. Williams raised an eyebrow. "Actually, I got a free cell phone too, my dear. You know me. I couldn't pass up one of those family plan deals where we share the minutes."

"Very cool, Mom," Scott said, nodding in approval.

"Now, I'm not too sure there will be coverage way out at the cabin," Mom said, "but if not, I'm sure there must be a pay phone somewhere on the campground. Why don't I call you on your cell? I'll just plan to catch up with you sometime during one of the session breaks."

"Becka, you can always program Darryl's home number into your cell phone too," Scott offered. "Of course, we may be too busy eating a double-cheese and 'roni pizza to answer."

"Thanks for nothing, bro."

"You can count on me." Scott tucked the coupons in the front pocket of his jeans.

Mrs. Williams called from the living room, "I'll drop you guys off on my way out. Let's leave in an hour, okay?"

"No prob," Scott said. He jumped out of his chair and headed to his room.

After her mom and brother left the room, Becka stared at the phone for a minute. Not only was she being forced to go to Julie's party, where she'd have to face Laura Henderson, but now she was spending her entire last weekend before the start of her senior year at Julie's. If anything, she'd like to get some time with her boyfriend, Ryan Riordan.

Becka picked up the phone and dialed Julie's number. What choice did she have? Julie answered on the second ring.

"It's me," Becka said.

"Hey," Julie said. "You coming?"

"Yeah, looks like I'll be spending the weekend too."

"Great," Julie said. "My mom said you might be, but I figured after our last conversation you might make other plans so you could avoid Laura."

"I still don't get it—why Laura?" Becka said, trying not to sound too frustrated. "I mean, I didn't know you guys were friends."

Julie laughed. "We're not. We just have a class together and have gotten to talk a couple of times. She's really not a bad person. Like I said, her dad is a lawyer and knows Sarina Fox's agent. When Laura offered me the chance to meet Sarina and learn about her TV show at the book signing, I figured the least I could do was to invite her. Come on, Beck, how many famous people ever show up in Crescent Bay?"

Becka took a deep breath. She knew she might as well try to smooth things over with Julie. "Listen, Julie. I want you to know I don't feel comfortable with Laura there, but I understand why you feel you should be nice to her. So don't worry, we'll work it out."

"Thanks for understanding. I know we'll have a blast," Julie said. "And guess what? There's two other girls coming."

"Wow. Who?" Becka said.

"Well, of course there's Krissi," Julie said, then added, "and my cousin Rachael—she's visiting from out of town."

"She's the one from Sacramento?"

"Seattle," Julie said. "She's totally into *The Hex* and is dying to meet Sarina."

Becka had heard about *The Hex*. Who hadn't? It was only the hottest TV show in the country. She didn't know much about the show, having never watched it herself. But somehow, if the name *The Hex* was any indication, Becka was pretty sure it wasn't the kind of show she'd want to see, and she was a little concerned that Julie sounded so excited about it. Then again, it was Julie's party and even Z said Becka should watch out for her. Maybe this was what he was talking about.

"It's gonna be so cool," Julie said. "Sarina Fox ... in person ... signing copies of her new book. WOW!"

"Uh-huh," Becka said, her palms starting to sweat.

"Laura is also gonna get us hooked up with Sarina for dessert or whatever afterwards. Fun, huh?"

Becka didn't say anything. Her mouth was too dry to speak, even if she could have thought of something to say. She switched the phone to her other ear.

When Becka didn't answer, Julie said, "Don't worry, Becka. Like I said, Laura's just going to the bookstore and dessert with us. That's all. I'm sure it won't be that bad for a few hours."

Becka cleared the tightness from her throat. "I ... I'm sure we'll ... be fine," she said. The truth was, she'd never forget the time Laura and several others from The Society attacked and almost killed her. True, Laura had just been acting on orders from Brooke, but it was a close call. "Hey, I better go. My mom's taking me to your place in an hour or so, and I've still got to grab my things."

Becka hung up and didn't move for a long minute. In the silence that followed, she remembered what bothered her about *The Hex*. Several days ago, she and Ryan had been riding to the airport in Ryan's Mustang. "Spellbound," the theme song from *The Hex*, filled the speakers. Although Becka couldn't recall the lyrics, the DJ made a comment that the song, like the TV show, was heavy into Wicca.

She didn't know much about Wicca.

She just knew Wicca had something to do with witchcraft.

And in a few hours she'd be face-to-face with what's-her-name from *The Hex*.

2

Laura walked to her father's study. Rather than march right in, she lingered by the French doors that led to the wood-paneled room. A grandfather clock in the corner ticked away the silence. Her mom had left for the beauty parlor several minutes prior, and her dad, a divorce attorney, was probably on the golf course. At least, that was Laura's guess. After all, it was Friday afternoon. As far back as she could recall, he always claimed he needed a round of golf to settle his nerves after a week of busting up people's marriages.

As a child of seven, Laura remembered standing in that very spot, wanting to rush in and give her dad a hug when he would arrive home late from work. The couple of times she had tried, she had been pushed away. Her dad had so much important stuff to do to establish his law practice. She just had to understand. Even her mother had said so.

"Dad's busy. Don't bother him." Even now that she was seventeen, her mother's words from ten years ago still echoed in her head. Come to think of it, not much had changed.

Laura's eyes scanned the room. The shades were drawn. The only light came from a small lamp with a dark green lamp shade on his desk. He had a habit of leaving it on. She walked into the office, circled around to the back of her father's massive mahogany desk, and eased herself into his big, high-back leather chair.

Once seated, the strong smell of tobacco greeted her nose. She noticed a half-smoked cigar resting on the edge of his ashtray. Her eyes drifted across the desktop. She dare not touch anything. Her dad had barked at the cleaning lady for disturbing his things. No, she didn't come to pry into his stuff. She just took comfort sitting in his chair.

It was about as close to him as she could get.

It would have to do.

Laura was about to leave when the phone on his desk purred. He had set the ringer on the lowest setting. On the second ring, the answering machine clicked on. Her ears perked up as the confident, deep voice of her father came on: "You've reached the home office of Les Henderson. Leave a confidential message at the tone. I'll return the call shortly."

The breathy voice of a woman whispered, "Les, it's me. I know you said not to call you here, but I just had to tell you what a wonderful time I had at lunch today."

Laura just about flew out of the chair. She leaned toward the answering machine. Who was this woman? What was she doing with her dad at lunch? Was she a client? If so, she sure sounded awfully friendly.

"I ... well, I can't wait to see you ... tonight ... I'll be sure to make it ... worthwhile." The caller paused, then added, "I feel positively naughty, don't you? Bye, dearest."

Laura was too stunned to move. For a second, she couldn't breathe. It felt as if a giant vacuum had sucked out all the air from her lungs. She brought a hand to her face. This wasn't happening. It couldn't be happening.

Her dad? Having an affair?

The walls of her father's study felt as if they were closing in on her, squeezing every ounce of life out of her world. It didn't make sense. Her parents didn't appear unhappy. As far as she could tell, they rarely argued. Then again, her folks rarely did much together aside from having brunch on Sunday at the country club.

The grandfather clock chimed four times. Laura focused on the clock through the tears now dampening her eyes. She remembered she had to be at Julie's by five. She'd have just enough time to do what she knew she had to do. She willed herself to leave the room, climbed the staircase to the second floor, and then made her way to her bedroom.

She closed and locked the door behind her, as if doing so would shield her from the knifelike betrayal she felt slicing away at her heart. Try as she did, she couldn't shake the voice of that woman echoing in her mind: *"Bye, dearest ... bye, dearest ... bye, dearest ..."*

She fell facedown on her bed, sobbing. Several minutes passed before she managed to pull herself upright. She sat on the edge of the bed and dabbed her tears with a corner of the sheet. Like a lost child, she sat, hands folded in her lap, waiting to be rescued.

In the stillness, a plan of action formed.

Slowly, Laura got down on her knees and withdrew a black, three-sided hat from beneath the bed. It was her Cone of Power, or, as her unenlightened friends called it, her witch's hat. She put it on her head and then walked to her desk.

She grabbed a piece of red construction paper and, with scissors, fashioned it into the shape of a tongue. Using a marker, she scribbled a few words on the paper tongue. Satisfied, Laura picked up a glass jar from the corner of her desk and then walked to the center of the room with the jar and the tongue.

As a Solitary, a witch practicing the craft of Wicca alone, Laura knew she had to create a magic circle, a holy ground in which she would cast a spell. Unlike Brooke, the leader of The

Society who was way deep into black magic, Laura viewed her private journey into Wicca as a less dangerous pathway to personal enlightenment.

She had pulled away from The Society last year after that horrible night at the park when she realized the control Brooke had over her. Laura shuddered, thinking about how she had taken part in terrorizing Becka. And while Brooke was still dealing with the police, Laura was required to have regular counseling for her part in the assault. Talk about an awful year.

That's when she discovered Wicca. As a Wiccan, her spell casting was a positive way to protect and provide for the people and things she loved. Or so she was taught.

She took a deep, cleansing breath and tried to quiet the restlessness in her spirit. As the calm settled upon her, she walked toward the North with her dominant hand leading the way. Her fingers pointed downward as she moved.

Laura began to pace in a clockwise direction around the room. As she walked, she imagined a hedge of tall trees emerging in the wake of her fingers as they floated through the air. She whispered these words:

"Circle of power, I call thee forth.

Be for me a boundary between this world and the spirits.

May it be a perfect place of peace, love, and power.

I look to the keepers of the North, the East, the South, and the West

To assist me now; consecrate this place

In the name of the lord and the lady."

Laura glided around the room three times as she spoke the words, stopping at the northern point. She bent over. With a slap of her hand against the floor, she added, "This great circle of power is sealed."

This done, she walked to the center of the circle, holding the tongue-shaped paper and jar. Laura opened the jar and then placed the tongue inside. She replaced the lid and tightened it with a twist. As she worked, she said:

"Speaker of evil, temptress of my dad,
I bind your tongue; I forever banish you
From this home, so you harm us no more.
May the spirit deal with you according to your evil intent.
May only love and positive energy encircle my home,
So mote it be!"

Laura closed her eyes. She envisioned the angels in the spirit world bathing her room with a warm light. She lifted the jar above her head, imagining the paper tongue inside scorched by fire. She lowered the jar, opened her eyes, and walked counterclockwise around the circle three times. With care, she put the jar in the bottom drawer of her desk and placed her three-sided hat back under the bed.

She glanced at the clock on her bed stand. She had thirty minutes before she had to be at Julie's house. It was then that a new idea came to her mind. She decided to cast a special spell of friendship for someone she'd be meeting later that evening.

She quickly retrieved the hat, grabbed a candle and a lighter, and then retraced her steps to conjure up a magic circle. This time, as she stood in the center, she pictured Julie's thick blonde hair. For a second, Laura considered how much prettier Julie's hair was than her own stringy blonde mane, but she quickly banished the negative energy that such comparisons generated.

Laura lit the candle and held it above her head. She said:

"I light my candle; my will be done.
Sarina Fox, kindred seeker,
Be drawn this day, to be at one
With me and with the lady.
All hail the goddess,
So mote it be!"

With a puff of hot breath, Laura blew out the candle.

3

"Hey, Mom," Scott said, picking up two large suitcases, "I thought you were only going for the weekend."

"I am," Mrs. Williams said, checking her hair in the mirror by the front door. She smiled. "One for each day."

"Gotcha." Slumping under the weight of a suitcase in each hand, Scott headed to the car. As he lugged them toward the driveway, Ryan Riordan pulled up. Scott turned and called toward the open front door of the house, "Becka, Ryan's here for the dog."

Becka bounded out onto the front lawn. "Hey, Ryan."

He gave her a hug. "Boy, is somebody moving?" he said with a laugh, pointing to the luggage.

"Actually," Mrs. Williams said, joining them, "it may look that way, but it's still just for the weekend."

Becka walked with Ryan toward the house. "Now, you're sure you and Muttly will get along?"

Ryan laughed. "You don't have to worry about a thing. I love dogs."

They headed to the kitchen, where Becka had Muttly's stuff. "Here's his food — just two scoops twice a day."

"I think I can handle that."

"And his toy, his blanket, his leash." She stopped mid-step. "Are you sure this isn't asking too much?"

Ryan gathered up the items. "I promise, Beck, we'll be fine. Besides, if Muttly misses you, I'll call you at Julie's, and you guys can talk on the phone ... deal?"

Becka blinked. "That reminds me. I've got a cell phone now."

"Imagine that," Ryan said with a sly grin. "The Williams have joined the rest of mankind."

Becka ignored the friendly jab and jotted down her new number on a napkin. "Here ya go," she said, tucking the paper in his shirt pocket. "Muttly's around back. Here, I'll get him—"

Ryan squeezed her arm. "No, I'll get him. You just do what you need to do to get ready."

"You sure?"

"Yeah, and let's plan on doing something Sunday night when you get home."

Becka liked the sound of that. "Thanks, Ryan." Her heart did a little flip-flop as he hugged her. Becka zoomed out of the kitchen and grabbed her bag.

"Come on, Becka," her mom said, switching off the lights in the living room.

"Mom, give me another sec, okay?" Becka said, plopping her overstuffed duffel bag by the front door. Beside it she placed Julie's present. An arrangement of colorful crepe paper sprouted out of the top of the bag. She was all set. Well, almost. She wished she had a better idea of what Wicca was all about, especially since she'd be meeting Sarina from *The Hex*.

"I just sent Z an email, and I'm hoping he'll see it before we leave," Becka said.

"We really need to get going, sweetheart," Mrs. Williams said with a look at the clock on the wall. "I don't want to be late for registration."

"I'll only be a sec, I promise." Becka sprinted up the stairs.

She rounded the corner and headed for Scott's room, where the computer screen glowed. She beamed when she noticed that a message was awaiting her. She clicked on the icon and opened the email. It was from Z.

> To: Becka
> From: Z
> Subject: Wicca
>
> Good to know you'll be spending the weekend with Julie. Regarding Wicca: on the surface it claims to promote healing, positivity, and oneness with nature. However, it's nothing more than a repackaged pagan belief system combining feminism, environmentalism, and spiritualism into a misguided and dangerous brew. Although Wiccans see Wicca as different from other forms of witchcraft, they rely upon spell casting, alignment of the stars and planets, and opening up one's self to demons—which they'll never admit. Wiccans believe there are many legitimate pathways to God, and they deny the concept of absolute evil as found in the person of Satan. They even deny that sin exists. Think about it. No sin, no need for Jesus. Nevertheless, the practice of Wicca is one of the fastest-growing religions in the world today.
>
> The Bible predicted this: "For the time will come when men will not put up with sound doctrine. Instead, to suit their own desires, they will gather around them a great number of teachers to say what their itching ears want to hear. They will turn their ears away from the truth and turn aside to myths. But you, keep your head in all situations, endure hardship, do the work of an evangelist, discharge all the duties of your ministry" (2 Timothy 4:3–5).
>
> The Wicca belief system is so popular, even the cartoon

series *Scooby-Doo* has promoted the notion that Wicca
witches are a good thing. Don't be fooled, Becka. There
is no such thing as "good" magic. Nor are there good
witches. All witchcraft is a perversion because it denies
the need for a Savior by suggesting there are many ways
to the Father.
Be careful. Be steadfast. Be true to the truth.
Z

Becka switched off the computer, thankful to have at least
some idea what Wiccans believe. At the same time, that hollow
feeling in the pit of her stomach whenever she was engaged in
spiritual warfare rumbled with fresh intensity.

Her thoughts drifted to Julie's birthday party. Maybe it
wasn't such a good idea for them to go to the bookstore and
meet Sarina. Sure, Sarina and *The Hex* were super popular. But if
Sarina as a practicing Wiccan was, as Z implied, into witchcraft
and casting spells, there was no way Becka, Julie, Krissi, and the
others should get near her.

Not after Julie and Krissi already had almost deadly encounters with demon possession several months ago.

But how could Becka stop them from going?

It was a few minutes before seven o'clock when the Suburban,
with Julie at the wheel, pulled around the corner and headed for
Borders. Becka sat in the front, and Krissi, Rachael, and Laura
were sandwiched together in the middle seat.

Although the girls were too busy talking to watch, a DVD
with three episodes of *The Hex*, a gift from Krissi, played on the
overhead TV monitor. Rachael had given Julie a beautiful jour-
nal, handmade in Indonesia. Laura gave her a crystal pendant on
a silver chain. And Becka's present—a gift set of Julie's favorite
lip gloss, eyeliner, and blush—was a hit.

Now that they were almost to the book signing, Becka's stomach was doing back flips. And her suggestion that they should maybe do something else—like go see a movie instead of meeting Sarina—went over like a lead balloon.

"It was just a suggestion," Becka said. She crossed her arms.

"Right, and miss seeing Sarina?" Krissi said, rolling her perfectly curled eyelashes. "Hey, Beck, control yourself; don't be so much fun," she added. She reached forward and gave Becka a playful tap on the shoulder.

Rachael snickered.

Although it wasn't mean-spirited, the mockery stung, but Becka let it pass.

"I don't get it, Becka," Laura said, turning toward Becka and then flipping her hair over her shoulder. "Why are you so down on someone you haven't even met?"

Becka held her tongue.

"I don't know," Krissi said, her forehead creased into a knot. "In a way, I can understand where Becka's coming from."

"How's that?" Laura asked. "If you ask me, Becka seems to be paranoid about stuff. Especially when it comes to all of that hocus-pocus Sarina does." Laura wiggled her fingers in the air as if casting a magical spell.

"Actually, I happen to think it's a whole lot more than hocus-whatever," Krissi said. "Then again, Laura's got a point too. Maybe we should wait to meet Sarina first before judging her."

Becka looked out the window. She regretted saying anything. Why should she care about Laura when she couldn't see something so potentially dangerous? Then again, maybe Laura didn't know she was flirting with serious stuff. Come to think of it, maybe now was a good time to use the earplugs from Z.

Julie cleared her throat. "Look, guys, let's drop it and have a good time. Okay? Becka's just trying to be helpful. Anyway, we're here."

"Check it out! The place is packed," Krissi said. "Even Channel 7 is here." She took out her compact and checked her lips.

"Check out the limo," Rachael said, pointing to a white stretch limousine that seemed to fill the street. "This is so cool!"

Julie found a parking space, and the girls piled out of the vehicle and raced to the door. As they entered, Becka figured there must be at least a hundred people. She had never seen the place so crammed. Some were sitting on chairs or on the floor. Others stood around the edges between the bookshelves.

A microphone mounted on a stand was positioned up front. To the left, stacks of books were piled high on a table. Becka was surprised—and a little alarmed—to see Priscilla Bantini, the Ascension Lady from the New Age Ascension Bookshop in town, approach the mike. Someone with a Press badge pinned to his jacket snapped a photo. The cameraman from Channel 7, his camera mounted on a tripod, panned across the room before positioning himself for a close-up of the Ascension Lady.

"Good evening," Priscilla said. Her salt-and-pepper hair complemented her thin frame. "And welcome. I'm so glad everyone could make it. You're in for a special treat tonight."

"Follow me," Laura said to the group just above a whisper.

As the Ascension Lady welcomed the crowd, Laura led them toward the front row. Much to Becka's surprise, five seats had been personally reserved for them. Laura sat on the end, and Julie took the seat next to her. Then Becka, Krissi, and Rachael filed in behind them like ducklings.

As they took their seats, Becka heard the Ascension Lady say, "I've asked Sarina to grace us with a few words and perhaps a reading from her new book, *White Magic: Wicca for Teen Seekers*." She held up a copy as if she were holding an original Picasso. The crowd burst into applause.

"These are great seats," Julie said to Laura over the hand clapping.

Priscilla tucked the book under one arm and said, "Sarina might even entertain a few questions. So join me in giving Sarina Fox a warm Crescent Bay welcome!" She clapped her frail hands together for all they were worth.

Everyone around Becka leaped to their feet as Sarina glided in from a side door. Becka's heart skipped a beat. There was no mistaking it: Sarina was the girl in the photograph from Z. She had a completely different look, but it was her.

The sensation, like the buzz of an alarm, started to ring at the base of Becka's skull. The warning spread to her forehead and resonated between her ears. The sudden ringing in her head was so strong, she was sure Julie could hear it. She glanced out of the corner of her eye.

Julie was too busy gawking to notice.

Sarina stood in front of the microphone, holding bottled water in one hand. The room exploded with flashes of light as camera-happy fans snapped dozens of photos. With a relaxed smile, she waited for the applause to subside. She appeared to be in her late twenties, and she wore little makeup. Her jet-black, shoulder-length hair framed her well-tanned face. Her black tank top hung loosely across her shoulders and revealed most of her trim midriff. She wore torn blue jeans, which hovered three inches below her pierced navel.

Becka noticed that her belt buckle was a circle with two fish-like images — one black, the other white — entwined. Becka was pretty sure the symbol was a Chinese design that had to do with a yin-yang philosophy. She'd ask Z to be sure.

Sarina took a sip of water, set the drink down on the table to her left, and then motioned to the fans to take their seats.

"You're too kind," she started to say.

Two kids in the back shouted, "WE LOVE YOU, Sarina!"

Several others did the same.

"I come to you in the name of the goddess," Sarina said.

"Tonight, if it's all right with you, I thought I'd start with a few words about my quest to bond with the Earth Spirit before I read from *White Magic*."

More applause. More ringing in Becka's ears.

"My story is simple," Sarina said. "I was twelve when a brave cousin introduced me to the fabulous world of Wicca. I say 'brave' because for years I was lied to by the so-called Christian church." Sarina scanned the faces in the room. She paused when she met Becka's eyes.

Becka felt her throat go dry.

"I . . . I discovered that Wicca isn't all that different from other spiritual paths," Sarina said after a moment. "God, whoever he may be, is like a diamond. There are many facets and many ways to view him. But there are a few truths worth pointing out. Wiccans don't believe in the silly notion of devils running around in red jumpsuits."

Someone giggled.

"We don't blame our problems on some mythical creature. And there's no such place as hell," Sarina continued. "Think about it. How could a loving God send anyone to hell?" She paused to take a sip from her water bottle.

Sarina's question prompted Becka's mind to drift to the death of her dad. *And why would a loving God take my dad away from me?* she wondered.

"No," Sarina said, placing the bottle down. "We make our own hell on earth when we ignore the opportunity to seek healing and peace. So, as a Wiccan, I've embraced a life-affirming religion, one that seeks to care for Mother Earth, desires harmony between all people groups, and gives me power to evolve to a higher level of spirit awareness."

A teen in the back row shouted, "You go, girl!"

A warm smile eased across Sarina's face. "And, for those nervous parents in the crowd, let me just say that we Wiccans practice white magic. Unlike those into black magic, we align ourselves with the lord and the lady. We strive to cast spells that effect positive change in us and in our world."

Becka stole a look behind her. Everyone appeared to be captivated by Sarina. As she spoke, her voice definitely had a magical, mesmerizing quality to it.

"There's one exception," Sarina said placing her right hand on her hip. Her voice became noticeably strident. "Wiccans will use their power to fight back against those who might try to silence them or do them harm."

Becka shifted in her seat. With a glance, she noticed Julie hanging on every word. Not good. This was exactly what Becka was afraid would happen. They'd come and get an earful of spiritual mumbo jumbo.

Sarina's tone softened. "Anyway, this is my first book. The first selection I'd like to read is called 'Celebrate the Craft.' May I?"

As the audience urged her on, part of Becka wanted to put as much distance between this place and herself as possible. On the other hand, Sarina's confidence and easygoing style sparked her curiosity. Becka bit the corner of her bottom lip as a question surfaced in her mind. Was it at all possible that there might be some truth in what Sarina was saying?

4

Scott propped his feet against the edge of Darryl's desk. They had migrated to Darryl's bedroom, where a TV was mounted from the ceiling. "This is the life," said Scott, reaching for his third slice. "Pizza ... a movie ... and my best friend. What could be better?"

"Uh, maybe if you could get your bird to shut up," Darryl said with a sniffle.

"Bite your tongue, heathen," Scott said.

"Why? What did I say?"

"You used the *S* word."

"I did not."

"Did too."

"All I asked was how to shut up that bird—"

Scott cut him off. "First rule of bird ownership. Never say anything in the presence of our fine-feathered friend that you don't want him to learn."

Darryl pushed his glasses up onto the bridge of his nose. "Okay, so I confess. I never went to bird-sensitivity training. What should I say?"

Scott finished a can of soda. "Try saying, 'Knock it off.'"

Darryl sniffled and then looked at Cornelius. "You heard him, Cornelius. Knock it off."

The bright green-and-scarlet military macaw bobbed his head up and down as he dashed from one end of his portable perch to the other. "I love you! Give me kisses!!"

"I can't believe I'm having a conversation with a bird," Darryl said.

"SQUAWK ... cowabunga, dude!"

When Scott and Becka first got Cornelius years ago, they had taught him some of the cool sayings from American TV they'd watched in South America. They learned the hard way that once a bird learned something, it rarely stopped repeating it. Worse, a bird like Cornelius could live sixty years—or more.

"How am I gonna watch my movie with that racket?" Darryl said. "Maybe it wasn't such a good idea bringing him here with you this weekend."

"Sorry. I didn't have much of a choice." Scott tore off an edge of his pizza and fed it to Cornelius.

"Mmmm. Is it good?" Cornelius said, his eyes dilating. He grabbed the crust with his powerful beak. Balancing on one foot, he used the other claw to hold it while he chowed down.

"Cornelius, just so you know ... we own a microwave," Darryl said, giving the bird an evil eye. "And I'm not afraid to use it."

"Make my day," Cornelius said with a squawk.

Darryl's eyes narrowed. "Hey, Cornelius, can you say, 'KFC'?"

"Very uncool," Scott said. He pitched his empty soda can into the trash. "You got any more soda?"

"Yeah, sure," Darryl said. He stood to leave. "Just pause the movie for me."

Scott fumbled with the remote control and pushed a button. The screen jumped to Channel 7. "Oops. Wrong button."

Darryl glanced at the screen. "Hold on."

"What?"

"I know that place. Isn't that the Borders bookstore downtown?"

Scott squinted. "Sure is."

"Who's that blonde lady at the mike?"

"Sarina Fox. I think she's a star in *The Hex* or whatever," Scott said. "Girls love that show—don't ask me why."

They listened for half a second to the report.

"So, you want another Dr. Pepper?" Darryl asked with a sniff.

"Shh—I'm trying to listen."

The reporter was saying, "... to sign her new book. Sarina describes *White Magic* as an intro to Wicca for teens. Now, Wicca is a fairly recent incarnation of an ancient version of witchcraft. What's more, Wicca is one of the fastest-growing religions in America today. Judging from the number of fans squeezing into the bookstore, it looks like this TV star has struck a responsive chord with the book crowd."

The camera panned the faces of the audience.

"I don't believe it," Darryl said, pointing to the screen.

"What happened? Did Elvis show up?"

"Isn't that your sister in the front row?"

Scott's eyes narrowed. "What in the world ..."

"I didn't know she was into witchcraft."

"She's not." Scott sat forward on the edge of his seat. He was certain he'd seen Sarina's face somewhere just recently. But where?

"Then what's she doing next to Laura?"

Scott blinked. Darryl was right. It didn't make sense. Last year Laura was part of the dynamic Brooke-and-Laura duo of The Society. Granted, they met in the back of the Ascension Bookshop. But Becka would never hang out with them. At least not to Scott's knowledge.

The reporter finished his commentary, and the program switched to a commercial.

At the sight of his sister, Scott felt a sinking feeling in his stomach. Didn't Z tell him to be praying for her? Instead, Scott had been too busy eating pizza and watching TV. He'd blown it, big time. He'd completely neglected his part of the assignment.

Scott shook his head in disgust. "I'm such a dunce."

"No argument there."

"Nice."

Scott fell silent. A heaviness pressed down on his chest. His mind raced as he scanned the bedroom for a clock. "Hey, what time is it?"

"I think it's about eight or so."

"Perfect. Can I use your computer for a minute?"

"In the middle of our movie?"

Scott wiped his hands on his pants. "I just need a minute to see if Z is online."

Darryl adjusted his glasses. "I'm kinda surprised Z even talks to you after what we did to find him." Several months ago and at Darryl's suggestion, Scott, with the help of Darryl's computer-hack cousin Hubert, had tried unsuccessfully to trace Z's identity.

Scott shrugged. "Can he blame us for being a little curious? I mean, like, he knows stuff about us that only someone in the family would know, you know?"

"Huh?"

"Never mind. Let's see if he's online," Scott said. "Maybe he knows what's up with Becka and all that Wicca garbage."

❧ ❧

Sarina finished her reading. She placed her book on the table and brushed her fingers through her hair. "I'd be happy to take a few questions, if that's all right with you all."

Several hands shot up. Becka had plenty of questions burning inside her, but she was more than a little frightened to speak up.

Sarina pointed to a girl two rows behind Becka. "Let's start with you. What's your name?"

"Um ... it's Jamie."

"Hey, Jamie. What's your question?"

"Yes, like, well, I'm a really, really, big fan—"

"Thank you," Sarina said with a soft smile.

"I'm wondering how you had time to write a whole book when you're on the set so much."

Sarina tilted her head to one side. "When something is as important to you as Wicca is to me, you just make time, you know?" she said. "You may laugh, but a lot of the time I'd have to scribble bits and pieces on scraps of paper ... or even a napkin ... whenever the spirit gives me inspiration, I have to get it down. It's almost like I'm channeling and taking dictation from the spirit world. Next question?"

"I'm Ami, and I love your show too. In your reading, you used the word *esbats*. What's that?"

"Good question, Ami," Sarina said. "Much of our power, as Wiccans, is associated with the movements and rhythms of the cosmos. We witches coordinate Esbats, which is a ritual of divination, with the thirteen full moons of the year. These moon phases contain sacred energies that flow from the Great Goddess through us to do good."

Becka worked to collect her courage. She was about to raise her hand when Sarina pointed to a fiftyish-looking woman in the back corner.

"Thank you. My name is Trisha. To be honest, I've never watched your show. Mind you, it's nothing personal—"

"No offense taken," Sarina said with a wink.

"Yes, well, I am favorably impressed with your presentation and positive outlook on life. I think you make an excellent role model for today's young people."

"Thank you. Was there something I could help you with?"

"What would you say to parents who might be tempted to

deny their children the chance to explore what Wicca has to offer?"

Sarina took a deep breath. "I'd have to ask them what they're so afraid of. What's wrong with a teen seeking to be empowered, to get the most out of this life? There's nothing evil here. Remember, it's the intolerant, oppressive Christian faith that murdered millions of people with their Crusades in the Middle Ages."

Several people clapped their agreement.

Becka was stunned that nobody took issue with anything Sarina said. She had tons of questions. At the same time, she didn't want to embarrass Julie or the other friends who had come with her. As she wrestled with the decision whether or not to ask a question, her heart raced so fast inside her chest she thought it might just explode.

"Who's next?" Sarina asked. She surveyed the crowd and settled on a woman in a stylish red dress. "Let's go with the lady in red."

"My name is Stacey," she said confidently, as if interviewing for a job. "Thank you for taking my comment."

"My pleasure," Sarina said with a tilt of her head.

"To be candid, I have been on what you might call a spiritual quest of sorts," Stacey said. "And, thanks to your TV show, Sarina, I was recently introduced to the benefits of Wicca."

"I'm glad to know that," Sarina said, obviously pleased with herself.

Stacey returned a smile. "I can only speak for myself, but in the months that I've opened myself to the Wicca faith, I've been amazed to watch my career soar. I've felt my sense of inner well-being increase. And I'm in a great new relationship."

"I'm happy for you. Those are just some of the benefits awaiting those who would give Wicca a chance to transform their life." Sarina shifted her stance. Smiling, she asked, "Was there a question I could answer for you?"

"Actually, no," Stacey said, bringing a hand to her expensive-looking necklace. "I just wanted to say I'm indebted to you for your inspiration. Thank you for having the courage to point us down this pathway of enlightenment. I look forward to reading your book!"

Priscilla stepped to the mike amidst a smattering of applause. Sarina took one step backward. Priscilla said, "I can see that we have time for just one more question. Who wants to have the last word?"

Sarina returned to the microphone.

Becka figured it was now or never. She slipped up her hand barely above her waist. She stopped breathing. Out of the corner of her eye, she caught a glimpse of Laura staring at her. Becka couldn't be sure, but it seemed like Laura wasn't too happy that Becka was about to ask a question.

Sarina cleared her throat. "How about right here in the front row."

Becka looked to her left and then to the right. She was the only one in the front row with a hand raised. With her left hand, she pointed to her chest and mouthed the word, *Me?*

"Yes, what's on your mind?"

Becka swallowed hard. "Um, I'm wondering how you can say there are many ways to God."

Sarina raised an eyebrow. "I'm sorry. What was your name?"

"Oh, right, it's Becka." She felt her face flush. How could she be so dumb as to forget her own name?

"Becka ... why don't you tell me what's behind your question." Sarina offered a thin smile.

"Well ... for example ... in the Bible, Jesus said, 'I am the way, the truth, and the life.'" Becka felt a bead of sweat forming on her forehead.

Sarina folded her arms together.

Becka continued. "He didn't say '*a* way' but '*the* way.' And he also said, 'No one can come to the Father *except through me.*'"

Someone in the back of the room groaned. Someone else said just above a whisper—but loud enough for everyone to hear—"Give me a break."

Sarina fidgeted with a ring. "Uh-huh."

Becka pressed the point. "So that seems to me to kinda rule out your theory that there are many ways to God." She felt as if every eye in the room was riveted to the back of her head. "I'm just wanting to . . . well, to get your take on that."

Becka could see Krissi leaning away from her.

Sarina remained motionless for several seconds of silence. She unfolded her arms. "What you just said is . . . well, it's a perfect example of intolerance." Sarina placed her right hand on her hip, then said, "You want to know something, Becka? The goddess has revealed to me that you are an angry young lady . . . with hatred in your heart."

"But—," Becka started to say.

A hollow darkness filled Sarina's eyes. Her voice went cold. "As to what your Jesus says . . . I'll just have to disagree. To me, all religious pathways are right in how they pursue the great Universal Spirit—as long as they respect the rights of everyone to seek the goddess in their own way."

Every inch of Becka's skin tingled. Not only did she strike a raw nerve with Sarina, she did a perfect job of alienating just about everyone in the entire room.

Priscilla took the mike from Sarina. "Well, I believe our time is up. Thank you for enlightening us, Sarina." The audience erupted in hearty applause. Priscilla gave Sarina a sideways hug and added, "In spite of the lone dissenter, you were a real hit. Thanks, everyone, for coming tonight."

More applause. Sarina took a seat at the table and prepared to autograph copies of her book. As she reached for the pen, Sarina glared at Becka.

If looks could kill, Becka would be dead.

5

Les Henderson, Laura's dad, inched his chair forward. He and the mystery woman, the one whose voice Laura had heard on the answering machine, sat at a quiet table in the back of an Italian restaurant, relaxing on a Friday night. The flame of a solitary candle danced between them. Off to their left, a wood-burning fireplace crackled. Les loosened his tie and sent a smile sailing across the table. She blushed.

"What looks good tonight?" Les said, glancing at the menu.

"Besides you?" she said, her tone as warm as the fire.

Les looked up. "You're only saying that because it's true," he said with a playful wink. "I hear the gnocchi is great."

"Ooh. You are positively intoxicating, Les," she said.

Their eyes lingered together. After a long moment, she looked away, carefully placed her napkin on her lap, and then picked up and scanned the menu. She stole a look over the top, where once again she met his gaze.

She raised an eyebrow. "What is it?" she said, fiddling with a diamond earring he had purchased for her twenty-ninth birthday several weeks ago.

Les placed his left elbow on the table and rested his chin on his hand. "I can't take my eyes off you."

"Well, if you don't, I may just melt right here."

A waiter approached the table with a loaf of warm, sliced garlic bread drizzled with olive oil and spices. He placed the wooden cutting board on the table, disappeared for several seconds, and returned with two full glasses.

"Have we decided?" the waiter asked. He cupped his hands together in anticipation.

"I'd like for this night not to end," she said, "but that's not on the menu." She pursed her red lips, pretending to pout.

"Ah, I see," said the waiter. "Very well, then. May I suggest the Passion Pasta for two? It's exquisite." With a gloved hand, he pointed to the Chef's Specials.

Without taking his eyes off his date, Les said, "I believe that will be perfect."

"I'll see right to it." The waiter gathered the menus and slipped away.

"Tell me," she said, tapping Les on the hand. "Where's your wife tonight?"

It was Les's turn to raise an eyebrow. "Not to worry. She went out of town for the weekend."

Her face lit up. She reached across the table and touched him on the back of the hand. "Oh, Les, that's just fantastic. We can stay out and dance the night away ... and no one will ever know."

"You were absolutely golden tonight," Demi said as she slid into the limo next to Sarina. The chauffeur closed the door and circled round the front to take his place behind the wheel. Within seconds, the limousine eased away from the curb and merged into the flow of traffic.

Demi pushed the intercom button on the overhead console. "James?"

"Yes, ma'am?"

She consulted her Palm handheld. "Caesar's ... on Third and Main."

"My pleasure."

For three years, the slender, forty-two-year-old redhead had served as Sarina's personal manager and literary agent. Having landed Sarina a lucrative, six-figure book deal, which she quickly farmed out to a ghostwriter, Demi was determined to push Sarina into as many personal appearances as possible. Tonight marked the tenth out of thirty in-store signings.

Sarina dug her hand into the leather seat between them. "Did you see what that ... that little *witch* in the front row did to me?"

"Coming from you, Sarina, I'd say that's an interesting choice of words," Demi said with a look over the edge of her designer glasses.

"You know what I mean," Sarina snapped. "The nerve. I'd love to pull out her stringy brown hair ... one strand at a time. *WITCH!*"

Demi squeezed her hand. "Definitely, without question, this was your best performance so far," she said, trying to smooth things over. "You know something, kiddo? You almost converted me to become a Wiccan."

"Who does she think she is?" Sarina fumed, ignoring the compliment. "Don't you get it, Demi? She embarrassed me in front of the crowd. I'm so mad, I could spit nails."

"You handled her perfectly."

Sarina continued as if she hadn't heard the affirmation. "But no ... the twerp had to challenge me. And, in case you forgot, that cameraman even got the whole thing on tape. Urrggg!" Sarina jabbed a finger in the air. "I could just *kill* her for that ..."

Demi cleared her throat. "You might just have your chance tonight."

Sarina froze. "What's that supposed to mean?"

"You're scheduled to have dessert with her and some of her friends in —" she consulted her watch — "fifteen minutes."

Sarina's eyes blazed. "No way. I'm not doing it."

"Yes you are, Sarina," Demi said. "We're doing this as a favor, remember?"

"Enlighten me," Sarina said.

"For the lawyer ... for the guy who handled my divorce."

A puzzled look crossed Sarina's face.

"Let me refresh your memory," Demi said. She turned slightly in her seat toward Sarina. "Les Henderson was my divorce attorney. He saved me a ton of money too. As a favor, I promised we'd do dessert with his daughter, Laura, and a couple of her buddies when we came through town."

Sarina released a slow breath like a leaking tire.

"We've already been over this," Demi added, "and you agreed to do it, remember?"

Sarina rolled her eyes. "Tell 'em I'm sick. I'm losing my voice. I can't make it. Regrets. Done."

Demi removed her glasses. "Sarina, I gave him my word. All I'm asking is for you to hold yourself together long enough to eat a scoop of spumoni with a group of teenagers. Come now, babe, do it for Demi."

Sarina crossed her legs and then folded her arms together. "I don't even like hanging out with the fans," she said, looking out the window at the passing streetlights.

"I know," Demi said. "But you're a great actress. You can pull it off. You always do."

"And I only agreed to these in-store signings because you guys said it would boost sales."

"And it has."

"But now," Sarina said, looking directly at Demi, "you want

me to sit across the table from some kid who gets her kicks out of trying to make a fool out of me? Where does it end?"

"Sarina, snap out of it," Demi said. "I'm telling you, you handled the situation perfectly. And the crowd loved you. Didn't you hear them? They were on your side the whole time. Just stick to the script. Go in there, smile, talk about the TV show. Kids love all of that behind-the-scenes stuff. Tonight will be over sooner than you think."

"I don't know. There's something about that girl ... Becka," Sarina said, staring into the night.

"I need you to do this for me."

They rode in silence for a minute. The only sound came from the muted rotation of the tires against the pavement.

"Demi ... I'll do this on two conditions."

"Name it."

"I want to sit as far away from her as possible," Sarina said. "And I want you to bail me out after fifteen or twenty minutes tops."

"Done."

👁 👁

"What came over you, Becka?" Laura asked once they were seated in the Suburban. "Of all the dumb things to do. I wanted to crawl under my chair."

Becka winced. "Sorry."

"Here I got my dad to set stuff up and you—"

"Laura, I said I'm sorry," Becka said, this time turning halfway around in her seat. It was going to be a long night, of that she was sure. Laura had avoided her during the book signing as if she had a contagious disease.

"I don't want to be mean," Krissi said, "but Sarina's only the hottest star on TV and you basically put her on the spot." Her eyelashes fluttered as she said, "It might be a good idea for you to go easy on the spiritual stuff, you know, at dessert."

"Don't listen to her," Julie said, turning her head to the side for a split second to face Becka.

"Really?" Becka said, a bit surprised.

"Yeah, I thought you were brave in there," Julie said.

"Really?" Becka's eyes widened.

"Yup, brave ... or do you mean *stupid?*" said Laura, cutting in with a laugh.

Becka's face flushed. Her heart sank to her feet.

"Like I said, to cross Sarina like that in public probably wasn't the best idea," Krissi said.

Rachael, who had been silent most of the night, spoke up. "Wow, I sure hope she doesn't plan to cast a spell on you for that."

"Naw. My guess is that Sarina has more class than that," Krissi said, her forehead wrinkled into a maze.

Laura softened her tone. "Hey, what do I know, Becka? You felt you did what you needed to do. Fine. But, honestly? I think I'll just die if you debate her at dinner."

"Okay, guys, how about we let it go," Julie said. "Becka just made a mistake, right, Becka?"

Becka looked out the window at the full moon. She bit her lip, trying to decide whether or not to defend herself. She *hadn't* made a mistake. She knew exactly what she had been doing. She wanted to make it clear that all paths don't lead to God. Some pathways are nothing more than counterfeits.

Becka brushed away a hot tear forming at the edge of her eye. "Julie," she said after a quick moment, "don't you remember how that demon posed as an angel and ended up possessing you?"

"Yeah, but Wicca is different," Julie said.

Becka studied her profile. "How can you be so sure?"

"Didn't you hear Sarina? She said so herself," Laura said. "Wicca is all about goodness and healing and wellness and personal prosperity—"

"I disagree," Becka said, cutting her off. "I believe that if we open ourselves to the spirit world through any kind of witch-craft, we're asking for trouble. Big time."

Laura laughed. "Open your eyes, Becka. If you haven't noticed, Sarina really has it together. I admire someone who's so in touch with herself. I'd say that means Wicca must be working for her."

Julie gave Becka a look. "Makes sense to me."

The Suburban rolled to a stop outside Caesar's restaurant, but Becka had lost her appetite a long time ago. It was bad enough that the others were on her case. But the thought of facing Sarina again, well, it felt as if a thousand panicked butterflies were flapping their wings inside her stomach.

Not to mention that Z wanted Becka to reach out to Sarina. But how?

6

Caesar's wasn't Becka's kind of restaurant. Not that she was opposed to going there once in a while. It's just that she and Ryan typically didn't hang out at places where tablecloths, fresh flowers, and real fireplaces were part of the ambience. It was, after all, the kind of place to go if you had lots of money and wanted to impress your date.

"Reservation for eight?" the head waiter asked in their direction.

The woman with red hair by Sarina's side nodded.

"Right this way," he said, holding a stack of menus.

Becka, avoiding eye contact with Sarina, trailed behind the others to a rectangular table positioned by the front window. As the last one in the group to arrive, Becka took the only seat available at the end of the table. That was fine with her. The farther from Sarina the better. Frankly, if she sat in the next room, that would be okay too.

The waiter took their drink orders. He bowed slightly, turned, and left.

The redhead, who sat on Sarina's right, was the first to get everyone's attention. "It's a pleasure to be with you tonight," she announced. "My name is Demi. I'm Sarina's personal assistant. It's been a long day, what with traveling, interviews, and the signing. I know Sarina is anxious to visit with you. Just so you'll know, we need to duck out a little sooner than originally planned. She has an early morning photo shoot. I'm sure you understand."

Somehow the speech felt a little rehearsed. Becka stole a look at Sarina. When Sarina glanced in her direction, Becka forced a grin. Sarina didn't smile in return. Instead, it felt as if Sarina was looking right through her. The dark, hollow feeling in Becka's stomach returned. The darkness she experienced had little to do with the dim lighting. It was as if she knew something dreadful was just around the corner.

Demi continued. "Feel free to ask anything you'd like about Sarina's book or the TV show."

Laura, who sat on the other side of Sarina, said, "I want you to know it was your show that really opened me up to become a practicing Wiccan."

Sarina seemed to relax a little at that. She smiled. "Is that so?"

Laura nodded. "I've always been interested in the occult. A group of us have really been into the supernatural. But I don't know ... when I started to watch *The Hex*, I saw there was a more positive way to connect with the spirit. That's when I sort of got into Wicca on my own."

"I'm glad to hear that," Sarina said. "We Wiccans have discovered that self-confidence, respect for the environment, and a deeper interconnection with the divine occurs when we align ourselves with the realms of the mighty Earth Spirit."

An awkward silence followed.

Rachael raised a hand just above the table.

Demi said, "Hey, feel free to jump in. This isn't a press conference."

That brought a laugh.

"Hi, Sarina," Rachael said with a hint of awe in her voice.

"I can't wait to read your book. But I was wondering if you ever thought of doing a movie?"

Sarina turned to Demi. Demi nodded. Sarina folded her hands together on the table. "I'll let you guys in on a little secret. We just landed a film deal, and we start production next month."

"No way!" Krissi said. "I can't wait to tell everyone at school."

"Uh, Krissi," Julie said, leaning toward her ear, "she just said it was a secret."

"Yeah, and if you let it out I'll have to put a spell on you," Sarina said. Her eyes narrowed.

Krissi froze. Becka watched as Krissi's face went as pale as a china doll's.

Sarina smiled. "I'm only playing with you."

Everyone but Becka laughed. Just sitting in the same space as Sarina was oppressive to her.

"Remember, Wiccans are into positive energy," Sarina said. "We only fight back if somebody or something strikes us first." She fixed her eyes on Becka as she spoke.

Becka almost jumped out of her skin when her cell phone vibrated in her pocket. She snatched up the phone, pushed Talk, and then pressed the phone to her ear. She turned away from the others toward the wall. "Hello?"

"Becka! It's me."

"Hey, Scott." Although she had hoped it was her mother, Becka's heart brightened at the sound of his voice.

"How's the witch?"

"Um..." Becka looked around, but the others were busy talking to the guest of honor. "I really can't talk. We're about ready to order dessert."

"Where?"

"Caesar's."

"Ooh. Fancy schmancy."

"Anyway, let's just say things are super intense. I feel so

outnumbered." She looked around again. Laura and Krissi were getting up to leave. She watched as they headed toward the restroom.

"I figured that," Scott said. "Darryl and I saw you on TV."

Becka swallowed. *Great. Now the whole world probably thinks I'm a jerk,* she thought.

"Hey, I talked to Z online," Scott said. "He filled me in on all that Wicca stuff. Pretty heavy-duty. He suggested that we pray together."

Becka sighed. "Boy, could I use your prayers, little bro."

"Put your hand on the phone and pray along with me," Scott said, imitating a radio preacher he once heard.

"Very funny, Scott," Becka said. She cupped her hand over the mouthpiece. "I can't quite tell you how I know this, but I think something pretty serious is about to happen."

"Really?" Scott said. "Like what?"

"I can't say for sure."

"Just remember that verse in Matthew: 'For where two or three come together in my name, there am I with them.' So, let's pray already."

"Um, Scott, maybe you should do the honors," Becka said, changing the phone to her other ear. "I don't think it's such a good idea for Sarina to hear me, you know, praying."

"Okay. Well, Lord," Scott began, "be with Becka tonight as she's with Sarina. We don't know exactly why things happen the way they do, but ... we know you have Becka there for a reason. Give her the strength and ... the wisdom to take a stand for you against the tricks of the devil. Help her to feel your presence by her side. In Jesus' name. Amen."

Becka hung up and put the phone in her pocket in time to take a glass of iced tea from the waiter. As she set it down, she noticed her hand was trembling.

Krissi leaned against the bathroom countertop to reapply her lipstick. Beside her, Laura washed and dried her hands. With a twist, Krissi closed her lipstick case, tucked it into her purse, and turned to face Laura. "So, did you see that woman with your dad? You know, I'm pretty sure she was at the bookstore."

Laura crumpled the paper towel. "What are you talking about?"

"Didn't you see them?"

"Here? Tonight?"

"Yeah, sitting in the corner. By the fireplace. I saw them when we walked down the hall."

Laura's forehead creased.

Krissi took her by the arm and steered her to the door. "Come on, I'll show you." Krissi opened the door and walked down the hallway with Laura on her heels. They paused where the hall joined the main dining area.

"Over there," Krissi said with a nod toward the rear of the restaurant. "The blonde with the hot red dress making serious eyes at that man. Didn't she ask a question tonight?"

An audible gasp escaped Laura's mouth.

"And isn't that your dad with her?"

Slowly, Laura began to nod.

Krissi faced her. "Sorry ... not good, is it?"

Laura pushed past Krissi and headed straight for the table. Krissi followed in her wake. As Laura approached, the woman stopped talking and sat upright in her chair. She appeared flustered.

"Dad?"

Les turned and, at the sight of Laura, started to stand. "Hey, sweetie," he said, looking as guilty as a kid stealing a cookie from a cookie jar.

"What are you doing here?" Laura said, maintaining a slight

distance from her father. She fought back the flood of emotion welling up inside.

Les dropped his napkin on the table and stood to his full height. He brought a fist to his mouth and cleared his throat. "Laura, this is a ... client. Stacey Young. We're ... uh ... working late. What brings you here?"

"Dessert, with friends." Laura spoke the words with about as much warmth as an Alaskan winter.

"Stacey, meet my daughter, Laura," Les said with a wave of his hand. "She'll be a junior at Crescent Bay High."

"Senior ... I'll be a senior this year, Dad."

He offered a nervous laugh. "My mistake. How time flies."

"I'm very pleased to meet you," Stacey said without standing. "You know, she looks positively like you, Les."

Laura's ears burned. This was no client, of that she was sure. This was the woman who had left the message on her dad's answering machine. She had the same breathy voice. Not to mention the way she pronounced the word *positively*.

"Who's your *little* friend?" Stacey said with a plastic smile.

"That's Krissi. She's a *senior* too." Laura spoke the words without a hint of graciousness.

"Care to join us?" Les said, swallowing hard. He took his seat again.

"No thanks," Laura said, in no mood for small talk. "We've got to get back to our table." What she thought of saying but didn't was *Fat chance. Sit here while Jezebel flirts with my dad? In your dreams.*

Instead, Laura turned away. Her heart hurt. Her head pounded. She had been betrayed by her dad and this home wrecker.

Something else bugged her. Why hadn't her spell worked on Stacey? Laura had done everything by the book, hadn't she? As she and Krissi marched away from the table, Laura knew exactly who to ask.

Sarina.

7

Claire Williams sat on a well-worn wooden bench under a tall pine tree. The coolness of the night was as refreshing as the opening session of the Free to Be conference. She pulled her knees up to her chest and studied the full moon. As her eyes adjusted to the meager light, she inhaled deeply of the pine aroma carried by the gentle evening breeze.

Claire couldn't recall the last time she'd treated herself to the luxury of an entire weekend away. After listening to tonight's keynote speaker, Claire realized how much her life had been put on hold since her husband died. True, life this past year had been filled with activity.

The relocation to Crescent Bay from Brazil.

Becka and Scott starting a new school.

Their endless adventures, thanks to Z.

Searching for work.

Volunteering at church.

It all added up to the simple fact that Claire had been on maximum spin since she could remember. No wonder she struggled to find time to feed her spirit and to discover what new direction God might have for her. She closed her eyes as she lingered in the stillness of the moment, basking in the tranquillity it offered.

Without warning, with the suddenness of a flash of lightning, the intense need to pray for Becka struck her. She didn't know why, but the prompting of the Holy Spirit was unmistakable. Her eyes flew open as she bolted upright and lowered her feet to the ground.

Somewhere in the depths of her spirit she had an overwhelming sensation that Becka was about to be confronted with a test of faith. And oddly, in the next instant, a picture of one of the items Z had provided came to mind: the earplugs. Her forehead creased. Why had he mailed them to Becka? Z always seemed to provide the perfect item for the adventures the kids were involved in. This one didn't make sense.

A moment later, at least one possible reason dawned on her. Maybe the earplugs symbolized something. Maybe Z was suggesting that Becka block her ears against the lies of the enemy. Was that it?

Claire began to pray silently. *Dear Lord Jesus, right now, in this moment, I commit my daughter Becka to you for protection. Be a shield against the schemes of the evil one. Be her strength. Be her confidence. And I pray that you keep her from listening to the lies and distortions of the great deceiver. May she stand strong for you. In Jesus' name. Amen.*

As she finished, Claire reached into her purse for her cell phone. She had to reach Becka.

❧　❧

Becka watched as Laura and Krissi hurried back to their seats at the table. She couldn't help but notice that something was definitely bugging Laura. But what? Laura's eyes seemed to shift rapidly between Sarina, who was answering a question about out-of-body experiences, and someone in the other room. Becka strained to see what Laura was looking at but couldn't tell, at least not from her current position.

For her part, Becka had taken about all she could handle from Sarina. "The goddess this" and "the goddess that" added up to a mountain of spiritual mumbo jumbo as far as Becka was concerned. Sarina really lost her when she rambled on about reincarnation as part of a Wiccan's quest.

The waiter appeared, carrying a tray. He began to serve the desserts when Demi spoke up. "This certainly has been a lot of fun, hasn't it?"

Rachael nodded. "It's really awesome that you made the time to meet with us, Sarina."

"Unfortunately," Demi said, consulting her watch, "we need to take off in another minute or so. Does anyone have a final question?"

It had taken Becka every ounce of restraint to keep quiet the whole night. No way would she risk ticking everyone off with another one of her "rude" questions.

Laura blurted out, "I've got a situation I really need your help with."

Sarina tilted her head. "What is it, Laura?"

"Okay, for starters my dad is in the other room," she said with a quick point of her forefinger. "He's over there in the back corner with … a woman. The blonde in a red dress."

Sarina's face maintained a blank look as if she didn't understand.

Laura said, "The problem is, she's not my mom. She's some young flirt. Actually, she was at the book signing this evening. I don't know if you remember, but she's the one who talked about how great Wicca has been for her, and how it helped her with her job and with some guy she's been seeing. I can't believe she was talking about my father."

"Well, I'm sorry to say that not everyone uses the power of Wicca the right way. Some people allow selfishness to destroy the good that Wicca can bring. I understand. Go on," Sarina said.

"Well, see, this afternoon I overheard that woman over there leaving a message on my dad's answering machine," Laura said. Her words ran together in her haste.

"Take your time, Laura. I can tell this is important to you," Sarina said.

Demi checked her watch.

"Uh, thanks," Laura said, taking a quick breath. "I had this feeling that if she's not stopped, she'll break up my parents' marriage. So I cast a spell on her to bind her tongue and to return on her the evil she's doing against our family."

Becka couldn't help but notice the others were riveted to Laura's story. Aside from the soft music playing in the background, she could hear a pin drop. Again, her feelings of apprehension returned. Somehow Becka knew something very dark and very evil was about to happen.

And she sensed it involved Sarina.

"Was I right in doing that?" Laura asked.

Sarina considered this. "Like I've said, for the most part Wiccans don't use spells against other people. However, in this case, I'd say you are perfectly right to defend what's important to you."

"So, why ... well, why didn't it work?" Laura said.

"I'd have to say that you allowed the anger in your heart to zap your kinetic connection with the goddess," Sarina answered.

Becka shook her head in disgust and said under her breath, "A case of bad karma, huh?"

"Quit it," Julie said with a kick under the table.

Sarina glared at Becka. For a second, Becka thought Sarina might leap across the table and strangle her. Instead, Sarina shifted her gaze back to Laura and said, "Why don't we try again — together."

"Really? Right now?"

A smile eased across Sarina's face. "Yes, but first I want you to release the negative energy that you're feeling. Can you do that for me?"

Laura inhaled deeply and released a long, continuous breath. She nodded.

"Good. Now, would you mind handing me the saltshaker," Sarina said, pointing to Rachael.

Rachael passed it to her.

"Salt represents the earth," Sarina said as she removed the top. She poured the contents out between her fingers onto the table. "Now, if someone would pass me the candle, which obviously represents fire."

Krissi passed the candle to Sarina.

Sarina took the candle and then reached for a glass of water. "This glass represents the waters of old," she said, stirring the liquid with a finger. She took her napkin and lit it in the fire. She blew out the flame on the napkin so that it smoldered, emitting a wisp of black smoke. "The smoke represents the air. Together we will call upon these elements to create a sacred space in our midst. Shall we?"

"Yes, yes," Laura said, her eyes wide with wonder.

Becka felt her heart starting to race out of control. Was Sarina actually going to cast a spell at their table?

Sarina raised the candle above her head, closing her eyes as she did. She tilted her chin up and said, "Holy goddess, we consecrate these elements to the use of thy service. We bind any negative forces that would obstruct their efficacy. In the name of the lord and the lady, empower us now. So mote it be."

Sarina lowered the candle and, with the slap of her hand against the table, said, "I seal this sacred space."

Becka almost jumped out of her seat.

"Now, Laura," Sarina said, her tone low and just above a whisper, "I want you to recast the spell you uttered this afternoon. Do you remember the exact wording?"

"Yes," Laura said.

"Then take my hand," Sarina said reaching out to Laura. Their fingers entwined. Sarina lifted their hands just above the spilled salt. "Where two or more are gathered in your name, oh, goddess of the moon, so art thou."

Becka cringed at the abuse of Scripture. She was tempted to point out the misuse when Laura began to speak:

"Speaker of evil, temptress of my dad,
I bind your tongue; I forever banish you
From this home, so you harm us no more.
May the spirit deal with you according to your evil intent.
May only love and positive energy encircle my home,
So mote it be!"

Sarina appeared solemn but pleased. She released Laura's hand. "May spirit be pleased. So mote it be."

"Okay, all right, there you have it," Demi said, starting to rise. "Sarina, we really do need to be heading back to the hotel. Remember the photo shoot in the morning?" They exchanged an impatient look.

"She's right. Enjoy the rest of your evening," Sarina said as she stood. "It's been a pleasure, especially being with a fellow true believer," she said to Laura. They shook hands. Sarina leaned forward and started to shake hands with Krissi when a bloodcurdling scream caught everyone's attention.

Becka's heart tried to leap out of her chest.

The sound of breaking glass and dishes filled the air.

CRASH! SMASH! CRASH!!

It sounded as if a tornado had touched down in the middle of the restaurant.

BAMM! CRASH! SMASH!!

Becka and the other girls jumped out of their seats.

"Oh ... my ... *word!*" they heard someone screech.

"HELP! Can't somebody help her?"

"Call 9-1-1!"

Becka and the others raced toward the source of the confusion, then froze as two dozen patrons pushed to get out of harm's way. Becka stared, momentarily numbed by the surreal drama unfolding before her eyes.

The woman in the red dress was flailing around, clutching at her throat with both hands.

"Oh no, that's Stacey!" Laura cried out.

"I–I ... had no idea," Krissi stammered. "The spell ... it really worked fast ..."

Stacey, driven by an unseen force, lunged headlong into another table. Plates, candles, and silverware flew in a dozen different directions. Shards of glass scattered into a million fragments as the dishes hit the marble floor.

Stacey's eyes bulged as she gasped for air. Her face, drawn as tight as a drum, was turning blue. An instant later, she hit the floor, where she gyrated in convulsions. Her face started to bleed, cut by fragments of splintered glass. She staggered to her feet, still clawing at her throat as if trying to scrape open a passageway to breathe.

"What on earth is going on?" Les shouted. With arms outstretched, he reached to contain her.

If Becka hadn't seen Stacey's reaction with her own eyes, she wouldn't have believed it. Stacey grabbed Les, throwing him against the wall with superhuman strength. He slumped to the floor. The next instant, Stacey threw herself face first against the table and then fell to the floor, where she flailed around like a wounded animal, knocking over chairs with her legs.

The crowd backed away as more tables and chairs were toppled.

As quickly as the confusion had begun, it stopped. Stacey's body tensed. With a lurch, she stumbled to her feet. Her face, red and puffy, twisted into a ferocious scowl, and a thin trickle of blood oozed its way down her cheek from a cut above her right eye. Her eyes, blazing with rage, scanned the crowd.

She locked eyes with Laura and started to hiss. A deep, guttural hiss.

Becka's skin crawled. She had an idea that the worst was yet to come.

Laura, who was just several feet from Becka, took a step backward. Then another. And another.

An agonizing scream escaped Stacey's mangled mouth. *"YOU! YOU DID THIS TO ME!"*

Laura gasped. She took another backward step.

"Don't think you can just walk away ...," a voice from somewhere deep inside Stacey bellowed. She raised her arms as if ready to attack. Her fingers twitched with anticipation. She snatched a knife from one of the few upright tables. With a shriek, she thrashed at the air in front of her with the blade. "Now it's my turn ... *witch!*"

"Someone call the police!" a waiter shouted. *"NOW!"*

8

I'm not so sure I agree," Darryl said with a generous sniff.

"With what part?" Scott leaned away from the computer, where they had been communicating with Z for several minutes.

Darryl blinked. "I ... I can't say for sure, but ..."

Scott jumped in. "Don't forget, Z's an expert in this stuff."

Darryl pushed his glasses up the bridge of his nose. "Okay, so I'm not an *expert*. But still ... maybe I don't see what the big deal is if someone wants to pursue a 'higher level of God consciousness' — or whatever Z called it — and they, like, use Wicca to get there."

"So you agree with Wiccans who think all that chanting, using herbs and incense, and setting up altars and shrines to channel the energy of the universe is the way to get to God?"

"Maybe. I don't see why not."

Scott reached for his soda. "Let me ask you this. When it comes to God and the supernatural world, you'd agree with the saying 'Whatever works for you,' right?"

Darryl took off his glasses and cleaned them with the end of his shirt. "I guess. Sure. Whatever floats your boat. I mean,

I haven't really studied all of this God stuff ... like you guys. It just sort of makes sense."

"Okay, look at it this way," Scott said, remembering something his dad used to say on the mission field. "If there are a bunch of different ways to get to God, why did God bother sending Jesus?"

Darryl shrugged. "Hey, maybe we should just forget about it and see what's on TV."

"Or not," Scott said. "Come on, this is important, Darryl."

"Maybe I don't want to argue about—"

"Who's arguing? We were just talking, at least the last time I checked."

Darryl sniffed.

"Think about it," Scott said. "The Bible says that Jesus was God's only Son ... and that his mission was to die on a cross for boneheads like you and me. Jesus even said he was the only way to God."

"Your point?"

"Jesus and Wiccans can't both be right, that's all."

"How can you be so sure there aren't other, well ... options?"

"You're a logical kind of guy," Scott said.

"I am?"

"I think so," Scott said. "So look at it logically. If there's more than one way to get to God other than Jesus," Scott said, scratching the back of his neck, "then I guess I could stand on my head ... or click my heels together three times ... or eat a pizza a day ... or do just about any other crazy thing I want to do and still get to God."

Darryl reached for the remote control. "You're losing me."

"Hold on," Scott said. "What I'm saying is that if clicking my heels together worked, then there wasn't a need to send Jesus. Get it?"

"I guess I see your point—kind of."

"My dad used to say that Jesus came because we were out of options. Nothing we do, except to have faith in him, works."

"Let's say I were to agree," Darryl said.

"Okay."

"Then what do you think happens when those Wicca girls do their thing?"

Scott cleared his throat. "I'd say they're opening themselves up to demons. And demons don't mess around. Sooner or later they'll destroy you."

Careful not to trip in the darkness, Claire hurried toward the lodge, carrying her conference notebook and Bible. As she had suspected, there wasn't cellular coverage in the remote location of the camp, but she remembered seeing a pay phone outside the front doors near the base of the steps. The uneasiness in her spirit was almost overwhelming. She started to pray with every step.

Jesus ... Jesus ... be with Becka. Protect my daughter. Put your guardian wings around her. Help her faith to remain strong no matter what comes her way. Give her the wisdom to rely on your power—not her own.

Claire was torn. On one hand, she realized that God had called Becka to be in the thick of spiritual warfare—especially since their move to Crescent Bay. On the other hand, she desired for Becka to be kept out of harm's way. Especially now.

Lord Jesus, Claire continued as she approached the phone, *she's my only daughter ... I've already lost my husband. I know you're sovereign. You promised not to give us more than we can handle ... but the thought that Becka may be in danger is really weighing on my heart. Be my peace too.*

Claire reached the phone, set her Bible and notebook on a bench to the left, and fished out her calling card from her pocket.

She squinted at the small print. The yellow bug light overhead did little to help her make out the number.

She snatched up the handset and discovered that the pay phone had probably been installed around the time Christopher Columbus discovered America. At least that was her guess. As she punched in the numbers, some of the buttons on the keypad stuck. She hung up and tried again. This time more slowly.

Several people walked out of the lodge as she brought the cracked earpiece to the side of her head. The phone rang.

Once. Twice.

According to Julie's mother, Becka would be at dinner right about now.

Five rings. Six rings.

Why wasn't she answering? "Jesus ... Jesus ... be with Becka," she prayed under her breath. The static on the line added to her growing sense of anxiety. It was then that she heard Becka's voice.

"Hey, it's Becka!"

"Oh, sweetie, it's Mom —"

" ... leave a message and I'll get back to you."

Claire's heart dropped, disappointed she couldn't get through. She heard the tone and then started to speak, her voice heavy with emotion. "Oh, Becka ... I just ... well ..." She swallowed. "I really wanted to hear your voice ... to know you're okay ... I'm praying for you, baby. I'll try again soon."

As she hung up, a chill swept over her. Her fingers lingered on the handset. "Jesus," she whispered, "be her protection." She leaned over, picked up her Bible, and clutched it to her chest. Behind her, the lodge door closed with a bang. Claire's heart jumped. She turned around as Susan Murdock, Becka's youth pastor, bounded down the steps.

"Hey, Mrs. Williams."

Claire wiped a tear from the corner of her eyes.

Susan studied her face. "You okay?"

Claire shrugged. "Mostly."

"That is *so* not the truth. What's up?"

Claire looked toward the moon. "I can't shake this feeling that Becka may be in real danger tonight."

Susan slipped her hand around Claire's arm and walked her to a nearby bench. Susan pulled her hair back over her shoulders as they sat. "You wanna talk about it?"

A nod. "Becka's at Julie's for the weekend," Claire said softly. "Tonight they went to a bookstore to meet that actress Sarina Fox."

"She's in *The Hex*, right?"

Claire nodded. "So you can imagine why I'm concerned."

"I can. And get this," Susan said, crossing her legs. "Most of the girls in youth group are all into that show."

Claire raised an eyebrow. "Really? *Christian* kids?"

Susan sighed. "You have no idea. I mean, Todd and I are having such a hard time getting them to see how dangerous the Wicca belief system really is. They say it's no big deal. It's just a TV show. But it's not. Wicca is another counterfeit that opens people up to the occult."

Claire took a deep breath. "Which is probably why I can't shake this heavy feeling inside."

"Maybe this will help," Susan said, reaching for Claire's Bible. "May I?"

Claire handed her the Bible.

"I read this in Psalm 121 this afternoon." Susan flipped to the passage. "Here it is: 'My help comes from the Lord, the Maker of heaven and earth … The sun will not harm you by day, nor the moon by night. The Lord will keep you from all harm—he will watch over your life; the Lord will watch over your coming and going both now and forevermore.'"

A smile found its way to Claire's face as the weight of the burden she was carrying began to lift. "Thanks. I needed to hear that."

"You want to know something else?" Susan said, handing the Bible back. "I've watched Becka. She's different. She takes her faith seriously. I wish more kids were like her. What I'm trying to say is that she's well grounded in the Word."

Claire searched her eyes. "I've seen that too. But I guess I'm praying Becka doesn't get arrogant and make the mistake of facing spiritual warfare without relying on the Lord. Not even for one second."

9

Becka's eyes snapped back and forth between Stacey, whose freakish ranting held everyone captive, and Laura, who would be the next target of Stacey's wrath if she wasn't stopped. Stacey's chest heaved. Her eyes bulged with a crazed intensity, and she waved the knife wildly.

Although Becka stood her ground, most of the patrons scrambled away from Stacey's menacing threats to the far recesses of the restaurant. Even the busboys, waiters, and cooks huddled behind the now-closed kitchen door.

No one moved. No one dared to attract Stacey's attention.

Somewhere along the edge of Becka's hearing, she picked up another drama unfolding not far from her. Keeping an eye on Laura and Stacey, Becka forced herself to tune into the heated debate behind her.

Krissi cried out, "Do something ... *anything*, Sarina!"

"Sarina, the car is waiting," Demi said, her voice strained but firm.

"What in the world?" Krissi said. "You can't just leave ... not now. We *need* you."

"Sarina, I'm telling you, don't get mixed up with this," Demi said, the impatience in her voice growing.

Becka's head spun around to steal a look. Sarina stood midway between the main exit and the standoff. Her eyes, wide as saucers, filled with indecision.

Or is it fear? Becka thought.

Krissi was all arms, waving and pleading. "Pleeease ... I'm begging you. Stop her. She's gonna hurt Laura."

Demi, no longer holding the front door ajar, stomped to Sarina's side. She grabbed her arm. "Are you hearing me, Sarina? The car. Let's go. You don't need this."

Sarina blinked as if having made up her mind. With a yank, Sarina freed herself from Demi's hold. Her eyes narrowed, filling with white-hot rage. She strutted toward Stacey, stopping ten feet short of the knife-wielding monster.

For her part, with the speed of a rocket, Stacey raced to Laura's side. Faster than light, Stacey's arm shot out. With one hand, she grabbed Laura around the base of her throat and then dragged her to the center of the room. The harder Laura resisted, the tighter Stacey's grip around her neck became.

Becka's heart drilled against her rib cage with the force of a jackhammer. She knew exactly what was going on.

She had seen this behavior before.

Stacey was possessed.

Becka also knew what she should do to stop it. But for an instant, she hesitated. She couldn't help but think back to the way Laura, acting on orders from Brooke, had held a knife to her throat several months ago, just as Stacey was currently doing to Laura.

Turnabout was fair play, right?

Why should Becka stop what Laura and Sarina had started? After all, everyone had spent this evening tossing their little jabs at her for confronting Sarina at the bookstore. Why get involved now? Sarina was a big-time TV star, right? And when it came to being a Wiccan, she talked a good game. Why not let her handle things her way? They'd just get what they deserved. Here was Becka's chance to be rid of at least one of her antagonists.

As if in answer to her questions, a single word surfaced in the back of her mind: *earplugs*. Becka sucked in a quick breath. Z had given her earplugs with a note. What had Z written? She strained to remember. Not five seconds later, it hit her.

Be careful little ears what you hear.

Z must have known that the devil would try to fill her mind with doubt. Maybe even with the idea of revenge — of getting back at Laura for all the pain she and The Society had caused Becka ever since she and her family moved to town. The earplugs suddenly made sense. They symbolized her need to block out the lies of the enemy.

Becka closed her eyes for half a second and prayed, *Forgive me, God, for letting my guard down. I'm embarrassed to think I actually listened to the voice of the devil and considered letting Laura get hurt. You love Laura ... and Stacey too. Be with me now, Lord, and may you have the victory here. In Jesus' name. Amen.*

Becka was about to swing into action when Sarina waved her arms through the air.

"RELEASE HER," Sarina commanded, her voice resonating as in an echo chamber. "By the power of the lord and the lady, I command you to cease your attack of darkness in this place."

For a quick moment, Stacey locked eyes with Sarina. Stacey's upper lip curled into a snarl. A low, hollow growl escaped her twisted mouth. "SILENCE! This is not your fight."

Sarina took one step forward, her eyebrows knotted into an angry line. Her right arm shot out. A long, slender forefinger jabbed at the space between them. "I call upon the air, the earth, the sea, and the fire to banish you — you spirit of barbarity — to outer darkness."

That brought a long, wicked laugh from the depths of Stacey's being. Still holding Laura by the neck with a viselike grip, Stacey placed the knife on a table and, with inhuman strength, seized a chair with her free hand and hurled it at Sarina.

Sarina brought her arms up to cushion the blow. On impact she yelped like a wounded puppy. The force of the airborne chair knocked her back several feet. Staggering, Sarina reached out to steady herself against a table. A vase of flowers toppled and crashed against the floor.

Stacey barked, "Be gone! This is not your fight. Now, *GO!*"

Sarina huffed, visibly shaken. As if on cue, she turned and marched to Demi. Sarina snatched up her coat, pulled it around her shoulders, and, seconds later, she disappeared through the door without saying another word.

Krissi dropped into a chair and buried her face in her hands. She started to cry. Julie and Rachael moved to stand near her, as if to share comfort in the confusion.

Becka turned and quickly studied the situation. Laura's dad, Les, was still slumped in a pile on the floor. No help there. In the confusion, she couldn't see exactly where Julie and Rachael were. Hopefully they'd head outside and away from danger.

Stacey's blonde mane, matted with sweat and food particles, framed her enraged eyes. She stood motionless, her stare lingering on the spot where Sarina had just left. Her fingers squeezed deep into the flesh of Laura's neck and showed no signs of easing up. If Becka didn't act fast, Laura would surely pass out — or worse.

Stacey blinked. She turned and shot a blast of fire at Becka with her eyes before her gaze moved to the fireplace.

As Stacey appeared to study the flames, Becka tried to speak, but her tongue stuck to the roof of her mouth. She discovered that her throat was as parched as hot sand. Her pulse maxed out. She tried to calm herself with a slow, steady breath, but her lungs burned as if she'd just finished a marathon.

Stacey dragged the helpless, doll-like body of Laura toward the fireplace. She picked up the fire poker. Still clutching Laura,

Stacey stoked the logs until the flames renewed their vigorous blaze.

Stacey looked directly at Becka, flinging her head back as her obscene laugh filled the air.

What's taking the police so long? Didn't anybody call for help yet? Becka thought. She managed to whisper, "Jesus ..."

The laughing stopped. Cold.

Stacey dropped Laura's body on the stone hearth of the open fireplace and spun around. The cut above her eye still bled, and her blackened eyes flared. "What ... was ... *that?* What did you say?"

Becka stood still. For a split second, a spark of doubt surfaced in her spirit. Who was she kidding? She was no match for this maniac. Every instinct told her to run. And fast. Becka silenced the restlessness with a verse she had memorized: *"My grace is sufficient for you, for my power is made perfect in weakness."*

Help me, Lord, she prayed. *Be my strength.*

Becka took a step forward. A piece of broken glass snapped underfoot. She cleared her throat. "By the power ... and by the blood of Jesus the Christ," Becka said, her voice growing stronger, "I command you to leave Stacey."

Stacey's eyelids twitched and fluttered like the wings of a butterfly. Her body convulsed as the voice within hissed. "I was summoned here," the demon said through Stacey's lips. "This is my vessel—leave me. Or must I destroy you too?"

Another bloodcurdling laugh pierced the air.

Becka stood her ground as the words of Romans 8 came to mind. *"For I am convinced that neither death nor life, neither angels nor demons ... nor anything else in all creation, will be able to separate us from the love of God that is in Christ Jesus our Lord."*

Becka said, "You're a liar ... just like your father, the devil. By the authority of Jesus of Nazareth, be gone from her!"

The demon hesitated.

"Now!" Becka demanded.

With a tormented scream, Stacey collapsed to the floor like a puppet whose strings were suddenly cut. Becka quickly moved to Stacey's side and knelt beside her still form. She felt for a pulse along Stacey's neck. Finding a faint pulsation, Becka looked toward the kitchen and said, "She's alive! Somebody call an ambulance. Hurry!"

Becka leaned close to Stacey's ear. "Hang in there. Jesus loves you, Stacey. You're gonna make it ... I promise."

"Becka!" Krissi screamed from across the room.

Becka's head jerked around. She looked at Krissi, puzzled.

"Laura ... she's on fire!"

Becka looked over at Laura, who wasn't making any effort to get away from the flames. Was she paralyzed? Had she blacked out? Couldn't she feel the fire burning her legs?

Was she dead?

"Julie," Becka said, "I could use a hand over here!"

Maybe Julie was in shock. Maybe she was scared. Whatever the reason, Julie bit her lip and didn't make a move to help.

There wasn't a second to lose. Rising, Becka sprinted to the fireplace and then pulled Laura by the arms away from the flames. Working as fast as she could, Becka yanked a tablecloth free from under a pile of broken plates, shook it out, and began to roll Laura in it.

Why weren't the flames going out?

A siren sounded in the distance.

Becka glanced around the room and spotted a table several feet away with pitchers of iced tea. She bolted upright, grabbed as many pitchers as she could carry, and doused Laura's body with the liquid. With the flames snuffed out, Becka dropped to her knees and cradled Laura's head in her lap.

Without warning, an overwhelming sense of compassion flooded Becka's heart. And for the first time since coming to

Crescent Bay, Becka felt a spark of love for this adversary. As she stroked Laura's hair, she couldn't tell whether or not Laura would make it.

Becka started to pray. *Not now, Jesus, not like this ... please, let her live.*

10

The full moon sent a gentle beam of dull light into the bedroom. With a squint, Becka looked at the radio alarm clock: 2:47. She yawned, stretched her back, and rolled onto her side. Although she, Julie, Krissi, and Rachael had stopped talking an hour earlier, Becka couldn't sleep. How could she?

The events of the day remained painfully fresh in her mind. The chaos. The paramedics. The police.

Becka actually found dealing with the police quite amusing. How do you explain a completely trashed upscale restaurant, three wounded bodies, and a missing TV star to police when, at the center of the investigation, was demon possession?

Who could they arrest for the damages to the restaurant?

Even now, she pictured the team of paramedics as they raced into Caesar's. Stacey had been the first to be carried out on a stretcher, while another team inserted a tube into Laura's throat so she could breathe before they transported her to the hospital.

Les was the last to go. According to the phone call she made to the nurses' station at the hospital before hitting the sack, Les had suffered a minor concussion and several scrapes. He had been treated and released. Becka figured he'd have a lot of explaining to do to his wife. She sure didn't want to be in his shoes.

Becka was especially thankful to learn that the burns to Laura's legs weren't as bad as anticipated. True, there were first-degree burns over 20 percent of Laura's legs, but that was minor compared to the damage to her vocal chords. Had Stacey's grip, under the demonic influence, remained much longer, the doctor was certain Laura's esophagus would have collapsed. Laura would be in the hospital at least several more days.

As of midnight, Stacey, however, remained in intensive care. Her situation was touch and go. Even after her vital signs stabilized, she'd have reconstructive work to undergo for the gash on her face. She'd most likely have to have psychiatric care, and she'd have to deal with the police as well.

Becka shuddered at the memory of Stacey's face.

Becka herself suffered only minor scrapes. The gauze wrapped around her left hand was uncomfortable, but she'd handle it. She was just glad the day was finally over. And after finally catching a quick phone call with her mom, Becka was happy to know that her mom would be heading home from the retreat early Saturday morning. They'd hook up around lunch. To think that it all started with that note and picture of Sarina from Z.

At the thought of Sarina, Becka cracked open her tired eyelids and spied the moon through the window. She was still unsure what Z had wanted her to do about Sarina. It wasn't like the two sat down for a quiet chat. Quite the contrary. Whatever it was, Becka was fairly certain she'd never see Sarina again.

But, hey, that's probably best, Becka thought.

She adjusted her pillow and closed her eyes.

Through the fog of exhaustion, Becka thought she heard a voice calling her name. There it was again. Closer now. Louder. Urgent. Pleading. Was she dreaming? Who would be calling?

Didn't they know she had been up half the night? Couldn't it wait?

"Becka ... telephone."

"Huh?" Becka rolled over.

"The phone. It's for you, Becka."

The voice sure sounded like Julie's. Becka blinked the bedroom into focus and noted its robin's egg blue walls. She squinted against the brilliance of the morning sun.

"I'm ...," Julie started to say. "Hey, I'm sorry to get you up, but it's Demi. On the phone." Julie, still wearing her pajamas, held out the cordless phone.

Becka pulled herself upright and then ran her fingers through her hair. The fog in her head started to lift. "What time is it?"

"Almost nine."

"Uh, Demi who?"

Julie plopped down on the bed next to her. "She's Sarina's agent person or whatever."

Becka took the phone and brought it to an ear. "Hello?"

"Becka? It's Demi. We met last night."

"Oh, right," Becka said. "Hi there."

"Listen, I'm sorry to call so early. I got Julie's number from the guest list last night and—"

"It's okay."

"Have you had breakfast?"

Becka chuckled. "I don't think my stomach's awake yet."

Demi was all business. "Great. Then you must join Sarina for breakfast ... we're at the Ritz."

"Me?"

"Just you, yes," Demi said. "Can you be ready in thirty minutes?"

That got Becka's attention. Suddenly awake, she felt her heart doing jumping jacks. "Sure thing, but—"

"Perfect. I'll send the limo around for you in half an hour."

"Okay, but what's this all about?" Becka said. "Hello?"

Becka and Julie exchanged a look.

"She hung up," Becka said flatly.

Julie grabbed Becka's arm. "Hey ... Sarina wants to have breakfast with you?"

"Looks that way. Wild, huh?"

"Big time," Julie said. She looked down at her hands. "I wish I were going."

"Fine. You're the birthday girl," Becka said, falling back against her pillow. "Go instead of me ... I'll just take a little nap."

"Yeah, in your dreams," Julie said, swiping the pillow.

Becka sat up. "What do you think she wants from me?"

"I dunno." Julie answered. "Maybe your autograph."

"Right," Becka said, stealing back the pillow and then hitting Julie with it.

Julie deflected the blow. "Yeah, well, she probably thinks you're a better ghostbuster or something." She paused for a moment before continuing. "Hey, Beck, I'm sorry for not helping you last night. I don't know what happened to me. I guess I just got freaked out by the whole thing."

Becka slowly smiled. "That's okay. I was pretty scared too. Do you think Sarina heard what happened, you know, after she left?"

Julie nodded. "I'd say so."

"How?"

"Hold on." Julie got up and darted out of the room. She reappeared, holding a copy of the *Crescent Bay Gazette*. "Right there. On the front page," she said with a point. "Looks like last night's little adventure at Caesar's is big news."

Becka's heart skipped a beat. A sharp pain flashed through her head. She never thought about the possibility of a reporter getting a hold of the story. Come to think of it, over the past year she and Scott had never attracted — nor did they want — any media attention whenever they were involved in spiritual warfare.

Not after the close call on Death Bridge.

Or the encounter at Hawthorne mansion.

But this was different. This involved Sarina Fox, a TV star in a town where stars didn't usually visit. Of course the press would be crawling all over the place. Becka wondered how she had managed to miss that not-so-little detail. Then again, what could Becka have done differently? It wasn't as if she wanted to confront a demon at an Italian restaurant. That's just the way things worked out.

Becka took the paper and read the headline: "TV's Favorite Wiccan No Match for the Devil."

"Oh, that's just *great*," Becka said. Her temples started to throb. "No wonder she wants to meet."

"Why is that?"

"Julie, don't you see?" Becka said, searching her eyes. "Sarina probably thinks I somehow staged the whole thing last night ... just to make her look bad."

"Now I *know* you're dreaming," Julie said.

Becka gasped as a new thought jumped to mind.

"What's wrong?" Julie said.

Becka's eyes widened. "I've got nothing to wear!"

11

The limousine, a late-model Mercedes-Benz, stretched the length of a full city block. At least that's the way it seemed to Becka as she slipped into the backseat. Once inside, the chauffeur closed the door, sealing out the outside world.

Becka's eyes darted around the luxurious interior. A TV. A stereo. A refrigerator. A wet bar. A sunroof.

Nice. Very nice.

Still, as nice as the limo was with its black leather seats, tinted windows, and fancy wood-grain trim, to Becka it felt strangely like the inside of a coffin.

Padded. And deadly silent.

She swallowed as she looked out the window. While the car eased away from the curb, Becka's emotions raced, especially now that the initial adrenaline rush gave way to reality. She was about to sit across the table from Sarina Fox, the Wiccan. A thousand questions crowded her already exhausted mind.

What was she getting into?

Why did Sarina want to see her—alone?

Would Sarina be mad? Probably. But how mad?

Becka had read stories about temperamental stars—how

they'd yell and bark out orders to bleary-eyed assistants and then snap the heads off anyone who didn't kiss the ground on which they walked. In the case of Sarina, Becka figured she'd be ten times worse, given the negative story in the paper.

How had the reporter put it? She thought back to the opening paragraph:

> TV's prime-time darling and star of *The Hex*, Sarina Fox, a self-proclaimed Wiccan, turned tail and fled in tears after a confrontation with an alleged manifestation of the spirit world. The altercation occurred at Caesar's, an Italian restaurant in downtown Crescent Bay. According to one witness, it took the actions of a former teen missionary, Becka Williams, to silence the hellacious encounter.

Becka cringed at the memory. While it was kind of cool to see her name in the paper, she never intended to draw attention to herself and certainly not to the exorcism.

Maybe this was a mistake. Maybe she should ask the driver to take her back to the safety of Julie's house. As she considered her options, Becka noticed a button on the overhead console marked CALL DRIVER. Fine. She'd just tell him she had a change of plans. Stuff like that happened all the time, right?

Becka started to reach for the button, then stopped.

Z.

There must be a reason Z had wanted her to connect with Sarina. But why? Whatever his reasons were, she was being handed another chance to reach out to her. Becka dropped her hand to her lap and turned toward the window. A moment later, she noticed a message on a signboard outside a church. It was one of those quasi-witty sayings pastors like to repeat. This one read "God Loves Knee-Mail."

Cute. But true.

In the haste of the morning, Becka had forgotten to bring

her concerns to God. She was about to pray when her cell phone started to play Beethoven's Fifth. She snatched it up and pushed the Talk button. "Hi, it's Becka."

"Becka?" She heard the caller say her name, but didn't recognize his deep, somber voice.

"Yeah, it's Becka."

"*The* Becka Williams?" the caller said.

Her skin started to crawl at his ominous voice. "Yes. Who's calling?" She looked at the phone number but didn't recognize it.

"Aren't you the witchbuster?" His tone darkened.

"Listen, *buster,*" she said, gripping the phone, "I'm in no mood for games. I'm hanging up."

The voice changed. "Hey, chill out. It's me. Your brother. Remember me?"

"Scott?" Becka said through clenched teeth. "You know you're being a real pain, don't you?"

"Isn't that great?" he said. "Darryl's got this new computer-based vocal harmonizer—"

"I should hang up on you right this second—"

"Okay, okay ... call off the dogs. I was just playing with you," Scott said with a warm chuckle. "So tell me, how are you? How was the party?"

She looked out the window. "I'm okay. Tired, mostly."

"How's that?"

She sighed. "Let's just say it was a long night."

"And ...?" Scott said, fishing for details.

Becka listened to the muted tones of the road noise through the thick leather padding of the limo as it cruised down the road. "Actually, can we talk later? I've got to—"

"Oh, that's right. I forgot," Scott said, cutting her off. "You're on your way to have breakfast with Sarina," he said with a hint of sarcasm. "Or let me guess, it's just 'my buddy Sarina'?"

"How'd you know I was—"

"I called Julie's ... they filled me in."

"Well, yes. We're gonna have breakfast."

"Hmm. Now that you're a big-time celebrity," Scott said, "I bet you're going to insist on driving everywhere in a limo." He laughed. "So where are you?"

"You'll never guess ..."

"Try me."

"In Sarina's limo." She had to laugh too.

"See, it's already happening, sis. Just remember us little people when you reach the top."

Becka noticed they were pulling into the parking lot of the Ritz-Carlton hotel. She asked, "Did Julie tell you what happened last night?"

"Yeah, but she didn't have to. I already saw it on TV."

Becka's heart lurched. "What do you mean ... *on TV?* You mean you read about it in the paper."

"Both actually. It's a really big story, Becka."

She bit her bottom lip. This wasn't what she wanted to hear.

"You still there?" Scott asked.

"Yeah, but—" Becka cleared her throat. "Listen, I've got to run. We just pulled up to the front doors. Pray for me, okay?"

"That's why I'm calling," Scott said. "You got two phone messages. Mom just called to tell me she's praying for you. She tried to reach you on the cell earlier, but it must have been off."

Becka's heart sank. She really would like to have heard her mother's voice again. Especially this morning. "Rats. I'll just see her when she gets into town. Who else called?"

"Ryan. He lost your cell number, wouldn't you know it, so he called the house. He misses you and is praying for you," Scott said. With a touch of sarcasm he added, "Isn't that sweet?"

Becka's face flushed. "As a matter of fact, yes. He's such a doll."

"Can I quote you?"

Becka's eyes narrowed. "If you do, you're taking your life in your hands, buster."

"Oh, and guess what?" Scott said.

"What? Hurry, I got to go."

"Got an email from Z today."

"Really?"

"Yeah. He said to ask Sarina about the mission field."

Her forehead knotted. "What does he mean by that?"

"Beats me," Scott said. "That's Z for you."

"Yeah, always mysterious. Well, I better go now. Bye, bro," Becka said, hanging up.

As the chauffeur came around to open her door, she noticed Demi standing at the curb.

And she didn't look happy.

12

"ight this way," Demi said, blasting through the front door
with enough force to almost bowl over the bellhop.

Becka scrambled to catch up.

"Thanks for coming," Demi said over her shoulder with
about as much warmth as an ice cube.

They walked so fast through the lobby toward the Ritz Café,
Becka hardly had time to let the posh surroundings sink in. She
did notice a handsome man playing a pearl white piano. The
sound of classical music filled the air. The piano, with its lid
up, was positioned in front of a commanding view of the rose
garden.

An enormous crystal chandelier dangled overhead. That was
hard to miss. And her feet — she noticed how they sank into the
most cushiony, well-padded carpet she'd ever stepped on. This
was definitely out of her league, not to mention way outside her
comfort zone.

Becka had spent most of her life on the mission field and
had never set foot in a hotel this elegant. She was already self-
conscious wearing Julie's clothes; as nice as they were, she felt

underdressed. The turbulence in her stomach wasn't helping matters either. She felt as if she had swallowed a squirrel.

Demi, still several feet in front, reached the café first. A second later, Becka breezed up alongside her.

"Table for two, ma'am?" said the hostess.

"We're already situated in the private dining room, thank you anyway," Demi said.

"Then you know your way," the hostess said with a broad smile and a wave of her hand.

Demi marched in, dodged several busboys, and snaked her way to a door on the far wall marked PRIVATE DINING ROOM. With a tug, she opened and then held the door for Becka.

Becka quickened her pace and stepped through the opening. "Thanks," she said, trying to be pleasant in spite of the growing sense of unease she felt with every second. Interacting with Demi was like talking to a tornado.

Demi blew past Becka and approached the table in the corner where Sarina was seated. Demi dropped into her chair and, with her forefinger, pointed to the seat opposite Sarina. "Have a seat," Demi said, sounding like a drill sergeant.

"Thanks." Becka pulled the chair out and offered Sarina a weak smile as she sat down. "Um ... good morning," she said, but the squirrel in her stomach had made its way into Becka's neck, causing her throat to choke off the words.

They were the only three people in the room. Cereal, juice, a pile of fresh-cut fruit, and a plate of assorted muffins were arranged between them. Sarina and Demi were drinking coffee, black.

Sarina, she noticed, had her hair pulled up into a clip. She wore blue jeans, a black shirt, and a jean jacket. Although the room wasn't particularly well lit, a pair of oversized sunglasses, like those provided by an eye doctor after dilating a patient's eyes, covered half of Sarina's face. Her cheeks appeared red and puffy. She wore little or no makeup and sat with her back to the window.

Becka detected a slight tremble in Sarina's hand as she brought a cigarette to her lips. She took a long, slow drag and exhaled a steady stream of smoke in Becka's direction.

Becka folded her hands in her lap. *Now what?*

After what felt like an eternity, Sarina took another drag and said, "I hope you're happy with yourself." She blew the smoke out the side of her mouth.

"Pardon me?" Becka raised an eyebrow.

"I guess you know you've just about ruined my career," she said with a wave of the cigarette. "The vultures in the press are circling. They can't wait to pick apart my flesh."

Becka couldn't believe what she was hearing. "I ... I—"

"It's true," Demi said, preoccupied with her Palm handheld. She glanced over the top edge of her glasses. Demi's phone rang. "Yes?" she said curtly and then listened for a second. "No ... no ... good *gracious,* no ... Sorry. Not a chance." With a snap, she closed the flip phone.

Sarina looked toward the ceiling.

Demi said, "That was the publicity department. They've received requests from *Good Morning America*, *The View*, and *Regis*—not to mention that all the major papers are looking for a comment. You see, Becka, they all want a piece of Sarina."

Becka managed to swallow. "All because of last night?"

Demi spoke. "As you can tell, we have a situation here."

Although Becka felt bad, she knew it really wasn't her fault. She figured she'd try to lighten things up. "At least it's not, like, the *Jerry Springer Show* calling," she said with a forced smile.

"They already did." Demi spat out the words.

Becka felt like crawling under the table.

"Obviously, you don't get it, do you?" Demi said, still looking over the top of her glasses. "Sarina Fox is an international phenomenon. She's the hottest thing going on television. She's worth millions. And last night she was upstaged by ... by a kid. No offense, mind you."

Becka's head hurt. Her neck ached. The room started to spin. She wanted to cry. It wasn't as if she had planned to wreck anybody's career. She didn't write the article that sparked the whole controversy. *This is so unfair,* she thought. *What am I supposed to do now?*

"Just tell me this, young lady. What did you think you were doing last night?" Demi said.

"I ... I was saving a friend's life."

"By the looks of it, you were trying to make a name for yourself at the expense of Sarina."

Becka shook her head. "No way. Besides, what was I supposed to do?"

"That's obvious," Demi said with a sneer. "You should have left well enough alone—"

"And let Laura die?" Becka could no longer hold back her feelings. She started to choke up. "You're being unfair. Both of you. And, frankly, I happen to think Laura's life is way more important than your career, Sarina—*no offense, mind you.*" Becka stood to leave.

Sarina removed her sunglasses. She took a drag and then snuffed out the cigarette butt in the ashtray. "Hold on, hold on. I can see this isn't going anywhere. Have a seat ... *please.*"

Becka hesitated. What was the point? Why hang around and get blasted? Becka looked at Sarina's dark, hollow eyes and saw something. But what? Sadness? Regret? Anxiety? Fear? Somewhere inside, Becka felt the gentle nudging of the Holy Spirit. *Be patient. This isn't about your feelings, Becka. It's about Sarina's life.* She sat down.

Sarina said, "Thank you." She reached inside her purse for a fresh cigarette. "There are a couple of things I need to know ... about last night."

Demi shot Sarina a look of warning.

Sarina waved her off. "I trust her, Demi."

Demi pulled off her glasses and tapped her teeth with the end of one earpiece. "You're making me nervous, Sarina."

"Not to worry. I can see it in her eyes. She's trustworthy."

Becka was unsure whether or not to believe her. Maybe this was part of a trap to get her to say something they could use against her. She took a deep breath. This was going to be harder than she expected. And although Becka had lost her appetite the moment she arrived, she wanted something to do with her hands. "May I?" she said, pointing to the muffins.

"Heavens, yes," Sarina said. She lit her cigarette. "Before I go on, I need you to promise me one thing."

Becka took a muffin, placed it on her plate, and looked at Sarina.

"Promise me that nothing we discuss leaves this room," Sarina said, tapping a finger on the table.

Becka nodded. "Sure thing."

"I'm serious. Not a soul."

"I understand."

Sarina held the cigarette in front of her mouth as she spoke. "For starters, I am *not* a witch. I don't really believe all of this Wicca stuff."

Becka's ears burned at that piece of information. "Excuse me?"

Sarina tilted her head. "That's right. It's just a part I play. I'm an actress, right?"

Becka couldn't believe what she was hearing. "No offense, but how can you live with yourself?"

"Welcome to Hollywood," Sarina said, brushing away a strand of black hair from her face. "That's the way it is in show business." She took a hard, long drag and then blew the smoke through her nose like a fire-breathing dragon.

"But . . . what about the book? What about the spell at dinner? What about—"

"Just smoke and mirrors." Sarina waved her cigarette in the air. "It's all part of the act."

13

"What's wrong?" Sarina said, peering at Becka through a cloud of smoke.

Becka, still trying to process Sarina's revelation, reached for her glass of orange juice. She paused, holding the glass in midair. "Sorry ... I guess I'm kind of in shock."

"What's the big deal? I'm an actress. I happen to play the part of a Wiccan," Sarina said, tapping the ash from her cigarette into the ashtray. "I could play Bozo the Clown. What difference does it make whether or not I'm really a clown?"

Becka considered this. "For starters, you don't have the nose for it," she said with a nervous laugh.

Sarina cracked a half smile.

"Besides, Bozo isn't messing around with the spirit world," Becka said as she sat back against her chair. "People who watch *The Hex* don't know whether or not you actually believe in it. With time they could easily start to think it's all true."

"Go on."

"Well, take Laura," Becka continued. "She said it herself ... she got into Wicca because of what she saw on the show."

Sarina bristled. "Don't try and pin her decision on me."

Becka flushed. "You're right. She made a choice, so that's on her. All I'm saying is that it's not a game. You can't just play around with this stuff. At least that's what God says in the Bible."

Sarina puffed away for a long minute.

Demi's phone rang again. She got up and walked to the corner of the room to answer it.

"I need you to explain something," Sarina said after another minute.

"Sure. At least, I'll try." Becka sipped her juice.

"What I don't get is," Sarina said, "last night I invoked a spell, a spell which, mind you, I didn't really mean."

Becka nodded.

"But after that woman—what's her name?"

"Stacey ... Stacey Young."

"Right. After Stacey got possessed, no matter what I said I wasn't able to undo it," Sarina said. "Seems it should work both ways, right?"

"Not really," Becka said, shifting in her seat. "At least, according to the Bible, only Christians have authority to cast out demons. And only in the name of Jesus."

Sarina didn't appear completely convinced.

"Okay," Becka said. "I'm not an expert, but demons in the spirit world are always looking for an invitation to break through to our world. When you and Laura cast the spell, you guys just happened to open the door."

Sarina tilted her head. "Let's say for the sake of argument I buy that. Then why couldn't we just send them back?"

Becka remembered an example her dad used back in Brazil. "It's sort of like toothpaste. You or I can squeeze the tube and the paste comes out. But only the manufacturer can put it back in."

Demi returned to the table. "That was the producer from *Oprah*. What did I miss?"

"We're talking about toothpaste," Sarina said with a touch of sarcasm.

Becka blushed. "Okay, so it's not the best example."

Sarina waved her on. "I'm just messing with you. Go on."

Becka swallowed. "Well, it's like the demons are the toothpaste. Once we release them, only God's Spirit has the power to put them where they belong."

Demi cut in. "I hate to do this, but Sarina's got to catch a plane in a hour."

"I do?" Sarina said, genuinely surprised.

"I agreed to do *Oprah*, Sarina."

Sarina started to protest. "Wait a second—"

"No. Listen to me, darling," Demi said, putting a hand on Sarina's arm. "I've thought of a way to spin this story. Trust me. We'll end up smelling like roses—and selling a ton of your books. Get serious. We're talking *Oprah* here. And if we don't come out and address the situation, I promise this story won't go away anytime soon."

Sarina took a long drag and then snuffed out the cigarette. "She's the boss." She put on her sunglasses, grabbed her purse, and started to rise.

Becka's heart pounded. She was forgetting something. But what? Yes. That's it. Scott had said Z wanted Becka to ask a question. But what was the question? She strained to remember.

Demi signed the bill for breakfast with a scribble. She tossed her Palm into her purse, slung the bag over a shoulder, and then stood.

Becka didn't move. "Um, Sarina?"

Sarina paused and checked her watch. "What's up?"

"I know this is gonna sound crazy, but do you know a guy by the name of Z?"

Sarina went pale. She lowered herself back into her chair. "I . . . I haven't heard that name in years. You know Z?"

Becka nodded. "Sort of. Anyway, for some reason he wanted

me to ask you about the mission field. Does that make any sense?"

Sarina removed her sunglasses. Her eyes narrowed. She focused intently on Becka's face. Slowly, she nodded. "In a way it does. My dad was a missionary most of my life. I guess you might say I was raised in a Christian home."

Becka hoped she didn't look too stunned. "Really?"

A faraway look clouded Sarina's eyes. "About nine, maybe ten years ago, my dad and Z had to rock climb their way to reach a tribe in the jungle with medical supplies." She swallowed. "On the way back, my dad fell about thirty feet. His harnessing, or whatever, broke loose. Z carried him on his back several miles."

Becka noticed even Demi seemed mesmerized by the story.

"I never knew this, Sarina," Demi said.

"Yeah, well, Dad died several days later from internal bleeding," Sarina said, looking away.

Demi circled behind Sarina and placed her hands on Sarina's shoulders. "I'm so sorry. Really I am."

When Sarina looked up, tears watered the edges of her eyes. "I was so hurt and mad. That's when ...," she said, wiping at the tears with the napkin. "That's when I stopped believing in God. I just didn't understand how God, if he was really loving, would take my dad. But what would you know about something like that, Becka?"

They stared at each other for several seconds.

Becka fought back tears of her own. "Actually, Sarina, I know plenty."

"How's that?"

"My dad died on the mission field too." Even as she spoke the words, Becka couldn't help the flow of tears that started to stain her cheeks. "He died last year. And believe me, I've had those same thoughts about God."

Sarina's gaze softened. "I'm ... sorry, Becka. I had no idea we had that in common."

"Yeah, but ... there's one big difference between us."

Sarina waited.

"I'm still placing my faith in Jesus."

Sarina's eyebrows narrowed. "I don't get it. Why?"

"Where else can I go if not to God?" Becka said, dabbing at her tears. "And the way I see it, Sarina, God is reaching out to you. Maybe that's why he brought us together."

Sarina shrugged. "Maybe."

"I could be way off here," Becka said. "Maybe he's giving you another chance to come home, you know?"

Neither spoke for a minute.

For her part, Becka was dying to ask Sarina a million questions about Z. What was his real name? What did he look like? How did they meet? Where did they meet? Who did he work for? How old was he? And most importantly, did she still know how to get in touch with him?

Demi broke the silence. She spoke softly. "Sarina, we really need to get a move on."

Becka bit her bottom lip. There was so much more she wanted to say. So much she wished she could talk about, especially about Z. After all, she and Sarina had so much in common. Time was slipping away. It was extremely difficult, but Becka forced herself to put aside her agenda and focus on what God would have her say in the seconds that remained.

"I know you've got to go, Sarina," Becka said. "But you've got a choice to make. You can go back to what your dad believed ... or keep messing around with the counterfeit."

Sarina swallowed. "I'm not prepared to make that choice," she said, lowering her voice a notch. "At least not yet." With that, Sarina stood to leave. As she came around the table, Becka reached out and touched her briefly on the arm.

"I'll be praying for you," Becka said.

14

Becka was thankful to be back at home later that morning. Sure, it wasn't as fancy as the Ritz. Nobody was playing the piano, and she wasn't surrounded by flowers and chandeliers. But Becka was convinced that nothing compared to lounging around in track pants, her feet up, at the kitchen table eating an early lunch with her mom. At the same time, a sadness settled on her heart.

"What's wrong, honey?" Mrs. Williams said, standing at the stove and looking over her shoulder.

"I'm not real sure," Becka said.

"Does this have to do with Sarina?" her mom said, walking to the table. She set a dish of spaghetti in front of Becka.

"I guess," Becka said, poking at the noodles with her fork. "I just wish Sarina had decided to change her heart."

Mrs. Williams sat down with her plate. She reached for the family Bible. "You know what, Becka?"

"What's that?"

"Let me read you something," she said, turning the pages. "Here we go. Listen to this. The apostle Paul gives Timothy, who was—"

"A young believer."

"Right," Mrs. Williams said. She put her finger on the page. "Paul warns Timothy, 'The Spirit clearly says that in later times some people will abandon the faith and follow deceiving spirits and things taught by demons.'"

"Really? That sounds familiar. Where's that?"

"First Timothy four, verse one," she said, closing the Bible.

"Wow, it's like he's talking about Sarina, huh?"

"Who's talking about Sarina?" Scott said as he bounded into the kitchen. He swung open the refrigerator door and foraged around for something to eat.

"The apostle Paul," Becka said, cutting her spaghetti.

"Wow, he knew Sarina?"

"Never mind," she said, shaking her head. "Anyway, Mom, I guess I'm also thinking about Laura."

"In what way?"

"Last night, for the first time, my heart went out to her," Becka said, putting her fork down on the plate. "It was as if God used that whole thing to cut through my ... well, my anger toward her for what she did to me in the park."

Mrs. Williams smiled. "I'm so glad to hear that. How is she?"

"She's got a long road ahead of her, but she'll make it. I don't know what's going to happen between her parents though." Becka took a bite. A moment later she added, "I was thinking that maybe I could bring her some flowers in the hospital this afternoon."

"Sounds like a good plan," her mom said. "I don't plan to go anywhere, so feel free to use the car."

"Thanks, Mom. That'd be great," Becka said.

"Boy, I wish I had another one of Z's pizza coupons," Scott said, drifting to the table. "That way you could pick up a pizza for me while you're out."

"How about I fix you a plate of spaghetti instead?" Mrs. Williams asked.

"Thanks, Mom. Hey, speaking of Z, we just got an email from him." Scott reached into his pocket. He pulled out and then unfolded a single sheet of paper.

Becka looked up. "What did he say?"

"I don't know. Haven't read it yet. I just printed it out."

She took the page from him and started to read out loud:

Regarding Sarina. Remember, Becka, not everyone will be open to you or to the Gospel. The Bible says some will harden their hearts to the things of God. It's not up to you whether or not they will receive your message. It's just up to you to be faithful to share the truth. And, as you've discovered, Wiccans like to say they don't harm anyone, that they're just trying to elevate the human condition. But to do this, they often engage in spell casting, which, as you know, is essentially calling on demons to do their bidding. That's all for now. May your fortunes be blessed.

Z

"What about that last line?" Becka said, dropping the note on the table. "I've never heard Z talk like that."

Mrs. Williams brought Scott his lunch. "Maybe this will help," she said, handing Becka a letter. "It's from Z. It came in today's mail."

"I don't suppose there's a return address?" Scott said with his mouth full.

"No," Becka said, already tearing into the letter. "Look, it's some tickets."

"Airline tickets?" Scott said, his eyes as wide as meatballs. "Where are we going? The Bahamas?"

Becka held up the tickets. "In your dreams, buster. Try Madame Theo's Fortune-Telling Palace."

Mrs. Williams reached for the tickets. "Isn't that that dumpy fortune-telling place downtown?"

Becka nodded. "Yeah. These tickets are for a free tarot-card reading. They look like something clipped out of a newspaper ad."

"Uh-oh," Scott said. "Why would Z send us there?"

"Wait," Becka said, spying a yellow sticky note inside the envelope. "I don't think he's sending *us* for a reading. This just says we're supposed to look for a friend there. Z says this person is in danger and desperately needs our help."

"A friend?" Scott said, puzzled. "I don't know anyone who hangs around that joint. Unless ..." He paused. His face became ghostly pale.

"Unless what?" Becka said.

"Unless ... it's Sarina Fox hoping to see what the future holds for an ex-Wiccan actress," Scott said, breaking into a cheesy grin.

Becka slugged him on the arm.

The Cards

Then we will no longer be infants, tossed back and forth by the waves, and blown here and there by every wind of teaching and by the cunning and craftiness of men in their deceitful scheming. Instead, speaking the truth in love, we will in all things grow up into him who is the Head, that is, Christ.

EPHESIANS 4:14–15

1

Philip reached between the folds of his mattress and retrieved the knife. He pulled it from its sheath and stared at its nine inches of cold, hardened steel. A thread of the November moonlight danced along the edge of the blade as if fearful of being slashed. Philip clutched the handle. The sweat in the palm of his hand almost caused him to lose his grip.

His tired eyes scanned the darkness around him and settled on the digital clock. With a squint, he noticed it was 2:27 a.m. Sleep had escaped him all night. He figured his bed must look as if it had been dumped into a blender. Hours of tossing and turning had created a jumbled maze of sheets and blankets.

Philip slumped to the floor and leaned back against his bed, careful not to accidentally slice himself.

At least not yet.

The knife had been a gift from his dad several months after his mother split and took his two sisters. Dad had promised they'd go hunting. Although that was years ago, at times the memories were still as fresh as the tears on his face.

Of course, they never went hunting. *Big surprise there*, Philip thought, placing the knife on the carpet next to him. He drew his legs up to his chest. His dad made lots of promises he never seemed to keep. Philip figured the knife and the promised hunting trip was just his dad's way of trying to smooth things over—or was it to buy his loyalty?

According to the judge during the divorce proceedings, once Philip turned eighteen, which he did next month, he could choose to live with either parent. Some choice. An oppressive dad or a mother who walked out on them in the middle of the night.

Philip missed his mom, no question. But he hated her for leaving—not that he completely blamed her. All his parents ever did was fight. If it wasn't one thing, it was another. When his dad got drunk, yelled, and threw things, that was the last straw. Mom was gone before the sun rose the next morning.

Even now, the memories flooded his mind with a fresh dose of pain. Why did life have to be so hard? The darkness of his room seemed to close in on him. He reached around and squeezed the base of his neck, which ached as if jammed into a vise. If only he could silence the voices in his head. Then maybe, just maybe, he'd find the peace that eluded him.

Sitting in the dark, tears staining his face, he wondered what the kids at school would think about Mr. Self-Confidence now. After all, most of his friends thought he had it all together. He had a cool car. His dad made tons of cash. They lived in a big house. And, when it came to clothes, he could buy whatever he wanted. No wonder his friends always came to him with *their* problems.

But where could he go with his?

If only his friends knew how close to the edge he had drifted. Sure, part of him wanted to show everyone he had it all together. He wasn't looking to blame someone else for the fact that he wore a mask. Like his dad, he didn't let anyone get too close. How many times had he heard his dad say, "Don't show them you've got issues, buddy boy. It's a sign of weakness."

But the game of being perfect was getting old.

He was tired of the charade.

He was tired of squirreling away his problems.

To make things worse, he couldn't take another day of fighting with his dad about where to go to college next year. Philip's dad wanted him to go to the same university that he had attended. Like father, like son. When the letters of acceptance from several big colleges came in yesterday morning, his dad had thundered, "Son, if you're smart, you'll go where I went."

Philip peered at the knife and his heart started to race.

Was this the way out? Would this silence the pain?

Why not put it all behind him right here, right now?

What if he did? Would he be missed? Would anybody really care? Sure, his girlfriend Krissi would be a basket case for a week. But she'd get over it once she found another popular senior to hang out with, right? Philip caught himself. *Why am I being so cynical about her?* Krissi, he knew, cared for him deeply. They had been together for years. She was the best friend he ever had. Why, then, did he write her off so quickly? Maybe he *was* losing his mind.

So why not end it all?

He reached for the knife and balanced it in his right hand. His lungs tightened as he considered the finality of this action. Maybe if the future was bright, maybe if he knew for certain it would be worth living, maybe then he'd reconsider. But, as far as he could see, nothing added up. His thoughts turned to Krissi. Even if things worked out between them and they got married someday, would she, like his mom, leave him at the first sign of trouble? Probably. So what was the point of pressing on?

He swallowed hard.

A new, more disturbing thought jolted him like a bolt of lightning. What if Scott and Becka were right about God? What if, as they claimed, there really was a God, a heaven, and a hell? What if those who didn't believe in him would spend forever burning in hell? Worse, what if Scott and Becka were right and there wasn't any way to change his mind?

He lowered the blade. Philip knew he wasn't ready for that final encounter with God — *if* there was a God.

Exhausted, he reached for the remote and flicked on the television. Maybe the drone from the box would help him numb the pain — or at least help him sleep. The TV, another gift from his dad, was complete with cable and sat on the hamper that he never used. The TV jumped to life with such brilliance, he had to slam his eyes shut until they could adjust to the light.

As his eyes blinked into focus, a woman, wearing a turban and sitting at a table, filled the screen.

Philip inched up the volume.

" ... we all possess this inner wisdom. The cards are just the gateway to the supernatural. They allow us to tap into our inner selves and can give us answers to life's most troubling questions."

Philip leaned forward. At the bottom of the screen he saw her name listed as Madame Theo, Psychic, Advisor, and Spiritual Counselor.

"Tonight, whether you're young or old, I know you have questions. I know you have problems. Don't be afraid to connect with the cosmic reality to find your personal answers."

Philip suppressed a laugh. *What a joke,* he thought. *As if Madame Theo knows squat.*

"Give the tarot a chance," she said. Her voice was as smooth as silk and as warm as the afternoon sun. The camera zoomed into her wrinkled face. "Yes, I have been used to help police solve crimes ... loved ones to find each other ... young people to find the right college — "

That got Philip's attention.

"And tonight," Madame Theo said as the camera zoomed in for a tighter shot, "I promise I can help you discover your destiny."

Philip tilted his head to the side. Several thoughts nagged at him. What if she's right? He had read somewhere about people who were missing who were found because of someone like Madame Theo. If she can help the police, maybe she's on to something, right? What harm could there be to check it out? On the other hand, he vaguely recalled a special on TV exposing psychic fraud. Maybe this lady was different.

"I'm so convinced that the tarot is a gift to us from the other side, I'll personally give you a free reading. Just call the toll-free number on the bottom of your screen ..."

Before he knew what he was doing, Philip reached over to his nightstand, tore a scrap of paper from a textbook, and jotted down the number and address of Madame Theo's Palace. He snapped off the TV and, in the darkness, decided to return the knife to its hiding place.

For now.

❧ ❧

"That's a wrap," a voice announced through the overhead monitor.

Madame Theo lingered at the desk where she had just finished another live, thirty-minute local broadcast. Her eyes, black as raisins, scanned the tiny setup. It wasn't much, just a desk, a chair, a dozen candles and, behind her, a backdrop of the city of Crescent Bay, California. But it was a start. After a month of broadcasting three nights a week, she noticed a significant jump in business.

She gathered her tarot cards, tucked them into an oversize handbag, and then eased out of her chair. At sixty-seven, she projected the air of a trustworthy grandmother, at least that's what Fred Stoner, her producer and chief financial backer, had said. She suppressed a sly smile at that memory. She circled around to the front of the desk and walked past two cameras mounted on tripods, careful not to trip on the thick cables that covered the floor like snakes. She headed for the exit.

Fred Stoner bounded through the door, almost bowling her over. "Big news!"

Madame Theo steadied herself and met his eyes, expectant.

Fred tucked a clipboard under his arm. "Listen, the station loves what you're doing."

She smiled faintly. "I'm gratified to hear that, Fred."

"You should be," he said, picking a piece of lint off the lapel of his navy blue suit coat. A patch of black hair poked out the front of his white shirt, unbuttoned at the collar. "You've made a huge sacrifice doing the graveyard shift."

She nodded. "It's been hard. You know I'm not a night owl."

He took her by the arm and led her to the hallway. "Here's the deal. They want to move your program to the 10 p.m. slot."

"Really?"

"I knew you'd be happy about that," Fred said. He smiled wide, revealing his perfectly straight, pearly white teeth. "There's more."

She raised an eyebrow. It almost collided with her turban.

"We're talking syndication, Madame Theo."

"Oh, my," she said, pretending to be surprised. She adjusted the handbag strap on her shoulder. "The cards said this would happen." That was an understatement and she knew it. Indeed, just the day before, while seeking wisdom from the cards, she experienced one of the more dramatic encounters with the spirit world. She'd keep that bit of information to herself. After all, Fred, she knew, wasn't a true believer in the divine forces at work. He was Mr. Businessman. Which was okay. One day he might come around to her way of thinking.

"I'm sure they did," he said with a slight smirk. "Anyway, if everything goes as planned, we're talking every major city up and down the California coast. The sky's the limit from there."

Madame Theo slipped her arm out of his and turned to face him. A worried, almost tormented look crossed her face.

"What is it?" Fred asked, appearing crestfallen.

She bit her bottom lip for a second before answering. "That means we'll be seen in Los Angeles too, right?"

"You bet," he said, rubbing his hands together as if in anticipation of a juicy steak. "Hey, it's only the largest market in the country."

She looked away. During yesterday's encounter, her new spirit manifestation never impressed upon her there would be such obstacles. Then again, direct contact with the spirit world was a whole new dimension for her. There was so much she didn't understand. If only she knew how to proceed. During her next contact she'd make a point to gain clarity.

Fred took her by the arm and, with a gentle yet firm tug, turned her back toward him. "What aren't you telling me?"

Madame Theo's eyes blazed with energy. "I think … well, that a show in Los Angeles might be a problem."

"Because?"

Her eyes narrowed. She lowered her voice a notch. "I can't tell you, at least not yet."

2

Philip bent over and plucked a pair of jeans and a T-shirt from his *almost dirty* pile on the floor, which meant he had worn the clothes at least once, maybe twice. With a quick sniff he figured they'd be good for another day.

He jerked the shirt over his head, jumped into the pants, and then rushed down the stairs, pausing for a split second to steal a look in the hallway mirror. He ran his fingers through his dark hair and noticed his bloodshot eyes looked battered. The nasty headache thumping between his temples didn't help matters.

He darted into the kitchen and flung open the cabinets, hoping to grab something quick. It was Monday morning and he wanted to cruise by Madame Theo's store to check things out. He knew the only way to squeeze that in before school was if he could escape before his dad cornered him. On the second shelf he spied an opened box of Pop-Tarts. Perfect.

"Oh, good, you're up," his dad said, coming into the kitchen from behind him.

Philip's heart sank. He snatched the Pop-Tarts, turned, and careful to avoid eye contact, muttered, "Um, hi, Dad."

"You're not going to school like that, are you?" he asked, adjusting his tie around his neck.

Philip's head pounded at the question. "Dad, since when did you become the clothes police?"

"Ah, watch it there, buddy boy," his dad said with a slight edge in his voice. "I guess you know your shirt looks like a wrinkled prune."

"It's the new style," Philip said with a little more sarcasm than he actually felt.

"When we were kids," his dad said, taking a step forward, "I'll have you know we had to wear a uniform to school. And our shoes had to be polished."

"Dad, that was before the flood."

"What's eating you?"

"Nothing," Philip said. He tossed the box of fruit-filled, rectangular, perfectly manufactured nutrition on the table. He spun around to face the refrigerator, yanked open the door, and strangled a bottle of milk. With a sharp twist, he wrenched off the lid, grabbed a glass from the counter, slopped the milk into the glass and, in his hurry, onto the counter.

"Oh, that's just great, buddy boy," his dad said, fastening his belt around his waist.

"Sorry—"

"What am I, the maid?"

"Dad, I *said* I'm sorry. I'll clean it up."

His father walked to the coffeemaker, reached for the coffeepot, and started to pour a cup. He cleared his throat. "Tell me, Philip, what are your thoughts about college?"

Philip spoke with his mouth full. "Dad, don't go there. I don't have time to—"

"We're talking about your future, son," he said, still pouring a cup of coffee. "Now listen. I spoke with the dean of students at the University of Berkeley and they—"

Philip cut him off. "Can't this wait?"

"I'm not just saying this because you're my son," he said, ignoring the remark. "But a kid like you, with your grades, can write your own ticket. I realize in many ways you're a lot like me. You're tall. You're handsome. You've got brains. And you especially want to keep your options open. I don't blame you for that."

Philip blew an impatient breath.

"Still, I know you'll love Berkeley, son." He took a sip of his coffee. "What I can't figure is what you have against it."

With each passing second, Philip felt hopelessly trapped in a conversation he didn't want to have, certainly not now. Couldn't his dad understand that maybe, just maybe, he wanted to go somewhere else? Somewhere where the teachers wouldn't be asking, "So you must be the son of blah blah blah." The jackhammers drilling between his temples didn't help. He wolfed down the rest of his Pop-Tart, spied the clock on the microwave, then stood to leave.

His dad looked up over the edge of his coffee cup. "Where are you going, anyway?"

"School, remember?"

"This early? You don't usually leave until—"

"Dad, please, give me a break here. I've got stuff to do."

"Let me guess ... you're giving Krissi a ride," his dad said, placing the cup on the table in front of himself. "She can take the bus, son. This is important—"

Philip almost snapped. "Dad, this has *nothing* to do with her."

"Then why can't you stay and talk for a few minutes? I thought you'd be interested to know what the dean said."

Philip snatched a paper towel and wiped up the spilled milk. "We'll talk later, I promise." Philip ducked out of the kitchen before his dad could say another word.

Upstairs, he grabbed his books, his car keys, and then snatched the paper where he had jotted down the address and number last night. He stuffed the note into his front pocket before racing out of the house.

Once outside, he jumped into his convertible and closed the door with a *wham!* If he hurried, he'd still have time to cruise by Madame Theo's Palace.

Maybe she could help him make sense of his life.

Maybe the cards would reveal where he should go to college.

Maybe they'd give him a reason to keep living with a hyper-controlling dad whose hyper-expectations of his brainy son were stifling.

Maybe.

Philip hesitated, putting the car in reverse as a new series of thoughts engaged his mind. He didn't know the first thing about tarot cards, telling the future, or Madame Theo, aside from what he saw last night. *Is this crazy or what?* he thought. *What if she's just another quack?* There was only one way to know for sure: he'd check her out for himself. Maybe good news awaited him in the cards.

If not ... well, he refused to think of the alternative.

Scott Williams worked his way through the lunch line, loading his plate with Monday's mystery meat, Tater Tots, creamed corn, a carton of milk, and a sickly cup of Jell-O 'd Crème, which was basically a square of red Jell-O with Cool Whip and a fancy name. He handed the cashier his student lunch card and then headed into the main dining area.

"Hey, Scott," Krissi said, batting her perfect, killer eyelashes. "Becka's got our seats saved ... over there." She nodded toward the back wall.

"Cool. Be right there," Scott said, scoping out the room.

When Scott and his sister, Becka, first started attending Crescent Bay High, after years of being away on the mission field in South America, he definitely had to learn about the seating dynamics in the cafeteria. Everybody had their place. True, the pecking order wasn't written down anywhere official. But anybody with half a brain couldn't miss it.

Many of the freshmen sat closest to the ice-cream bar.

The nerd types next to them.

The upperclass jocks hassled anyone who dared to approach their table by the windows. The coolest jock, of course, sat at the end. While the cheerleaders were an exception (they could approach the jocks without being tackled), cheerleaders usually filled a table of their own.

The corner opposite from the jocks was home to the druggies and fringe kids, and those who wore black everything. The honor students and those in chess club or on the student council took the center two tables. And, while the most popular kids sat wherever they wanted, they usually picked a table by the far wall.

He started to walk in that direction.

The seniors, he noticed, always parked their trays on the table nearest to the faculty lounge as if to imply they would be next in charge if the faculty decided not to show up one day. Scott sat down next to his sister.

"So, Becka," Krissi said. She placed her tray on the table and then removed the items, one by one, organizing them into positions as if setting the table for the queen of Sheba. "Did you see Philip today?"

"Yeah, for something like a half second," Becka said. "He looked pretty, um ..." She paused, as if to think of a kind word.

Scott butt in. "Just say it. He looked like he had a close encounter with a herd of cattle."

"Really?" Krissi flipped her auburn hair over her shoulder.

"Yeah," Becka said, nodding. "I can't say for sure, but I'd say he seemed really stressed too."

Scott poked at his dessert. "His eyes were all puffy and red like this gross Jell-O."

Krissi appeared to be considering that. "I bet his dad's been riding him about college again," she said, placing her napkin on her lap.

"Could be," Becka said. "I don't know. I kind of think there's something else bugging him. So what about you guys? Is everything cool between you two?"

Krissi blushed. "Of course. We're doing great. I mean, sometimes ... well, when we talk about the future, he, like, gets this faraway look in his eyes."

Scott tossed a Tater Tot in the air and scarfed it down. He swallowed. "Speaking of your man," Scott said a little too loudly, "there he is."

Krissi and Becka turned around as Philip approached their table. His hair looked as if it had been caught in a tornado. Shirt wrinkled. Eyes bloodshot. He plopped down next to Krissi without saying a word.

"Hey, there," Krissi said. "I missed you. You okay?"

"I'm fine." Philip started to shovel lunch into his mouth.

"Could have fooled me," Scott said with a cheesy grin.

Philip glared at him. "Who asked you?"

"Excu-u-use me for living," Scott said, raising both hands as if surrendering to the police.

Nobody spoke for a long minute. Becka swallowed a bite of lunch and said, "So, Philip, what's the latest on your college scholarship—"

He cut her off. "I really don't feel like talking about it."

Krissi and Becka exchanged a concerned look. Krissi turned to him, her eyes softened. "Are you sure you're okay?"

Philip didn't answer.

"I mean," Krissi said, putting her arm around the back of his chair, "you seem so tense—"

He brushed away her arm. "What's this? Pick on Philip day?"

Krissi pulled her arm back and dropped her hands to her lap. "Nobody's picking on you, babe."

Scott wiped his mouth with the back of his hand. "I know. You're worried about the big debate tomorrow, right?" Scott, although two years younger than Philip, was on the debate team with him.

Philip's eyes reddened. "Wrong-o, Scott."

"Then what's up?" Becka said softly.

Without warning, Philip jumped to his feet. "Can't you guys take a hint? I don't feel like talking. And if you *must* know, I'm tired of everybody sticking their nose in my business."

A low whistle escaped Scott's lips. "Speaking of being tired, dude, maybe you should get some sleep, you know?"

Philip pointed a finger at Scott. "Don't start with me. You know, you're just like my dad ... always telling me what to do with my life."

"Hey, it was a joke," Scott said, shocked by his friend's over-reaction. "I didn't mean to start World War three."

"Come on, guys, just give me some space," Philip said, then hustled out of the room.

👁 👁

"Mom, I'm telling you," Becka said that evening at the supper table, "I've just never seen Philip with such a short fuse."

Mrs. Williams dabbed at the corner of her mouth with a napkin. "In what way?"

"Well, he's always been a really nice guy. And just about everyone at school likes him," Becka said. She was momentarily distracted as her dog Muttly started to beg for a treat. "No, Muttly, you've already had enough for one day." She scratched him behind the ears instead. "Anyway, he was really kind of abrupt with all of us at lunch. Not his usual self and all that."

"I'm sorry to hear that," her mom said. "What does Krissi think?"

Becka sighed. "She says Philip's dad is bearing down on him

about college. Plus, there's a bunch of stuff going on between his parents. You remember they're divorced, right?"

Mrs. Williams nodded.

"Well, it has something to do with where Philip will live next month," Becka said. "Krissi thinks the pressure has been really getting him down."

"That's got to be tough," her mom said, reaching for her cup of coffee.

"News flash!" Scott said, barging into the kitchen.

Becka and her mom turned toward him.

"You've got to come and see this," Scott said, beckoning with a wave of his hand.

"See what?" Becka asked.

"I just got an email from Z," Scott said, his face glowing with excitement. "Something's up, big time."

Z was a buddy they had met in a chat room on the Internet. Z always seemed to have a mission for Scott and Becka to undertake, usually involving some level of spiritual warfare. But it had been several months since Z sent them on a new adventure.

"So tell me," Becka said, starting to get out of her chair. "What was his message?"

"You'll never believe it," Scott said. "Z sent a link to a psychic website and told me to download a video clip of that lady called Madame Theo."

"Really? Why?" Mrs. Williams asked.

"Z said we need to help a friend trust God for the future or something like that," Scott reported. "Who knows, maybe this person is mixed up with a fortune-teller. Does anybody come to mind?"

Becka walked over to Scott. "Well, Mom and I were just talking about Krissi and Philip's situation."

Scott looked puzzled. "You think the friend Z is talking about is Krissi?"

"Could be," Becka said. "Or Philip."

3

Madame Theo sat alone in the near darkness at a small desk. The desk, cluttered with assorted papers, books on astrology, notes, and a receipt book, was tucked away in the cramped back room of Madame Theo's Palace, a ground-floor, two-room storefront at the edge of downtown Crescent Bay.

She folded her thin, bony fingers together and rested them in her lap. Although it was three o'clock Monday afternoon, the drapes were drawn tight. She preferred candlelight to sunlight.

Her forehead was a wrinkled knot — not from age, but from the concern that had troubled her ever since Fred Stoner mentioned syndication into the Los Angeles market. While his excitement was unmistakable, he didn't know about her past. How could he? She had never told him about her years in Los Angeles.

It wasn't really any of his business, right?

Besides, that was decades ago.

When she agreed to work with Fred, she never guessed the past would come back to haunt her. Now, like a frightened cat, she found herself backed into a corner. Fred was a natural promoter. One of the best she'd ever seen. He wouldn't stop until Madame Theo was on national television.

How, then, could she insist she didn't want to be seen in Los Angeles? Fred was sharp. If she made up some phony reason, he'd press her until he knew the truth. That was the kind of guy he was. And, since the local television station was interested in syndication, she knew she'd have to confront the demons of her past sooner or later.

Unless she decided to drop the whole thing and not agree to the syndication. Of course, Fred would be furious. He'd say she could forget about her TV show. He'd say the station wanted rat-ings—especially with the revenue that ratings and syndication would bring.

Either she went all the way or not at all. She closed her eyes and whispered, "Spirits, speak to me as you did before. I'm lis-tening. Is this the direction I should take?" She opened her eyes and followed the flame of a candle as it danced to the cadence of an unseen current of air. Watching the movement produced a trancelike state. In the tranquility of the moment, a name from the past came to her mind. He was the one person who might know what to do—if she could reach him.

"Yes, thank you," she said, excited at the inspiration from the other side.

She reached down and opened the bottom desk drawer. Under a stack of papers, she found what she was looking for: a well-worn sheet of paper. Although it had yellowed around the edges with time, the list of phone numbers was still discernible. She laid the page on the desk and smoothed it out with the palms of her hands.

At the bottom of the page she spotted a handwritten name and number scribbled in pencil. At the sight of his name, a fount of memories gushed to mind. Had it really been thirty years since she had first jotted down his name? She picked up her phone and then dialed. What choice did she have?

She brought the receiver to her ear.

"Law offices of Jacobs, Barnes, and Zimmerman," the voice of a young woman announced after the second ring.

"Yes, I'm calling to speak with Zack Zimmerman."

"Who may I say is calling?"

Madame Theo hesitated. "Just tell him ... an old friend."

"I'm sorry, ma'am," the receptionist said, her voice professional but clipped. "Mr. Zimmerman is very busy. Can I take a message?" As she spoke, Madame Theo heard the ring of other phones in the background.

"I ... well, listen, can't you tell him it's urgent?"

"I'm sure it is," the receptionist said with a touch of contempt. "All of his calls are urgent. But if you won't give me a name, I can take a message—or put you through to his voice mail if you'd like."

Madame Theo considered that. She knew Zack's style. If she left him a message—voice or otherwise—he might not get it for days. High-profile defense attorneys were usually juggling more cases than they could handle. Zack was no different. He'd be swamped. But she needed him now, not in a week. She just had to speak with him directly.

Madame Theo took a long, slow, cleansing breath. "Okay, then, please tell him ... Rita Thomas is calling."

"I'll see if he's available. Please hold."

Afraid she might drop the handset, Madame Theo squeezed the phone against the side of her head as tightly as her crooked fingers could handle. She was so focused on what she was about to say, she paid little attention to the nondescript sound of Muzak playing in the background.

Thirty seconds later, the familiar, thick voice of Zack Zimmerman filled the earpiece. "Rita? Is that *really* you? I thought you were dead."

👁 👁

Philip pulled his car to the curb, turned off the engine, and then sat for a long minute. Although he was as motionless as a mannequin, his heart raced to keep up with the questions flooding his mind. Was he really going to do this? What were the odds that a little stack of cards could give him the answers and the hope he craved?

What would his dad think?

Philip had parked under a tall oak tree several doors down and across the street from Madame Theo's Palace. From where he was positioned, he had a clear view of the front door and was surprised not to see anybody going in or coming out.

Maybe he needed an appointment.

Maybe she was closed on Mondays.

Maybe she was at a late lunch.

Maybe I should just leave and get my head examined, he thought. One thing was certain. No way did he want to be seen going inside by a friend, especially not Krissi. As much as he liked her, he knew Krissi sometimes had a tough time keeping her mouth shut. If word got around school that he went to have his cards read, his friends would dog him for days, maybe the rest of the year—if not his entire life.

After all, Philip was the brain of the bunch. Under most circumstances he relied on logic, on reason, and on his intellect to sort things out. How could he explain that he went to some palm-reading, fortune-telling, card-dealing woman for answers? Even *he* found that notion hard to believe. Then again, last night, this woman seemed so caring, so in touch with something she had called "the cosmic reality."

He had come this far, why not go for it?

He slipped on a pair of dark sunglasses.

With a squint, he read the sign on the door: Open. Walk-Ins

Welcome. He checked his rearview mirror before cracking open the door. The coast was clear. It was now or never. With his heart in overdrive, he gulped a quick breath, jumped out, and then darted across the street.

His steps slowed as he approached the doorway. With a glance over his shoulder, he reached out, turned the knob, and slipped inside. As the door opened, a little cowbell sounded, announcing his arrival. He removed his sunglasses. It took a second for his eyes to adjust to the darkness.

As the room came into focus, he noticed it wasn't much bigger than his bedroom and was lit by candles mounted on metal stands. A card table and two chairs were in the middle. Thick, red curtains hung from the walls, and a velvet black cloth, like dark clouds, hovered overhead covering the ceiling. He felt as if he had stepped into another world.

He had hardly taken a step forward when the odor of strong, cinnamon incense filled his lungs. To his left, he observed the source: an incense pot puffing away. Directly across the room, he noticed an open doorway covered with strings of beads. He couldn't see beyond that to the next room.

Puzzled, he waited a moment. Now what?

As if in answer to his unspoken question, Madame Theo parted the beads and glided into the room. "Welcome," she said. With a wave of her hand, she motioned toward the chair closest to him. "Please have a seat. I can sense you are troubled in spirit."

Philip's heart jumped into his throat. How did she know that?

Catching himself from leaping to conclusions, he figured she probably said the same thing to everyone who came in. Why else would they be here if they weren't troubled? Most folks wouldn't come to her for a tea party, right?

"I . . . I saw you last night," Philip said, his voice almost breaking. "On TV, that is. I thought you might be able to help me with … um … the future and stuff." He pulled the chair out and sat down. His eyes darted around studying her every move.

Madame Theo smiled as she eased into the other chair. Her turban, like a massive bandage, was wrapped tightly around her head. She wore a floral-printed muumuu. The one-piece gown floated around her as she moved as if caught in a gentle breeze. She placed her hands on the edge of the table like a dealer at a casino waiting for the players to place a bet.

When she didn't immediately start to speak, Philip said, "This is the first time I —"

She brought a finger to her lips. "Please, not a word. Before we begin, I must focus on the energy you brought into the room."

Philip swallowed. Was she serious? What energy? He wasn't aware that he had brought anything with him besides his pounding heart. He crossed his arms and waited. The silence that followed was almost as thick as the incense.

After what felt like an eternity, she spoke. "Tell me your first name." She closed her eyes in anticipation.

"It's Philip."

She nodded as if he had uttered something profound. She opened her eyes and gave him a penetrating look. "I sense that you are impatient, Philip. Do you know anything about the gift of the tarot cards?"

He shook his head. "No, ma'am."

"But you believe in their power?"

"I … well, let's just say I'm open to learning more." No way would he let on about his skeptical nature. She had a lot to prove if she was going to sway his thinking.

Another nod. "It's a start," she said softly. "The tarot cards allow us to tap into the well of our inner wisdom."

"Cool." Philip forced a smile.

She raised an eyebrow. "It would be best if you didn't interrupt the process."

"Sorry." He dropped his hands into his lap.

"You must understand, Philip, that this is a sacred moment," she said, lowering her voice. "Tarot cards are not a game. They are connected to, and take us to, the cosmic treasury of knowledge passed down from before time itself."

Whatever that means, he thought, but didn't say it.

"Each of us is on a journey," she said, placing the deck of cards in front of her. "Tarot cards reveal the energies and life forces which are in motion at the time we conduct a reading."

Philip nodded, as if this made sense to him.

Madame Theo laid a hand on top of the deck as if touching a holy relic. "There are seventy-eight tarot cards divided into three groups: the major arcana, of which there are twenty-two. You might look at them as trump cards."

Trump card. At last, something he understood.

"The minor arcana, with sixteen cards, appear much like the king, queen, knight, and page cards in a regular deck. The third grouping is the forty pip cards."

Philip watched as she shuffled the cards. For all he knew, the cards were marked.

"Let us begin," she said. "May the spirit guide move into position the order of the cards." Madame Theo placed the deck in the center of the table. She continued to speak after a brief pause. "There's one more thing, Philip, before we proceed further."

"Yeah?"

"Do you know what divination means?"

"You mean, as in the *occult?*" He hoped his voice didn't betray the panic he felt at the word. He had seen the effects of the occult before when Krissi fooled around with channeling and wanted nothing to do with it.

She nodded. "Again, I sense your apprehension. Please, Philip, the word only means 'hidden.' There is nothing to fear here. Tarot cards are a systematic form of divination that allow us to divine the future course of our lives. You do want to know about your life, don't you?"

He swallowed hard. Maybe yes, maybe no. Certainly not if he ended up possessed by some crazy spirit, thrashing around the room like Krissi. But Madame Theo said there was nothing to fear, so why not? He managed a nod.

"I will conduct a basic three-card spread this afternoon." She peeled off the top card, followed by the second and third cards, laying each in a row, face up.

Philip leaned forward. As far as he could tell, the first card looked like a bunch of stars. The next card had a picture of people leaping from a building that had been struck by lightning. The image bothered him. He felt the overwhelming impression to leave. At the sight of the third card, a skeleton in a suit of armor riding on a horse, a little voice at the back of his mind told him to leave.

Madame Theo pointed a long, thin finger at the first card. "This represents your immediate future," she said. Shifting her finger to the second card, she said, "this points to your near future. And this," she added, lowering her voice just above a whisper, "represents your distant future ... unless circumstances change."

Philip scratched the side of his head. "So ... what do they mean?"

The pupils of her eyes narrowed to the size of a pea. "Let me just say I rarely see three trump cards in a row. That means you are a special person."

He liked the sound of that. Maybe there was something in the cards for him after all.

"The first card," she said, resting a finger on it, "is the star. Your star is on the rise. You will be successful sometime very soon."

Philip smiled. "In the immediate future. Cool."

"This second card is the tower," she said. "Although it may appear frightening, it actually means in the near future you must make some drastic changes."

"Like, what kind of change?"

"Maybe in a friendship or relationship or situation." She leaned forward. "Does anything come to mind?"

Philip searched his thoughts. Maybe it meant he needed to break up with Krissi. Or maybe he needed to avoid Scott. Or perhaps he was supposed to move out of his house and away from his dad. He shrugged. "I guess there are several things I can think of."

Madame Theo brought a hand to her chin. "Don't jump to conclusions. Keep in touch with your inner voice. Allow the forces of the universe to speak to you. You'll know what to do at the right time."

"All right," Philip said, growing a little weirded out by the whole experience, yet somehow he was drawn to know more. "But what does this last card mean?"

Madame Theo hesitated. She adjusted her turban and then rested her hands in front of her. "That, Philip, is the death card."

His heart spiked.

She raised a finger. "I can tell by the look on your face that you are filled with fear."

Yeah, and I can hardly breathe, he thought. "What does—"

"Don't let it disturb you, son. While it may suggest that death awaits you in the distant future," she said, reaching across the table to touch the back of his hand, "it also points to the need for transformation."

Philip's heart almost exploded inside his chest. "But it *could* mean I'll die ..."

"Young man, just remember, the death card was dealt last. That's a good sign."

"How so?"

"Death is not, shall we say, inevitable. There's still time to change your course."

"But how?"

"By heeding the warning of the tower," she said, pointing to the center card with a single tap. "Change the relationships that are holding you back, that prevent you from growing. Then, and only then, will you avoid the consequences of the death card."

Philip wanted to run as fast as he could from this place, this woman, these cards, and that awful incense. He wanted to make whatever changes he needed to avoid the death sentence. For some reason, he couldn't move. He remained helplessly frozen in place. He felt as if an anchor had been tied around his waist and he had been tossed into the bottom of the sea.

4

So where's your brother, Becka?" Ryan Riordan asked, tapping his ring against the steering wheel of his Mustang.

"I thought he'd be here by now. I wanted to see how they did in debate class." She scanned the parking lot, hoping for a glimpse of Scott.

They sat in Ryan's car parked against the back wall of the school parking lot where the seniors always parked. Although the spaces weren't reserved for the seniors, the juniors knew better than to park there. It was just one of those unwritten rules of high school life.

"Nothing personal, but I've got stuff I've got to do on my project," he said, checking his watch. "I think the library closes early on Tuesday, right?"

"Yeah, I think so," Becka said, looking at her boyfriend. She could tell he wasn't upset, just pressured to get to work on his senior project. "I'll tell you what. I'll just catch up with Scott at home," Becka said, finding it hard to stop gazing into his eyes.

"In that case, I say we hit the road." Ryan reached over to the ignition and, with a wink, fired up the engine.

Ryan's thick, black hair framed his killer, sparkling blue eyes.

As usual, Becka's heart skipped a beat when he smiled at her, that smile with the little upward curl at the corners.

No wonder Ryan was one of the most popular kids at school.

And, while she always found him attractive, she was at a complete loss as to what Ryan saw in her. Take Krissi. She could double as the Miss Perfect Barbie doll. Or Julie Mitchell, her best friend on the track team, with her beautiful blonde hair.

By comparison, Becka saw herself about as nondescript as a houseplant. What could be so attractive about her thin, mousy brown hair and equally thin, nearly nonexistent body?

Whatever his reason, Ryan seemed to enjoy her company. A lot.

And lately, Becka couldn't help but wonder what would happen next year after he left for college. Would they still keep in touch? Would they go deeper in their relationship even though they'd be apart? Like her mom always said, "Absence makes the heart grow fonder."

Or . . . to wander, Becka countered.

What if he met some college girl with a million talents, who'd found a cure for cancer and whose dad was a wealthy president of some big company? Becka was afraid he'd forget all the great times they had had together and be married to Miss Wonderful his first semester at college.

They drove a few minutes in silence. Ryan was the first to speak. "So what's on your mind?"

"Me?"

He flashed a grin. "Do you see anybody else in the car?"

Becka blushed. "I . . . I was just thinking . . ."

"About?" He turned the car toward the Sonic several blocks from school, the drive-in burger-and-shake joint where the waitresses skated to the car with your order. "I missed lunch. Thought we'd grab a shake."

Becka was glad for the distraction. "Sounds great."

He pulled the car to a stop in one of the parking spaces next to a menu board. "What looks good?" he asked, scanning the colorful list of choices.

"How about a strawberry slush for me," Becka said.

Ryan pushed the Call button.

"May I take your order?" a cheery voice asked.

"One medium strawberry slush and a number-two combo, please." Ryan pulled out his wallet. He looked at Becka and said, "It's my treat."

"We'll have that right out," the voice said. "Your total is $4.57."

"Thanks," Ryan said. He turned to Becka. "So what were you saying?"

Becka's heart did a somersault. She wasn't planning to talk about her feelings, at least not yet. She fidgeted with an earring as she struggled to find the right words. "I was just thinking, um, about ... the future."

Ryan stretched. "I know what you mean."

"Really?" Her eyes widened. She wondered if he was feeling the same thing she was feeling.

"Yeah, kind of," he said. "I mean, wouldn't it be cool to know what will happen before it happens? Like, where we'll go to college, who we'll meet, what we'll do with our life and stuff like that."

"Oh." Becka was thinking more specifically about *their* future. "But don't you ever think about—"

"Hold on," Ryan said, reaching for his Bible in the backseat. He flipped through the well-worn pages. "I know what you're about to say. It says in Matthew somewhere ... here it is in Matthew 6." He held the Bible between them.

Becka leaned forward.

Ryan pointed to verse 27. "Right here Jesus asks, 'Who of you by worrying can add a single hour to his life?'" Ryan paused as his eyes skimmed further down the text before he continued with verse 31. "'So do not worry, saying 'What shall we eat?' or 'What shall we drink?' or 'What shall we wear?'"

Becka cleared her throat. "Actually, what I'm trying to say is that sometimes I worry about—"

"Hold on a sec, there's more," he said. "'For the pagans run after these things, and your heavenly Father knows you need them. But seek first his kingdom and his righteousness, and all these things will be given to you as well.'"

Becka blew a short breath. *Sometimes guys are just so dense,* she thought. "Ryan, that's great. And I believe it. But what I'm trying to say is … is that sometimes … well, honestly, I worry—"

"Did you hear what I just read?"

"Okay, so it was a poor choice of words," she said. Her heart danced wildly in her chest. She just had to get her feelings out in the open. "Sometimes I'm … *concerned* about, you know … *us.* About our future … together … do you know what I mean?"

Ryan's eyes met hers. Neither spoke for a long moment. Becka was sure he could hear her heart banging away. A big, melt-your-heart grin appeared on his face.

"What?" Becka said, her forehead creasing. "What are you smiling about?"

Before Ryan could answer, a teen on skates wearing a Sonic apron rolled to the edge of their car with a tray of food. "Hey, guys, sorry to interrupt. Here's your order."

Philip was stunned. Even now, sitting in his car outside of a local gas station, a cold chill ran down his spine as he rehashed the events of the afternoon. He was exhausted from a fitful night's sleep. His mind was distracted by pressure from his dad. Even Krissi kind of bugged him with her questions about their future together. And yet, against the odds, he had led his school to win the regional debate championship. In fact, he had clobbered schools with much better debate teams; teams who seemed to always win. Not today.

Today, Philip blew away the competition.

What's more, the victory had come "in the near future" just as Madame Theo had predicted. But how did she know that his "star was on the rise"?

Was it a coincidence? A fluke?

Somehow he couldn't shake the feeling that there was a definite connection. Sure, at first he was skeptical about Madame Theo. But now, an hour after winning the trophy, he wasn't so quick to dismiss the messages in the tarot cards.

That's what excited and scared him the most.

Especially with that death card hanging over his head. He looked over his shoulder and spotted Scott heading toward the car. They had stopped at the mini mart for a bag of chips and a couple of sodas.

"Scott, what took you so long?" Philip reached for the keys in the ignition.

Scott jumped into the front seat of Philip's convertible. "Just this," he said. He handed Philip a strip of paper about the size of a fortune cookie fortune.

Philip started the car and then read the message.

"If that isn't the dumbest thing I've ever seen," Scott said, snatching the paper back.

Philip grunted. "What makes you say that?"

"Didn't you read it? It says, 'You will rise to the challenge today.'"

Philip appeared puzzled. "Yeah, so?" He drove away from the gas station.

"Duh," Scott said, making a face. "Rise to what challenge? Don't you see? These stupid messages are so general they could mean a million things to a million people. I can't believe people fall for this stuff."

Philip was silent for a moment. "Where did you get it?"

"Actually, I was checking my weight," Scott said, glancing out his window. "Didn't you see that scale by the door? When I stepped on it, it gave me ... *my secret message for the day,*" Scott said in a deep, affected voice. "What a joke. As if a dumb machine is going to predict the future."

Philip clenched his jaw. He didn't like Scott's attitude. Who was to say for sure that the cosmic forces—or whatever Madame Theo had called them—couldn't communicate through that scale? If they could make contact through the cards, why not the scale too?

"So," Scott said, guzzling his Dr. Pepper, "where did you say we're going?"

Philip hesitated, unsure what Scott would say. He was starting to regret offering Scott a ride home. No way would Scott be cool about their next stop. Then again, what choice did Philip have? He just had to know more about the second card. He tried to sound as casual as possible.

"Um, it's just a place called ... Madame Theo's Palace."

5

"Here's what I'm thinking," Fred Stoner said. He folded his arms together and, in the candlelit semidarkness, leaned against the wall next to Madame Theo's desk. "If we're gonna boost the ratings in our new time slot, we need a fresh angle."

Madame Theo, sitting at her desk, appeared puzzled. Without warning, she felt the presence of the spirit world swirling around her. Her eyes narrowed as she attempted to process this new sensation. Who—or what—was trying to reach her? she wondered.

"Angle?" she asked, trying to remain focused.

"Yeah, you know, something to spice things up," he said.

Feeling a draft, Madame Theo glanced around the room to see if someone had entered. Again, she felt the vaporlike spirit energy drift through the air around her head. She wondered if Fred felt it too. By the look of intensity on his face, she was pretty sure he was oblivious to the unfolding mysterious phenomenon. She tried to concentrate.

"And what do you have in mind? A guest?"

He shrugged. "Can't say for sure. Maybe." He paused to think about that for a second. "Actually, nix the guest idea. Too risky. If they're boring, we'll lose the audience."

"I see," she said, distracted by the compelling force that seemed to tug at her inner spirit. In a way she wasn't surprised that the spirit world would bypass the cards and attempt to make direct contact with her. Still, this was unlike anything she had experienced so far, and it both thrilled and, to a lesser degree, frightened her.

A moment later he snapped his fingers. "I got it. We get one of your clients to give a testimonial on camera. Yeah, that's it. We put someone on whose life has been changed or whatever from a reading. We can pre-tape the whole thing. I love it."

Madame Theo studied him without saying a word. The other world was there in the room. No question. The cosmic forces were trying to break through and speak directly to her consciousness. But how? What did she need to do? She closed her eyes for a long second, took a deep breath, and thought, *I'm listening. Speak.*

You have been chosen!

Madame Theo's eyes shot open. Her heart raced. The spirit guide had spoken to her. To her! Now what?

"I'm telling you, this is brilliant. There's nothing like putting a face on the benefits of the tarot," Fred said, obviously pleased with the idea.

Her head rotated slowly, from side to side, like an oscillating fan. She waited for something more, but nothing came. The presence in the room started to fade. "Wait!" she shouted as the spirit faded.

Fred almost jumped. "Excuse me?"

Madame Theo realized she had spoken out loud. "Um, sorry, it's just that ... I'm not so sure, Fred. My clients value their privacy."

He laughed. "Have you watched TV lately? People will do just about anything for a few minutes of fame. They'll eat worms.

They'll travel halfway around the world to live on an island where cameras videotape their every move. They'll even marry a complete stranger."

"Fred," Madame Theo said, her voice now quiet. Whatever had contacted her was gone, of that she was fairly sure. "I appreciate your enthusiasm. But this isn't a game show. This is very serious business."

He held up a finger. "Say no more. I agree. We'll take the high road. Don't worry. I'm not looking for cheap thrills. Just something to ... to maximize the power of your gift."

She tapped a finger against the surface of her desk. Now, more than ever, she knew this was a gift. The spirit even said she had been chosen. "Okay, let's say I can find someone willing to go on camera. Then what? What happens if we get too much business? Have you thought of that?"

"Not to worry."

"I'm serious," she said. "I'll have you know, my schedule is already almost full with the clients I have right now."

He flashed a grin. "I know. I've got this all worked out."

She raised both eyebrows.

He rested a hand on her shoulder. "Sweetie, this is way bigger than you can imagine. Once we syndicate, thousands—maybe millions—of people will want what you have to offer."

"And, pray tell, how do you propose I handle that?"

"You don't." Fred rubbed his hands together. "As of tonight, we start pushing a toll-free number for personal consultations. I've made arrangements with a phone bank in Salt Lake City who will field the calls."

Madame Theo squinted. "I ... I don't know. Readings by phone?" Would the collective spirit world be offended by such a thing? she wondered.

"Exactly." Fred started to pace. "The first minute of the consultation is $5.95 and then $1 a minute after that. If the average call is ten minutes, we're talking almost $15 per call. Do the math. A thousand ten-minute calls is $15,000. At that rate, we're talking $90,000 per hour."

She whistled, warming to the idea. Surely there was nothing wrong with introducing people to the supernatural, right? If she made a lot of money along the way, the spirits would have to guide her on how to use it for the greater good.

"That's just the start," he said. "People who want a personal reading from you will have to pay more."

"What's the catch?"

"No catch." Fred suppressed a cough. "But, as you might guess, I do need the green light to syndicate into Los Angeles for the deal to work."

Madame Theo fell silent. In the other room, the bell above the front door jingled, indicating someone was entering. Besides, she needed time to process what had just happened. Never before had she been spoken to by the other side so directly.

"Fred, I have a client. I ... I better go."

He circled around and faced her. "What's the problem? I thought you'd be thrilled."

"I am, it's just—"

"Los Angeles," he said, finishing her sentence. "I don't get it. What is your objection to doing TV in L.A.?"

She pushed herself back from the desk and then stood. "I wish I could tell you, Fred. But I can't. Maybe later."

"Like, when? I've got a show to run."

"Soon."

☙   ☙

Scott tagged behind Philip as they headed into Madame Theo's Palace. Once inside, a heaviness of heart, like a dark cloud, settled over Scott. He couldn't shake the distinct impression that they shouldn't be there. He wasn't able to pinpoint the source of his uneasiness. He didn't know the first thing about Madame

Theo, her store, or tarot cards. But the restlessness in his spirit was as distinct as the cinnamon incense that filled the air.

"This place gives me the creeps," Scott said just above a whisper.

Philip, standing inside the door, turned around and shot him a look. "Like I said, you can wait outside if you're going to make a bunch of comments."

"Hey, it's your show," Scott said, scanning the room. As his vision adjusted to the meager light, he noticed the table situated in the center of the room, the candles, the thick blood red-colored drapes, and the incense pot. What really caught his eye was the array of crystals displayed on the end table in the far corner. *Not good,* he thought.

Scott and his sister, Becka, had been engaged in enough spiritual warfare to know the warning signs early on. Anybody who turned to crystals for guidance was asking for trouble, and he knew it. Scott looked at Philip and was about to caution him when a woman appeared through the beaded doorway.

"Welcome," she said, offering a polite smile.

"Uh, hi," Philip said, inching forward. "Remember me? From yesterday?"

She nodded. "I do. Please have a seat, Philip. And who is this with you?"

Scott cleared his throat. He remained standing close to the door, unwilling to venture too close. The alarms in his head seemed to grow with each passing minute. "I'm Scott. Scott Williams."

Madame Theo drifted like a phantom to her chair. She floated into place and rested her hands on the table. "I take it, Scott, you're not here for a reading?"

He shook his head. "No, ma'am. I'm here with my friend."

She closed her eyes. When she opened them several seconds later, she appeared agitated. "I'm sorry, Scott. I need to ask you to wait outside."

"Me?" he said, raising a hand to his chest. "What did I do?"

"Please," she said firmly. "We won't be long."

"I don't get it," Scott said, his face flushed. "Why can't I stay right here?"

Philip's head spun around. "Don't make a scene, Scott. Just do what she says."

Scott felt his pulse race. It wasn't that he wanted to stay, but he didn't like being asked to leave for no apparent reason. Besides, what right did she have to judge him? Scott fumed, "Let me guess, I've got *bad karma?* Is that it?"

Madame Theo tilted her head to the side. "In a word, yes. Your karma is competing with the cosmic realities necessary to offer a proper reading of the cards."

"Whatever," Scott said, shaking his head. With a turn, he opened the door and stepped outside. He yanked the door shut with a sharp thwack. Almost instantly, he regretted leaving Philip alone with that woman. Philip wasn't a believer, and Scott knew full well that he would be putty in the hands of the great deceiver. Now what? Should he go back inside? What would he say?

Scott sat in the front seat of the car, troubled by what had just happened. He knew he probably ticked Philip off inside of Madame Theo's. He didn't mean to, but he couldn't help himself. For the life of him, he couldn't think of a single reason why Madame Theo asked him to leave.

In fact, for the last fifteen minutes, he'd replayed the brief sequence of events. The only thing he remembered saying was his name—and that Philip was a friend. That's it. After Madame Theo had closed her eyes, she told him to leave.

Talk about weird, Scott thought. But on second thought, Scott felt convicted for acting so selfishly. He had been obsessed with staying on Philip's good side. Instead, Scott realized he should be more concerned that Philip felt the need to go to such a creepy place.

At that moment, he watched Philip storm toward the car and braced himself for the worst.

"You wanna know something?" Philip shouted as he reached the side of the vehicle. He jumped in and then slammed the car door shut with enough force to rattle the rearview mirror.

"What's that?"

"*Sometimes* you can be such a *complete* jerk." That said, Philip jammed in the key and stomped on the gas pedal.

"That's good," Scott said with a smirk. "For a second I thought you were going to announce that I was *always* a jerk."

"Back off, Scott," Philip said. He gripped the steering wheel and looked straight ahead.

Scott let out a low whistle. "Hey, I'm just playing with you. Now who's got the bad karma?"

Rather than say another word, Philip cranked the volume on the radio until it was almost deafening.

"Hey, you want to turn that down?" Scott shouted.

"No."

"Come on, man. Let's talk."

Philip turned the music up a notch.

Scott reached over and snapped it off.

Philip's eyes narrowed into a glare, but he didn't say a word.

"Listen, Philip, I'm sorry that—"

He cut Scott off. "I don't want to talk about it."

"Okay ... okay. Chill out, man."

They rode several minutes in the silence. Scott had never seen Philip so on edge. Yesterday in the lunch room had come close. But this was different. Philip's whole temperament was changing. He had a wild, faraway look in his eyes.

A new thought came to mind. Maybe Philip had heard something inside that frightened him. Maybe. But what? What could possibly be so disturbing that it would cause Philip to be so on edge? If only he knew more about tarot cards, then perhaps he'd know what Philip was getting mixed up in.

One thing was sure. Scott would ask Z when he got home. Although Scott didn't know much about Z, it seemed that Z had tons of advice about these kinds of things, especially if it had to do with the spirit realm.

"You know," Scott said, trying to start a conversation, "I actually think it would be kind of cool to know the future ... and all of that stuff."

Philip clenched his jaw and stared straight ahead.

"I'm serious," Scott added, trying to sound sincere. "You know, that would make it easier to figure out what to do before you had to do it, right?"

Philip looked the other way.

"But if you ask me—" Scott started to say.

Philip's head snapped around. His eyes were as dark as his hair. "I didn't *ask* you."

"Still," Scott said, ignoring him, "there's something not right with that lady. Her whole deal is so ... weird, you know? I mean, the candles, the crystals, the turban thing around her head—what's with that, anyway?"

Philip slammed on his brakes. The car skidded to a stop. "Get out."

"What?"

"Now."

"Here? Why?"

Philip barked, "You just don't know when to shut up, do you?"

6

Becka hummed a tuneless melody as she, gliding through the kitchen, stacked the spaghetti-soiled dinner plates in the sink. Nothing could dampen the feeling of euphoria. Not the pile of homework awaiting her in her bedroom, not the fact that she had to study for two tests, not even Scott's sour mood.

Today was an exceptional day. Her mom, who needed to rush out after dinner for a meeting at church, had asked her to do the dishes. Becka didn't mind. All she cared about was what happened that afternoon at Sonic.

With Ryan.

As she remembered every little detail, she was amazed that her heart didn't go into cardiac arrest when Ryan had said he too was thinking about their future *together*. True, they had always taken their relationship slowly. Still, he had feelings for her. What more could she want? Knowing that was enough to put the spin in her world.

Her spirit soared somewhere above the clouds at the memory.

From some faraway place, she thought she heard a voice calling her name ... *Becka*.

Gazing at the sunset, its golden glow perfectly framed through the window over the sink, she lowered a dish into the warm water. As her hands slipped into the soap bubbles, her mind drifted miles away to the ocean. She imagined herself on the beach walking along the seaside with her toes leaving little tracks in the sand.

With Ryan.

"Becka..."

This time, the voice was much clearer. She blinked and found herself in front of the sink. She sighed as reality set back in. Out of the corner of her eye, she spotted her mother by the front door, purse and keys in hand. "Oh, hey, Mom."

"Didn't you hear me calling your name, sweetheart?"

"I ... I guess I was lost in my thoughts," Becka said, blushing.

"I've got the cell phone in case you guys need anything, okay?"

"We'll be fine, Mom," Becka said, noticing her hands were dripping onto the floor. She quickly placed them over the sink.

"I'll be back in about two hours," Mrs. Williams said. "Thanks for doing the dishes, Becka. And, Scott?"

He grunted, "Yeah, Mom?"

"Don't forget tonight is trash night—"

"I know, I'll handle it."

Mrs. Williams hesitated with one hand on the doorknob. "Well, better run. How do I look?"

Becka tilted her head. "Great, Mom. I really like your new dress."

That brought a smile. "Thanks, sweetie. I love you both," she said and then left.

Becka's attention drifted from the front door to the lump of humanity hunched over his plate at the kitchen table. From experience, she knew something was seriously wrong if Scott refused to eat. Especially if he was ignoring something as awesome as Mom's homemade spaghetti and meatballs.

Ever since their father had died in a plane crash while on the mission field in South America, she and Scott had drawn closer. In many ways, they were the best of friends even though he was two years younger. When he was hurting, Becka hurt with him.

She forced herself to put her daydream on hold, dried her hands on a towel, walked to the table, and pulled up a chair. "So what's up, bro?"

Scott noodled his spaghetti with a fork. He shrugged.

"Come on, Scotty," she said, pulling her hair back. "Are you bummed out that Philip won first place in the debate?"

He looked up. "No way. I'm happy for him."

"Then why the long face?" As she waited for Scott to respond, Muttly wandered into the room and rested at Becka's feet. Becka leaned over and rubbed his belly.

Scott leaned back in his chair and folded his arms. "Philip's being a dork, big time."

"Okay, like how?"

Scott shook his head in disgust. "Get this. He kicked me out of the car and made me walk almost halfway home."

Oddly, that actually struck her as funny. She bit her bottom lip to suppress a laugh. "You're kidding, right?"

"For real. The guy's nuts in the head," Scott said, making cuckoo circles next to his ear. "He slammed on the brakes, which just about killed us. Then he yelled and told me to get out of the car. He's so messed up."

Becka, still fighting back a snicker, said, "Mom and I wondered what took you so long to get home."

"Actually, we stopped at that Madame Weirdo's place first."

"Huh?" Becka watched as Muttly stretched his legs and then strolled out of the room, apparently losing interest in the conversation.

"She's a lady that tells the future with tarot cards—whatever they are," Scott said. He reached for a roll. "At least that's what Philip claims." He munched on the bread for a second.

Was Philip the person Z wanted them to help? No matter what, Becka didn't like the sound of Philip getting mixed up with a fortune-teller. Although she was no expert on the subject, she knew enough about the Bible and had come face-to-face with demonic powers to know that stuff like palm reading and fooling around with contacting spirits was a bad deal. "Do you think that this what's-her-face—"

"Madame Theo," Scott said, as a picture of her turban-bound head came to mind.

"Yeah, that this Madame Theo might have something to do with Philip's reaction?"

"I don't know. Probably." Scott popped the rest of the roll into his mouth. "At least, it looks that way, now that you mention it."

Becka sat cross-legged on the chair. "I know. Why don't you just call and talk to Krissi? Maybe she knows what's up with Philip."

"You think so?"

"Sure. I mean, this involves Krissi too."

"How's that?"

"Think about it," Becka said. "Philip was so not himself yesterday in the cafeteria, right?"

"Yeah. So?"

"I say there's a connection between what happened today and what was going on yesterday. See?"

"I . . ."

"Trust me," Becka said, starting to stand. "Just call it a woman's intuition."

"But what do I tell Krissi?" Scott said, scrunching his nose. "I don't know the first thing about tarot cards."

"Why not ask Z first?"

Scott smacked his forehead. "I knew there was something I forgot to do. I'll see if he's online."

❧ ❧

Scott walked into his bedroom and quietly turned on the small desk lamp. Cornelius, his pet military macaw, stood asleep on a perch near his desk. With one foot drawn to his chest, his powerful beak was buried in a patch of bright green and scarlet plumage. Scott scratched the back of his bird's neck before taking a seat in front of the computer.

Scott tapped the space bar to wake the monitor from its sleep mode. He typed in his password—Dirty Socks—and logged on to the computer. After many months, they were no closer to knowing much about the mysterious Z, even though on several occasions they had tried to discover Z's true identity.

One thing was certain: Z was an expert on the supernatural and for some strange reason had taken an interest in Scott and Becka's efforts to fight the forces of darkness. Whenever they had a question about the occult, they'd send Z an email. Often Z would be online in the evenings. Scott noted the clock on his menu bar: 8:47. His fingers danced across the keyboard.

Hey, Z. Are you there? It's Scott.

As Scott waited, he couldn't help but think of all of the things Z knew about them ... personal family things. In a way, it was unsettling. Z knew stuff that only somebody really close to them could know. So far, Z had never steered them wrong or done anything to make them uncomfortable.

Still, the fact that this stranger knew about him and seemed to care about him was difficult for Scott to process. In an odd sort of way, Z made Scott long for his dad. His dad, after all, was someone who, like Z, knew a lot about the Bible and who always helped him figure stuff out.

Scott watched a response form on the screen.

Great to hear from you, Scott. How's your friend?

Scott swallowed. He assumed Z was referring to Philip. *How in the world does Z know about him?* Scott thought. He hadn't said anything about Philip, at least not yet. That eerie sensation returned, but Scott shrugged it off. Z just seemed to have his sources. Scott typed:

Z, Philip is really stressed out. He's using tarot cards to figure out the future. What do you know about tarot?

After several seconds, a message from Z appeared:

Tarot cards are nothing more than a tool of divination used to foretell events, much like crystal gazing, palmistry, or soothsaying.

Is it dangerous?

Indeed. On several levels.

Like how?

Scott waited as his cursor blinked impatiently on the screen. No response.

Z, I have to know. What's Philip getting into?

After a pause, an answer appeared:

People who promote tarot cards claim it's an innocent way to discern the future. They use words like spiritual development, inner knowledge, life forces, and cosmic energies to explain what you're tapping into with the cards.

So what's the danger?

Another extended pause. Scott took a deep breath. He knew sometimes Z wouldn't answer a direct question, at least not immediately. And other times, Z would answer a question with a question. A question formed on the screen:

Who holds your life in his hand?

That's easy. Jesus does.

Who knows everything about your future?

Jesus.

How does he invite you to communicate with him?

By talking with him. Through prayer. What's this got to do with tarot cards?

As Scott waited for a response, Becka walked into the room and leaned over his shoulder. "What's Z saying?"

"I'm a little confused," Scott said, scratching the side of his head. "I don't think he really answered my question."

"Let's see," Becka said, reaching for the mouse. She scrolled back and read the conversation thread. "Hey, I think I get what Z's trying to say."

"Okay, if you're so brilliant, what's he saying?"

"You've got to read between the lines, Scott. Look here." She pointed to the screen. "We're supposed to talk to Jesus through prayer, right?"

"Right ... but ..."

"Which means we don't need tarot cards," Becka said. "We already have a direct line to God. So who, then, are people talking to when they use stuff like tarot cards to communicate? It sure can't be God. Get it? That's Z's point."

"I guess ... but ..."

Becka nudged Scott to the side and typed a question:

Z, it's Becka. Are you saying that tarot cards can open up a person to satanic activity?

They waited several seconds before one word appeared on the screen:

Exactly.

Scott felt a sudden chill creep up from the base of his spine. If tarot cards were really just another form of spiritual counterfeit, one with roots in the occult, then Philip was in more danger than he probably knew. Even though Scott was still hacked off at Philip for kicking him out of the car, there was no way he'd stand by and let his friend get sucked into a trap.

Scott pounded out one last question:

Z, it's Scott. I've got to know. How dangerous are they?

Nothing. Scott exchanged a look with Becka. He checked the screen again. After what felt like forever, Z's response scrawled across the screen one letter at a time:

Can be lethal.
Z

7

S peaking of lover boy," Scott said, lowering his voice to Krissi the next day before study hall. He nodded in the direction of the door.

Krissi, who sat next to Scott, looked over his shoulder as Philip shuffled into the crowded study hall. His T-shirt was partially untucked in the back, his jeans wrinkled, and his hair had a bad case of static cling.

He took one of the remaining available seats in the front right corner of the room close to the door. Not that he had much of a choice. All of the seats in the back were already taken. Philip flopped into his chair, plopped his stuff on the desk in front of him, and leaning forward, dropped his chin onto the stack of books.

"I'd say he had five minutes of sleep last night," Scott said, leaning closer to Krissi. "Five minutes, tops. I told you something's up with him. I bet he was up in the middle of the night watching that Madame Whacko I was telling you about."

Krissi's eyelashes fluttered. "Really? Okay, you've got to tell me all about this place you guys, like, went to after school. And don't skip anything."

Last night, at Becka's suggestion, Scott had planned to call Krissi to talk about Philip. As usual, Scott got distracted and forgot. After first period, he caught up with her and made a plan to talk with her during this study hall.

The bell sounded and, as Scott started to answer, the librarian stepped into the room. "What's Mr. Lowry doing here?"

Krissi tossed her auburn hair. "Beats me. I almost never see him doing study hall duty, you know?"

Scott nodded. "Well, he's cool. The last time I was in detention, he let us talk as long as we didn't cause a riot."

Mr. Lowry stood at the front of the room tapping a thin, black attendance book against his thigh. Scott noticed most of the other students ignored his presence. This was, after all, a talking study hall. Unlike the silent study hall in room 305, where conversation was forbidden, Scott knew the students here were normally allowed to talk as long as they kept the general noise level lower than a sonic boom.

"May I have your attention," Mr. Lowry announced, mustering up a commanding voice.

A girl with thick glasses turned in her seat and started to shush the others.

"As you may have guessed, I'm a substitute teacher for this period." He circled around the teacher's desk and leaned against the front edge. "I understand that this is usually a talking period. Today, however, will be different."

Several students groaned.

Mr. Lowry started to pace back and forth at the front of the class as if addressing the troops. "As of this moment, there will be no talking—"

More groans.

"No talking ... no eating ... no sleeping—"

Another round of whines and moans.

"And there will be no passing of notes," he said, pointing with the black attendance book like a battle-ax.

One of the jocks on the basketball team blurted, "Mr. Lowry?"

"Yes?"

The jock leaned back in his chair, legs sprawled as if in a lounge chair at the beach. "Um, sir. In case they didn't tell you, this isn't junior high."

Several of his buddies snickered.

"What's next? No gum chewing?" he added with a laugh.

Mr. Lowry stared at him as if torn between ordering him to do five hundred push-ups or settling for a swift boot to the seat of his pants. "Young man, what is your name?"

He looked around as if Mr. Lowry were addressing someone else and then said, "Who, me?"

He marched forward three steps. "I'm waiting."

Every eye in the room was on him. The student cleared his throat. "Jordan Bolte."

"Thank you, Mr. Bolte, for that wonderful idea." Mr. Lowry turned to face the others. "At the suggestion of Mr. Bolte, there will be no gum chewing either."

"Oh, that's great, Jordy," one of his buddies said, with a punch to his arm.

"For those students with PDAs, cell phones, or any kind of instant messengers," he said, scanning the faces through narrowed eyes, "if you want to keep them, I'd suggest you turn them off and put them away. Thank you. I have a pounding migraine headache and will not tolerate any extraneous noise." Mr. Lowry took a seat behind the desk and opened the roll book. He started to take attendance.

Scott exchanged a look with Krissi. Scott whispered, "What came over him?"

Krissi shrugged and then silently mouthed the words, *Now what?*

Scott threw up his hands. He hadn't planned on this curveball. Whatever Mr. Lowry's reason, which, for obvious reasons, Scott wouldn't dare question, the option of talking was nixed.

Krissi took out a sheet of paper and a pen. She motioned to him to do the same.

Scott wasn't sure that was such a good idea. Without speaking, he mouthed back, "Pass a note?" What if they got caught? If only he had remembered to call her last night.

He looked into Krissi's pleading, green eyes and guessed that if he didn't tell her what he knew, Krissi would nag him through the entire forty-five-minute period. What harm could there be in telling her the basics? Besides, Mr. Lowry, he reasoned, was a substitute study-hall teacher—a tough one, sure. But he was a seasoned student. He knew all the tricks of silent communication.

What were the odds of being noticed in the last row?

He slipped out a piece of paper, clicked open his pen, and began to write in large block type, stealing quick glances in the direction of the teacher. As he worked, his heart started to pound. The last thing he needed was another detention. When he finished, he propped up a textbook and, with a suppressed cough, signaled to Krissi.

Krissi, trying not to be too obvious, tilted her head. She squinted. Scott lifted the paper for a better view behind the book. She squinted again but couldn't read it. Frustrated, Scott pretended to look at the ceiling and then the bulletin board before scanning the front of the room.

Mr. Lowry's head was down as he called names and scrawled marks in the attendance book.

Krissi tapped her pen twice. Scott looked at her as her eyes widened, as if to ask, "Are you going to give that to me or not?"

Scott's heart tapped away. He knew he was taking a risk. A big risk. No way would he want anybody but Krissi to see what he had written. Against his better judgment, he carefully folded the paper several times. His movements were slow and deliberate so as to attract as little attention as possible. When finished, the paper fit in the palm of his hand.

He stole a final look at the teacher and then sniffled.

As if on cue, Krissi pretended to accidentally knock her pen onto the floor between them. It rolled toward Scott. As smooth as a well-rehearsed play, Scott picked up the pen and handed it to Krissi, slipping the note into her hand in the same motion.

Although the adrenaline was pumping through his veins, Scott lowered his book, satisfied that they had pulled it off. He exhaled a slow, long breath.

Several seconds passed when, from across the room, he thought he heard someone say, "I'll take that."

Scott's heart skipped a beat. No mistake about it. Mr. Lowry's eyes, like two laser-guided missiles, zeroed in on Krissi.

"Excuse me?" Krissi said, playing dumb. She tried to smile.

With a wave of the hand, Mr. Lowry beckoned. "I may spend most of my time in a library, but I wasn't born yesterday. Hand me the note."

"I ... I just—"

"Now, please."

Krissi looked at Scott and winced. Her otherwise fair complexion reddened. As she walked to the front of the class, he knew they were busted. Big time. Talk about a bad dream. Make that a nightmare. Krissi dropped the note on the desk and turned to leave.

"Don't move. Remain by my desk," Mr. Lowry said, promptly unfolding the page.

The clock on the wall ticked away a painfully long minute. *If only the floor would open up and swallow me,* Scott thought, burying his face in his hands.

With a jerk, Mr. Lowry stood up and faced the class. "I'd like for the person who wrote this to join her."

Scott tried to swallow, but his throat was as dry as sand.

At first, he didn't move—couldn't move was more like it. His feet felt as if they were encased in cement. What choice did he have? Every eye in the room was on him. He inched out of his seat and sulked his way to the front. The room was so quiet, Scott could hear the blood throbbing along the edge of his earlobes.

"People," Mr. Lowry said, obviously delighted to enforce the rules, "this is how we handle those who can't follow basic instructions."

Scott took his place alongside Krissi, drooping his shoulders as if waiting to be court-martialed. From the corner of his eye, he couldn't help but see the angry scowl on Philip's face. Scott looked away. He tried to focus on a spot on the floor instead. His mind ran wild. *Whatever you do ... starve me ... use Chinese torture on me ... just don't read that out loud.*

Mr. Lowry raised the note for all to see, as if holding the scalp of someone from a warring tribe. He lowered the paper and held it at arm's length. "I now have something to share with the group."

Scott stopped breathing. *Oh, great, I'm so dead,* he thought. *Looks like for once Krissi won't be blamed for starting the rumors.*

Mr. Lowry adjusted his reading glasses. He began to read the note out loud. "'Krissi, you know how much Philip is changing? Well, I think he's depressed. Like, big time. He tries to look like he has it together, but I think he's losing it. He even went to a psychic yesterday. That's messed up. As if a lady in a turban really knows anything about the future. That just shows you how desperate he must be. I think he needs you now more than ever ...'" Mr. Lowry stopped. "I think that's about enough," he said, crumpling the note in his hand.

Yeah, Scott thought, *enough for Philip to want to skin me alive.*

8

The white FedEx truck stopped in the middle of the road, its flashers on. The driver, wearing shorts, clutching a clipboard and an eight-by-ten flat envelope, hopped out. She hustled to the building and rang the bell.

The door opened. "Yes?"

"Hi. Package for—" The driver paused to scan the label, then added, "For a Rita Thomas."

At the sound of Rita's name, a brief spike of fear surged in Madame Theo's heart. Instinctively, she peeked up and down the street to see if anyone might overhear the conversation. She knew she couldn't be too careful.

"Yes ... thank you, that's me," Madame Theo said, reaching for the clipboard. She kept inside the door, her heart still jumpy.

"I'll need your signature right there," the driver said, pointing toward the bottom half of the form. "And, if you would, print your name next to it ... on the second line."

Madame Theo carefully filled in the required information with the pen attached to the clipboard.

"Nice day, isn't it?" the driver said, making small talk while

Madame Theo took her time signing the document as if she were creating a work of art. "I hear they're calling for rain."

"We could use some, couldn't we?" Madame Theo said, putting the finishing touches on her masterpiece. She looked up. "Here you go."

"Thank you very much," the driver said, retrieving the clipboard. Using a handheld scanner, she swiped the bar code on the label, typed in the date and time on the side of the scanning device, and then holstered it like a gun on her belt. She started to hand over the envelope when, for no apparent reason, she stopped and took a good look at Madame Theo.

Madame Theo, her hand extended to receive the package, returned the gaze. She raised an eyebrow wondering what was wrong. Why didn't the FedEx lady give her the envelope?

"You want to know something funny?"

Madame Theo pretended to be interested. "What's that?"

"It's just that your face looks really familiar." The woman tucked the clipboard under an arm. She made no further effort to release the envelope. "Aren't you on TV?"

Madame Theo felt her face flush. *Where is this going?* "Yes, such as it is," she answered, her posture matter-of-fact. "We're on in the middle of the night, for now, that is."

"That's it," the driver said with a broad smile. "The other night I couldn't sleep. My husband was out of town, and I always have a hard time falling asleep when he's away. Anyway, that's when I must have seen you on TV."

Although not an impatient person, Madame Theo was growing restless. She was dying to review the material from her former lawyer. She kept an eye on the package, like a vulture eyeing its next meal, and forced a smile. "I'm glad to know there's at least one person in the audience watching. Now, if you don't mind, I had better get back to work."

Perplexed, the driver tilted her head to one side.

"Is there something wrong?" Madame Theo asked.

"Actually, before I can leave this with you," the driver said, withholding the envelope, "I'll need to see some form of picture ID from you, ma'am."

"Excuse me?" Madame Theo's heart skipped several beats. "I … is that necessary?"

"You see this little orange sticker?" she said, holding up the package as if presenting evidence to the jury. "I can only leave this with the person who's named therein."

"So?"

"You signed this as Rita Thomas."

"Indeed. That's me."

"But last night, on TV, you were Madame Theo."

Madame Theo tucked a loose strand of hair back underneath her turban. She was beginning to see where this was going and started to steam. Why did her lawyer put Rita's name on it? He, of all people, should know a move like that would cause complications. Now what?

"You see," the psychic said in a soft, confidential voice, "Madame Theo is my … my stage name. So I'll just take that and we'll move on, okay? I'm expecting a client any moment."

"I still need to see some form of ID," the woman said, her tone pleasant but firm. "Driver's license. Passport. Just something with a picture. It's company policy."

Madame Theo sighed.

"I'm sure you know we do this for your security. Must be important stuff if it's got one of those orange stickers."

What was the point of arguing? Madame Theo ducked back inside the room, fished her wallet out of her frumpy, oversize bag, and returned to the door. With a flip, she opened the flap and presented her California driver's license.

"Nice picture," the FedEx lady said, studying the two-by-three plastic card. "Says here you're Theodella Smith."

A nod. "Naturally, in my line of work, I go by Madame Theo. But, yes, that's my full name."

The FedEx service woman handed back the license.

"What about the package?" Madame Theo asked, expectant, trying not to sound too anxious.

"I'm really sorry, ma'am. Unless you have another picture ID bearing the name of Rita Thomas, I'll need to return this to the station."

Madame Theo shook her head in disbelief. She was jammed between the desperate need to get that package and the reality that she, decades ago, had erased all traces of her former self, the lovely Rita Thomas. She didn't have a single item with Rita's name on it. Certainly not a picture ID. What if somebody broke in, snooped through her stuff, and stumbled on it? She'd be through. Or what if she were raided by the police?

Like the last time?

Still, Madame Theo had to find a way to put her hands on that information. With it, maybe she'd be able to convince her producer, Fred Stoner, to end his relentless push to syndicate into Los Angeles.

She tried another approach. "I ... well, can't you make an exception? After all, I am on TV. You can trust me."

"You could be one of the Beatles," the driver said with a guarded smile. "Still, as long as there's an orange sticker, we have no choice but to verify your ID."

Madame Theo started to feel dizzy. "Are you sure?"

"I'll tell you what," the driver said, extending a business card. "That's the dispatcher's number. Call him. I doubt it, but maybe you can work something out. Sorry. Gotta run." With that, she turned and dashed to the truck.

Within seconds, Madame Theo was at her desk. She dialed a private number and waited for an answer.

On the fourth ring, her lawyer muttered, "Zack Zimmerman."

Madame Theo clutched the phone against the side of her head. "What kind of stunt are you pulling, Zack?"

The bell sounded, signaling the end of fourth period. Contrary to what he had envisioned, Scott discovered he was still alive. The floor hadn't swallowed him. The walls hadn't crushed him. And he hadn't been publicly stoned for what he had done — at least not yet. Somehow he managed to survive the snickers, the catcalls, and the sneers from the students while Mr. Lowry read his note.

Philip was another matter. The instant the bell rang, he ducked out the door and, like a phantom, disappeared into the crowded hallway. Scott, with Krissi in tow, pushed his way through the mass of bodies and headed for the cafeteria. Getting there was like trying to make his way through rush-hour traffic.

Krissi tapped Scott's arm. "You think he's mad?"

"You're kidding, right?"

"Well, it wasn't like we were trying to be mean —"

"Doesn't matter," Scott said. "Didn't you see the look on his face while Mr. Lowry started reading?"

Krissi sighed. "Yeah, I feel really bad for him."

A moment later, they reached the food line, grabbed trays, silverware, and napkins, and then slinked forward to select their lunch choices. Philip, coming from the opposite direction, walked toward them. With a shove to Scott's shoulder, he said, "Boy, you sure can't be trusted, can you?"

Scott knew he deserved the rebuke and didn't shove back. As a kid, whenever Scott would get into a scuffle, his dad would say, "Remember, son, blessed are the peacemakers." Now was one of those times he needed to practice a healthy dose of grace.

"Did you ever think," Philip said, his eyes puffy, "about asking for my permission before talking behind my back?"

Scott held his tongue. For one of the first times in his life, Scott had nothing to say.

"Well, did you?"

Krissi, however, spoke up. "Come on, Philip. I asked Scott about yesterday because I'm concerned about you. How did we know the teacher would do that?"

"Krissi," Philip said with a sigh, "I really do think this is between Scott and me. You and I can talk about things later, okay?"

Scott started to apologize. "Man, I ... I'm—"

Philip cut him off. "A creep, that's what you are, Scott Williams." Philip inched closer. "In fact, you're the biggest chump in the world." With that, Philip turned and started to leave. Three steps away he paused, then turned back around. "What kind of Christian are you, anyway?"

9

The sun struggled to poke a hole through the gray clouds that hung, like a thick blanket, low in the sky. It would be raining before long, of that Philip was sure. He pulled his convertible to a stop and parked directly in front of Madame Theo's Palace. Thanks to Scott and Krissi's blunder, he no longer felt the need to hide what he was doing from friends at school.

By the time lunch was over, the buzz in the hallway was about Philip and the TV psychic. The rumor mill was working overtime. Everywhere he walked, he heard whispers and felt as if people everywhere were now talking behind his back. And once, while using the bathroom, he had overheard some punk telling his buddy a joke about Madame Theo:

"Knock knock."

"Who's there?"

"Madame Theo."

"Madame Theo who?"

"If you were psychic, you'd know too."

It wasn't even funny, Philip thought, dismissing the memory.

He raised the top on his convertible and, checking his watch, noticed he was right on time for his hastily scheduled appointment. After today's meltdown at school, he knew he needed to get some clarity. And so far, in spite of what the others might say about her, Madame Theo was right on the money. His mind drifted back to the three-card spread she had dealt during his initial session.

According to the first tarot card, she predicted his star was on the rise. The next day he won the debate against the best team in the region. At first he had wondered if it was a mere coincidence. In light of the current developments, he wasn't so sure. Last night, he was contacted by a recruiter from one of the colleges he was really interested in. Somehow they had gotten wind of his performance and quickly arranged an increase in their scholarship offer.

The second card, the one with people leaping from the tower, indicated he should make some drastic changes. *That's easy,* he thought. After today, he could see that he needed to cut things off with Krissi and especially with Scott. Philip was convinced they'd do nothing but hold him back. Or worse. Their friendship could keep his star from rising further and might even contribute to his downfall.

But it was the third card, the death card, that worried him at the moment. If Madame Theo was right about the first two cards, then she was most likely on target with the third. Was he going to die? Was someone close to him going to die? Or, as she had hinted, was there something in his world that needed to end for him to advance in his climb to the top? He needed to know. He needed someone to talk with who wouldn't mock his desire to know the future.

He needed Madame Theo. Or did he? So far, she seemed to have all the answers. Maybe that was part of what was bothering him. Maybe he was giving her too much credit. What if everything she had predicted about his future was just a coincidence?

Then again, what harm was there in giving her another chance? Philip reached for the handle and let himself in.

"Please, Philip, come in. I've been expecting you," she said, already sitting at the table.

It took a moment for him to adjust to the blast of scented air and the darkness of the room. He took a seat across from Madame Theo and, with a sigh, slumped forward.

"I see a young man with a heavy heart," she said. Her voice was soft and airy as a feather.

Philip took a deep breath. "I ... I hope I'm not late."

She shook her head. "You're right on time, my friend. Now give me your hands." She extended her hands, palms up, across the table. "Why don't you start by telling me what's troubling your spirit."

For a split second, Philip felt a little alarm go off in the back of his brain. It warned something wasn't right, a warning that he promptly dismissed. He slipped his hands into hers and tried to think where he should start.

In the quiet that followed, he felt moved to come clean. He confessed his original doubts about her, about the cards, about the whole idea that she could actually discern future events. He told her about winning the debate, about losing his girl-friend—and the fallout with Scott. And he told her about his fears of the death card.

As he spoke, Madame Theo's eyes remained closed, her grip steady and firm. She seemed to be in a trance. Without warning, she released his hands and looked him straight in the eyes. "This evening," she announced, dropping her arms below the table, "I believe you're ready for the next level."

"Come again?"

"At first, by your own admission, you didn't believe with your whole heart. Your mind refused to give way to your deeper, inner connection to the spirit realm. I see that has changed."

Madame Theo reached for the deck of tarot cards. "This change is good. This is very good, Philip."

He smiled at the affirmation.

"I knew when I first saw you, you were destined for greatness," she added, covering the deck with the palm of her hand.

Philip straightened up in his chair. He liked the sound of her validation. "Um, thank you," was all he could think to say.

"Now keep in mind," she said, "each reading relies upon the kinetic forces operating in the universe at the time of the reading."

"Got it." Philip vaguely remembered this from their first session.

"Which means your concerns about the death card will either be validated, deepened, or changed, depending on the ebb and flow of the unseen divine forces."

"Okay," Philip said, unsure if this was good news or bad.

"Before we begin, let us invoke the goodness of the eternal spirit guide," she said, closing her eyes, her hands still hovering over the cards.

"Huh? Oh," Philip said, figuring out that he, too, should probably bow his head. Once again, a little alarm sounded in his mind, although less strongly this time. He shoved it aside.

"May the highest powers be pleased by our desire for good, not harm, to come of this revelation. We stand against the negative forces that might thwart a blessing. So be it."

Philip peeked with one eye, unsure if it was okay to look. "Uh … amen," he said quickly, uncertain what the right response should be to her quasi prayer. He watched as Madame Theo dealt five cards in a straight row, facedown in the center of the table.

"This is a five-card spread," she said, setting the balance of the deck to one side. "The meanings are similar to the three-card spread. But there are differences."

"How so?"

"We start with the past influences," she said, turning over

the first. It revealed a man and woman standing in a garden. "Hmm. These are the lovers. In the past, you've been close to someone special. She has held much influence over you. And now you must decide if you will remain under her influence. Can you think of someone who this might represent?"

Philip immediately said, "Krissi."

"Your girlfriend, the one you're broken up with, at least in your heart?"

A nod.

"Good. It appears the cards are confirming your need for a change." She turned over the second tarot card. "This is your present influence."

"Looks like a dude in a chariot," Philip said, tilting his head for a better view.

"Strictly speaking, yes. What it represents has much to do with the tension of opposite forces at work."

"I ... I ... what's that mean?"

"Could be pointing to a divorce," Madame Theo said, carefully eyeing Philip's reaction.

"Wow. My parents are split up ..."

"That, Philip, must be the opposite forces at work in your life. The cards are saying you must remain steady in the midst of the struggle."

"I see." Philip felt his heart racing. He had watched her shuffle the deck. How, then, did the cards know his situation? With each second, Philip found himself longing to understand and to connect with whatever was at work behind the cards.

When Madame Theo dealt the third card, Philip gasped. "That guy looks like he's been hanged," he said, his voice cracking midsentence. "What in the world—"

"Not to worry," she said, her voice warm as a summer breeze. "The hanged man, which is a hidden influence, simply means you need to put to death outdated ideas or influences or thought patterns and embrace a new, liberating frontier."

One word popped into his mind. He said, "Christianity."

"I'm not surprised," she said. "For centuries we've been persecuted by those of the so-called Christian faith. The tarot is speaking, Philip. You must flee the prison which those ideas hold you in."

Philip's brain was on maximum spin. If true, if Christianity was holding him back, then everything Becka and Scott, and more recently Ryan and Julie, believed was a lie.

"Are you still with me, Philip?"

His eyes flickered. "I'm sorry, yes. It's just ... just so much to take in all at once."

Madame Theo smiled. "I know, son. We're almost there. The fourth card is what I like to call the counselor, for it is in the position to provide advice," she said. She brought a finger to the side of her head, adding, "You may elect to follow this advice or ignore it at your own peril." She flipped over the card.

A dry swallow and then Philip spoke. "What's ... uh ... the old guy with the lantern mean?"

"That's the hermit." Her fingers lingered on the surface of the table.

Philip waited for the implication. "And?"

"The other side is trying to reach you, Philip." Her voice wavered ever so slightly, as if treading on sacred ground. "Hear me, son. You must meditate and open yourself up to the divine spirit guide that's active in the other world."

"Then what?"

She shook her head. "I can't say for sure. Only you can identify the direction in which the streams of life forces move you. But you must listen ... listen ... listen."

Philip blinked. Open himself up to what? Or better, listen to whom? And what if he did? What then? Before Philip could answer his own questions, he heard a knock at the door.

Madame Theo looked up, startled. "I'm sorry. This is most unusual." She crossed the room and opened the door.

Philip looked over his shoulder. As far as he could see, it was a delivery service of sorts. He strained to hear the conversation. The voice on the outside said something about an exception had been made even if she didn't have proper ID for Rita Thomas, whoever that was.

Thirty seconds later, Madame Theo set a white FedEx envelope on the end table next to the incense pot. "Our time is almost gone," she said, quickly returning to her seat. Her mood appeared significantly impatient. "Uh, now where was I?"

Philip raised an eyebrow. "The fifth card, I think."

She exhaled. "Yes. Thank you. I view this as the likely outcome of future events, if you follow the advice provided by the hermit."

"It's a sun," Philip said, noticing a line of perspiration forming across Madame Theo's forehead. "Are you okay?"

She seemed startled by the question. "Yes, fine. Now," she said, fiddling with the edge of her turban, "the sun is a sign that your future … will be bright, filled with joy, warmth … uh … and good things. It's all there for the taking."

"But?"

"But," she said, her eyes darting toward the package and then back to the table. "But … you must rely solely on your own energies, insights, and … uh, on your inner strength if you are to succeed."

Philip felt a growing sense of uneasiness spread across his chest. Something had put Madame Theo on edge. But what? She seemed fine, until, that is, the package arrived. Why? Why the sudden restlessness?

"There you have it," she said abruptly. "That will be twenty-five dollars."

"Sure thing." Philip reached into his pocket and clutched two bills. "Got change for thirty?"

Madame Theo took the money and then disappeared into the back room. Once she was gone, and in spite of the fact it was none of his business, Philip leaned to his side to inspect the package. Maybe it held a clue that would explain the change in her behavior.

With a squint, he made out the name Rita Thomas on the shipping label. *That's odd,* he thought. *Why did somebody draw a red line through the name and cross it out?*

Beneath the red line, a message had been scrawled: *a.k.a. Madame Theo — okay to deliver per district dispatch.*

10

Wednesday night, a hard, steady rain fell from the darkened sky, accented occasionally by streaks of yellow lightning. Krissi, Ryan, and Becka sat in a booth in the back corner of a local hamburger joint. A handful of stray fries and several crumpled sandwich wrappers stained with special sauce was all that was left on their trays.

Becka drained the last of her chocolate shake. She eyed the clock on the wall: it was almost 8:30 p.m. "Looks like Philip is a total no-show," she said, wiping her hands on a napkin. "What's with that? He knew we were getting together at 6:00 for the movie, right?"

Krissi sighed. She looked away and said, "I guess he completely bailed on me."

"You try his cell phone?" Ryan asked.

"Yeah. I even called and left a message after school reminding him," Krissi said, playing with a burned fry. She tossed it onto the pile. "No answer at his home, either."

"Can you blame him?" Becka asked. "I mean, Scott told me all about what happened at study hall. He's got to be pretty upset."

"Still, he should have called," Krissi said, miffed. She swiped a loose strand of hair from her face. "It kind of makes me mad, you know? I mean, how rude is that for him to just blow me off like this?"

"So," Ryan said after a long moment, "what's with Philip going to see that tarot lady, anyway?"

Krissi shrugged. "Beats me. I know his dad's been putting tons of pressure on him about college—"

"But ... a fortune-teller?" Becka interjected. After school, Scott had caught up with her and told her everything—Philip's angry meltdown in the cafeteria, the crazed look in his eyes, and how Scott had never seen Philip so nervous and flipped out.

"Sounds bogus to me too," Ryan said. "I just don't picture Philip, you know, falling for such a ridiculous—"

Becka jumped in. "Ryan ..."

He winked. "Okay ... let's just say, something else must be seriously wrong with him to see, um ... Madame Whacko."

"Ryan!" Becka said with a punch to his shoulder.

Krissi thought about that for a second. She shifted in her seat. "Well, honestly, maybe he's confused about ... about us too. Like, about our future together. I mean, with his dad putting on the pressure for college and all that, maybe he's been afraid of making a commitment."

Becka stole a look at Ryan. She knew the feeling. She had tons of questions about what would happen between her and Ryan. She also knew there were better ways to deal with those concerns than to consult a psychic. The occult was nothing to mess around with. After all that had happened—at the mansion, with Krissi, in the park—surely Philip understood that much, didn't he?

Something else was bothering her about Philip's strange behavior. Z had said that fooling around with tarot cards could be lethal.

Was Philip in danger?

Becka glanced across the table, framing her next question as carefully as she could. "Krissi, you don't think Philip is ... like ... suicidal do you?"

Krissi paled. "I ..."

As if on cue, her cell phone rang. Krissi almost jumped out of her seat. Flustered, she snatched it from her purse, pushed Talk, and said, "It's Krissi."

Krissi noticed Becka watching her as if studying her face to figure out who the caller was.

"Philip!" Krissi said, her eyes darting between Becka and Ryan. "What's going on? Where have you been? We missed you at the movie. I've been so worried—"

Krissi fell silent as she listened, imagining her face morphing into a picture of disbelief, hurt, surprise, and then anger.

"Whatever!" Krissi said a little too loud. She bolted upright and then scrambled out of the booth. She stood, her back to the table, with her right finger pressed against one ear and the phone against the other ear.

"I don't know what's wrong with you ..."

"Listen, Krissi, I'm just really confused about so much these days," Philip said.

"As if I hadn't noticed."

Philip cleared his throat. "I ... I just need some time to sort stuff out."

"Yeah, but what about us? You know, you and me against the world and all that stuff?"

"You know that hasn't changed—"

"Right ..." Krissi rolled her eyes. "Then why didn't you show tonight? I'm really hurt if you want to know the truth."

Philip remained silent for a moment. "I'm sorry, Krissi. I don't ever want to hurt you, really I don't. But I guess I needed to be alone ... for a while."

"And meanwhile, what am I supposed to do?"

"Well, I kind of hoped you'd understand my need for some space."

Krissi's voice raised a notch. "Sorry, Philip. I'd like to understand, but I don't."

"Why not?"

"Just tell me this. How long do I need to stick around to find out if this relationship is going to go somewhere?"

"I don't know," Philip said, his voice growing distant. "And I guess I don't know why you're coming down so hard on me."

"Why? Because you're not the same guy I used to know ..."

"How's that?"

"Where's the Philip who used to make me laugh and cry at the same time?"

Philip hesitated. "He's just a little lost right now."

"Still," Krissi said, stealing a look at Ryan and Becka. She lowered her voice. "As far as I'm concerned, our relationship is as good as over!"

Krissi snapped the phone shut and collapsed into her seat.

Philip had been driving aimlessly in the rain for hours. He had a vague awareness that it was a little after 8:00 at night. Parked under a railroad bridge, he sat somewhere out in the country away from the problems back in Crescent Bay. His eyes were drained of their tears, his mind was filled with confusion, and his heart was running on empty.

He squeezed the phone against his ear until it hurt. Did Krissi really hang up on him? Was it really over? Numbed that she had, in fact, cut him off, he sat in a daze thicker than the fog blanketing the road ahead. The phone slipped from his hand onto the front seat next to him.

He had just lost his best friend.

The one who stuck by him when his parents were breaking up.

The girl who always seemed to lift his spirits.

The person who seemed to know and care so much about him. A hole formed in the pit of his stomach. Krissi refused to understand—or couldn't understand—his situation. Either way, she was leaving him in the dust.

Maybe breaking up was for the best. Wasn't that what the tarot cards pointed to? According to Madame Theo, Krissi was in the way of his growth, his future fortunes, and his destiny. She was holding back his rising star. Or was she?

Could the cards be wrong?

The more he tossed the situation over in his mind, the more the whole tarot thing seemed so subjective. Even Madame Theo said that he needed to listen to the divine cosmic forces or whatever. Maybe that's where he made a mistake. Maybe he didn't do a very good job of listening. Worse, if he had heard wrong, then he had just played the fool and burned the bridge to the most important friend in his life.

Philip slapped the dash with his right hand.

Several painfully long seconds passed. It seemed to him that the more he struggled to take control of his future, the worse things were starting to become. Fighting back a fresh round of tears, he decided to get home. Besides, having noticed it was 8:34, if he hurried, he'd be able to catch Madame Theo in her new time slot on TV.

He reached for the keys to start the car. With a whine, the engine conked out. He tried again. Same thing. On the third try, the engine caught. He engaged the transmission, flipped on the wipers, and pulled onto the two-lane road, where he hadn't seen a car in the last thirty minutes.

Philip leaned against his door and drove with one hand draped over the wheel. The wipers flopped from side to side as the lightning flashed across the night sky. He had gone about two miles when the convertible sputtered, stalled, and stopped. The wipers continued their rhythmic thump as he coasted to the curb. Now what? He scanned the gauges and spotted the problem.

He had run out of gas.

Philip pounded the steering wheel with both hands. "Why? ... Why me? ... Why now?"

He snapped off the lights, hopped out of the car, and slammed the door so violently the windows shook. He started to wander home in the pouring rain. What choice did he have? He wasn't about to call his dad—or Krissi for that matter.

Within minutes he was soaked through to the skin. His shoes were waterlogged and his hair matted against his forehead until he could have passed for a drenched rat. The deluge of anger surged within him with each step.

Philip lifted his face against the wet blackness and screamed, "God ... I need answers!"

Nothing but the jagged flash of lightning answered him.

Figures, he thought. Where was God when he needed him? Where was God when his mother decided to split in the middle of the night? Where was God when his dad was bearing down on him? Where? Nowhere, that's where, he decided, shrugging off a chill.

As he strained against the storm, he realized he didn't have the strength to press on. He'd never make it. Furious, Philip kicked the ground, turned, and headed back to the car where he had left the cell phone. Once inside the car, he swallowed his pride, dialed a number, and prayed for a small miracle.

Come on, Scott, answer the phone.

❧ ❧

Scott sat at his desk in his bedroom and suppressed a yawn. He stared at the computer screen. He had just finished telling Z about the disaster with Philip at school and was waiting for Z's take on the situation. Z's answer finally appeared.

Scott, keep in mind, not all tarot readers know what

they're doing. It's a highly subjective field. Many are simply guessing about possible outcomes based on what they perceive the client wants to hear.

But I thought you said tarot cards were lethal.

Yes, they can be. Turning to tarot opens a person up to very real dangers.

See. So I was right to have warned Philip.

This time, Z answered Scott with a question of his own. The words crawled across the screen:

Scott, the Bible says unbelievers will know we are Christians by our what?

By our love. But that's so unfair, Z. Philip's fooling around with tarot cards. They're dangerous. You said so yourself.

When we are wronged, what does Jesus want us to do?

I guess turn the other cheek.

Scott shook his head, upset by the direction of the conversation. After all, Philip was the one who kicked him out of the car. Philip was the one who yelled at him in front of everybody in the cafeteria. Philip was the one who was being a jerk. Still feeling defensive, he fired off another response:

Yeah, but, Z, Philip is the one who's gone off the deep end. Not me.

Scott waited. After a long pause, Z typed back:

You can be theologically correct about tarot cards, Scott, and still have no heart in it. Maybe what Philip sees in you is judgment and condemnation.

What am I supposed to do?

Just love him.

How?

Scott waited for a response, but none came. That was like Z too. Half the time it seemed Z wanted Scott and Becka to figure things out on their own. Scott yawned, stretched his arms, then signed off and folded his arms. This wasn't what he wanted to hear. Secretly, he had hoped Z would have at least applauded him for trying his best and then told him to drop the whole thing. The clock next to his bed indicated it was 8:44. With another yawn, he shut down the computer.

Scott scratched the back of Cornelius's head for several seconds. It had been one of the longest days of his life, at least emotionally. First, the study hall fiasco. Then the confrontation in the cafeteria, not to mention all the little jabs he had overheard in the hallway throughout the rest of the day.

He covered his mouth as another yawn emerged. He still had a pile of homework to do, but that would have to wait until he grabbed a few minutes of rest. He turned out the lights and then crashed against his pillow. He closed his eyes as the dull patter of rain against the roof serenaded him to sleep.

Within seconds, he heard a window on the other side of the bedroom blow open. He propped himself up on one arm. He quickly scanned the darkness. Against the flash of thunder, he saw a faceless intruder sneaking across the room. It was just steps away, moving in his direction. Scott's heart spiked.

The figure, hunched over and cloaked, made no noise as it drifted like a phantom to the edge of the bed.

"Who's there?" Scott asked, suddenly feeling fully awake.

No answer.

A crack of lightning lit up the intruder's features. For a split second, Scott caught a glimpse of her face. He knew this woman, but he had no idea why she had trailed him home.

Scott found his voice. With a croak, he said, "What ... what do you want with me?"

11

Her long, bony forefinger was as thin as a twig. With a jab, she punctured the night air in Scott's direction. A harsh crackle roared in the distance followed by several flashes of light. The drapes by the open window flailed about like two sails in the wind, beating against the mad rush of angry air.

The ghostlike figure leaned over his bed. Her eyes glowed like two hot charcoals. Her skin, a washed-out mixture of ashen and gray, seemed to hang from her bones. Her breath smelled of rotting garbage, and the wraps of her turban appeared mummy-like.

Scott's heart zoomed as his mind raced to find answers. All he managed to say was, "Madame Theo?"

"Silence!" She poked his side with her bony finger.

Scott jumped backward, rubbing the spot she had pierced. It burned as if her finger had been dipped in acid. "What in the world—"

"He's mine ... all mine."

"Who ... who is?" Scott asked, still dazed by the encounter.

"Philip." Madame Theo circled the bed, running, floating,

flying. With each revolution, she poked Scott again and again, shouting, "Philip … Philip … Philip …"

Try as he did, he was unable to avoid the piercing sting of her fingertip. He felt as punctured as a pincushion. His lungs began to constrict as he tried to catch his breath. Somewhere in the distance, a bell started ringing. The hollow clanging echoed in his head until it throbbed.

Scott tried to sit upright — had to sit up — but Madame Theo knocked him down with a blow to the chest. The force of her hand compressed the remaining air from his burning lungs. He felt a prolonged pressure crushing against his rib cage as if caught in the jaws of a giant invisible vise.

"Stay away from Philip," she bellowed. She reached out and grabbed the corner of the bed. With a jerk, she sent the bed spinning in a circle. Scott held on for dear life.

Like a wounded animal, Madame Theo howled, "He's mine … all mine."

Just as quickly as the ordeal had started, it stopped.

The bed came to a rest. Madame Theo was gone.

With the exception of the thunder and the rain pelting the roof, the room was deadly silent. In the thick silence that followed her stormy appearance, the ringing inside of Scott's head grew louder and louder, more intense with each second until he could no longer bear it. Covering his ears with the palms of his hands, Scott yelled, "Stop it!"

With a blink, Scott woke from the nightmare. Drenched in sweat, his heart hammering against his chest, he sat up and tossed his legs over the edge of the bed. The windows were closed. The drapes hung in place.

The phone was ringing.

Scott fumbled in the dark for the portable handset. "Hello?"

"Scott?"

The voice was familiar, but the connection was so bad he didn't recognize it at first. "Yeah?"

"It's Philip."

Scott sat upright, alert. Was this part of the nightmare too? After all, Philip was the last person he expected to hear from. Scott switched on a lamp. He was awake. This was no dream. "What time is it?"

"Like, 9:45," Philip said. "Sorry. Did I wake you up?"

"I ... I must have dozed for a minute," Scott said.

As he regained consciousness, Scott was about to give Philip a piece of his mind for yelling at him at school when Z's words — *just love him* — came to mind. Scott blew a short breath. He really wasn't in a mood to be loving. Then again, maybe this was one of those divine appointments Z always talked about.

"Scott?"

"I'm here," Scott said, rubbing the spots where Madame Theo had poked him in his dream.

"I've been trying to get through, but your line was busy."

See, Scott thought, *he's already trying to pick a fight.* Instead of jumping to conclusions, Scott said, "I was online. Um, that is, before I fell asleep. So what's up, man?"

"I ... I could really use your help."

👁 👁

"Mom, can I borrow the car?" Scott asked. Although he had turned sixteen a month ago and had been taking drivers ed, he knew it was a long shot if she agreed. He stood in the doorway to her bedroom where she was reading a book in bed.

"Isn't it kind of late?"

Scott resisted a yawn. "Yeah, but Philip's car broke down. He needs a lift. I figure it's the least I can do for him."

She placed a finger in the page where she had been reading and then partially closed the book. "I don't know. It's raining pretty hard out there—"

"I'll be careful."

She studied his face. "I know you want to help, but can't Philip just call a tow truck?"

"Yeah, he might have been able to, but I think his battery went dead or something," Scott said, leaning against the doorjamb.

"I don't know," she said, placing the book in her lap. "Maybe I should get up and take you."

"I really don't think that'd be too cool," Scott said. "I mean, thanks for the offer and all that, but I think we've got some stuff we need to hash out."

Mrs. Williams nodded. "Okay, son. Just be home by eleven. Remember, better safe than sorry."

Scott kissed her on the forehead, grabbed the keys, and headed for the car.

Scott followed Philip's directions until he spied Philip's car by the side of the road. He pulled alongside of the convertible and, reaching across the seat, Scott unlocked the passenger door.

"Thanks, dude," Philip said, once inside.

"Hey, what are friends for." Scott handed Philip a towel to dry his face and said, "Here, my mom suggested I bring this for you."

"Your mom's cool. Thanks." He started to towel down his hair. "You know, I should have asked you to just bring a gas can. Guess I wasn't thinking."

"Even if you had," Scott said with a smile, "I passed the gas station and it was already closed." He carefully made a U-turn and headed back to town. He considered telling Philip about his bizarre dream with Madame Theo but figured he might just get defensive. "So what happened to the big date? I thought you were going out with Krissi, Ryan, and Becka tonight."

Philip dried the back of his neck. "Honestly?"

Scott tossed him a look. "Sure."

"I'm pretty confused these days, you know?"

Scott thought of a wisecrack but decided against saying it.

"Anyway," Philip said, toweling down his arms, "I just didn't see the point, at least, not after what Madame Theo said today."

At the mention of her name, Scott's heart flinched. "You saw her again?"

Philip cautiously eyed Scott.

"Look, about today … I am so sorry, man," Scott said. "I shouldn't have talked about you behind your back. I mean, it's not like I was gossiping. It's just that some of us think you're changing. We care, that's all."

Philip wrapped the towel around his neck. He leaned an elbow against the passenger door. "Can I trust you not to blab?"

Scott nodded. "I promise."

For the next several minutes, Philip told Scott about the five-card spread, Madame Theo's interpretation, and the changes he thought he needed to make—including putting some distance between himself and Krissi. After he was finished, Philip fell silent.

For his part, Scott wanted to warn him about the dangers of getting involved with tarot cards. He couldn't shake the feeling that Philip was walking on very dangerous ground. Instead of giving him a lecture, he tried a different approach.

"You're taking this tarot stuff pretty seriously, huh?" Scott said, stealing a quick look at his passenger.

"I don't know what to think," Philip said. "But—"

"But what?"

"Something happened today that was kind of weird."

Scott raised an eyebrow. "Like, how?"

"She got a package. One of those overnight deals," Philip said, looking out his window. "It came during my session."

"What's so weird about that?"

"I could be wrong, but she started acting really different afterward," Philip said. "It was like she had lost interest in the cards and wanted me to leave."

Scott wrinkled his nose. "I don't get it. What's wrong with that? She probably had stuff to do."

Philip shook his head. "Actually, the weird part had to do with the name on the package."

"How's that?"

"Just that it was addressed to somebody called Rita Thomas."

"So?"

"Well, she's the only one there," Philip said with a shrug. "Maybe it's nothing. But Rita's name was crossed out and it said a.k.a. Madame Theo or something like that."

Scott looked at Philip and waited for an explanation. "What's a.k.a. mean?" he finally asked.

"That means 'also known as,' " Philip said.

Scott allowed the information to sink in. Then it hit him. "So Madame Theo is *also known as* Rita Thomas."

"I knew there was something going on with her," Philip said.

They rode in silence for half a mile, when Scott asked, "Why the different names?"

"That's what I don't get," Philip said, wiping his face with the towel again. "Why doesn't she just call herself Madame Rita? Unless—"

Scott finished his sentence. "Unless she's hiding something."

"But what's she hiding?"

12

Philip ducked inside the kitchen door, hoping to dash up the back staircase to his room without being detected by his dad. He could tell his dad was still awake by the bluish flicker of light in the den. Philip figured he had probably fallen asleep with the TV on, but he didn't take any chances. He removed his waterlogged sneakers and started for the steps.

A voice from the den called out, "Do you have any idea what time it is?"

Philip swallowed hard. "Just after eleven."

"May I ask where you've been all night?" his dad asked, appearing at the door to the kitchen. A beer dangled from the fingers in his right hand.

"I kind of ran out of gas, sir."

A pained look crossed his father's face. He took a sip from the can. "You what?"

"I ran out—"

"I heard you the first time. Now sit down."

Philip took a seat at the kitchen table. He had an idea of what was coming and desperately wanted to avoid another argument.

But how? Once Dad started drinking, it was impossible to have a rational conversation.

"You expect me to believe that story, buddy boy?" his dad said, staggering toward the table. "Well, I don't. I wasn't born yesterday. You were out with that ... that Missy girl."

"It's Krissi, and no, I wasn't out with her, Dad. Actually, can we talk about this tomorrow?"

His dad waved him off. "How come you're soaking wet?"

"It's raining, remember?"

"Hey, watch it, buster." His dad finished the beer and reached for another from the refrigerator. "I want to talk to you about ... about your college plans."

Philip shook his head. "Please, Dad, not again. I—"

His dad smacked the table with his palm. "We're done talking when I say we're done. Got it?"

"Dad, cut me some slack here," Philip said, starting to rise. "It's late and I'd like to get some dry clothes on."

"Shut up ... and sit down."

"Dad, come on," Philip said, moving toward the stairway. "You're drunk. Let's talk in the morning, okay? I promise."

His dad swore and then threw an empty beer can in Philip's direction. It ricocheted off a cabinet and, falling to the floor, flipped several times before coming to a stop. A trickle of beer leaked out. "You're just like your mother ... always looking for a quick exit. Go on. Get out of here. I can't stop you from ruining your life."

Glad to make his getaway, glad to distance himself from his drunken father, Philip ran up the stairs two steps at a time. He tossed off his wet clothing, dried himself off, and pulled on shorts and a T-shirt. He snapped off the lights and jumped into bed. He exhaled a long, tired breath.

Alone in the darkness, Philip tried to sleep but couldn't stop thinking about Krissi. On the one hand, he was dying to call her, to hear her voice, to know that everything would still work out between them. Maybe if he, like Scott, apologized, they'd get back together.

On the other hand, maybe Madame Theo was right. Maybe Krissi was holding him back. Maybe she wasn't good enough for him and she, like his mother, would dump him when things got tough. Then again, it bothered him that Madame Theo might be hiding something. But what? Was she really who she claimed to be? He had been so quick to believe everything she had been saying. What if she was just another scam artist after a quick buck?

Philip rolled over onto his side and thought about the hunting knife hidden between his mattresses. Why did life have to be so hard? Why was he under such pressure to perform? To please his dad? To get good grades? Why couldn't he get a grip? Would anybody really miss him if he were gone? The more he thought things through, the more depressed he became.

In the darkness he slipped out of bed, sat on the floor, and reached for the knife. He rested the blade across his lap and slumped against the bed. With this final desperate act, he could settle his struggles once and for all. Death would free him from the heavy burden that had weighed him down for years.

No more encounters with a drunken parent.

No more upset girlfriends.

No more unanswered questions.

No more uncertainty about the future.

Death was the answer. Or was it? His heartbeat quickened.

There was something about the finality of death that scared him. What happened when he died? Did he just cease to exist? Or was there something or someone out there? He couldn't shake the feeling that he wasn't ready to face the great unknown. It was then that a face came to his mind.

Becka.

Of all the people he knew from school, Becka seemed different. There was an irresistible warmth behind her smile.

A brightness in her eyes. A self-confidence that didn't appear forced. Sure, she had problems. She made mistakes. But there was something about Becka that he couldn't ignore.

Becka had peace.

That's it, Philip decided. No matter the circumstances, she seemed at peace. And she wasn't afraid to stand for what she believed, even when battling evil spirits. Why? What was it about Becka that gave her the strength to carry on—even after the untimely plane crash involving the dad she loved?

He knew Becka claimed to be a Christian and that she believed in Jesus. But he couldn't figure how that would make any real difference. In fact, Philip remembered a time when he had been curious about Jesus too. But his interest was sidetracked by other important stuff—like Krissi and school and his car.

Now, hanging on to the end of his rope, there was a part of him wishing he had been as thorough in his investigation of Christianity as he was of Madame Theo's tarot cards. Was it too late to reconsider Jesus?

In the cold, dark shadows of the night, Philip broke into a sweat. His breathing was hard and labored. His head ached as if he'd been clobbered by a baseball bat. More than anything, he wished he had someone to talk to. Someone who might pull him back from the cliff. Someone, anyone, who cared.

God, if you're there ... I need a sign ... a friend ... just something—

Philip hadn't finished his prayer when the phone by his bed purred. His heart leaped. *Probably a wrong number,* he thought. It rang again. And it rang a third time as he reached for the phone. He cleared his throat. "Hello?"

"Dude, it's Scott."

Philip's heart skipped a beat. "Hey, Scott."

"Hope I didn't wake you up. You okay?"

"Sure, why do you ask?"

"I don't know. Just felt this need to call you," Scott said. "I mean, I know this may sound far out—"

"No, go ahead," Philip said, hoping he didn't sound as shocked as he felt.

"Well, ever since I got home, I've had this impression like God wanted me to call." Scott paused.

Philip held the phone between his shoulder and his ear as he studied the knife. "Uh, everything's okay. I'm just kind of burned-out. You know how that goes."

"I do," Scott said. "Hey, I'll be praying for you."

Philip swallowed. "Thanks, Scott."

"By the way, I sent an email to Z tonight and told him about the whole Rita Thomas thing," Scott announced. "Maybe he can dig something up on her. Hope you don't mind. He's amazing. I bet he'll come up with something."

"That's cool," Philip said.

"See you tomorrow?"

"Uh, sure."

On Thursday morning Madame Theo sat in the stuffed leather chair facing the desk of Fred Stoner, her producer. The new time slot worked great. Her guest was wonderful. The phone bank in Utah was swamped with callers looking to get a peek at their future. The money was starting to roll in. The first round of syndication was working. But, at the moment, none of that mattered.

She studied Fred's face like a hawk as he flipped through several documents—secret papers sent to her from Zack Zimmerman, her lawyer in Los Angeles. As far as she could tell, Fred was unmoved by what he saw. He showed about as much emotion as a houseplant. He flipped over another page and, scanning the contents, shook his head.

"This is what you were concerned about?" he said after a prolonged silence.

"Shouldn't I be?" Madame Theo asked, puzzled by his indifference.

"Not in the least," he said, dropping the papers to his desk. "It's old news. I'm no lawyer, but it seems to me that the statute of limitations has run out on these ... these—"

"Crimes," she said, adjusting her turban. "I'm not proud of what I did, but I'm not offended to use the right term."

"Listen to me," he said, massaging his temples. "That was then. This is now. And you're hot. Do you understand that?"

Madame Theo tried to appear surprised.

"I'm telling you," Fred said, flashing a mouth full of highly polished teeth, "you're about to step into the big time. I'm talking hyperspace. I'm talking mounds of cash once we ramp up to full syndication. This ... this stuff is old news. In my view, you don't have anything to lose sleep over."

Madame Theo folded her arms. "Really? You think so?"

"Really." Fred Stoner walked to her side, helped her up, and guided her toward the hall. "It's late. Get some rest. Tomorrow I'll pull out all the stops. We'll go live in Los Angeles. Nothing can go wrong."

"But—"

Fred put an arm around Madame Theo's shoulders. "Trust me. Who's gonna know our little secret, anyway? Right?"

13

Scott raced through the halls between classes. He had an idea of where Philip would be — or should be was more like it. So far, four periods into Thursday morning and still no sign of Philip anywhere. None of Philip's friends had spotted him either. Scott was getting anxious after what had happened last night.

All morning, Scott replayed the phone conversation from the previous night in his mind. Something in Philip's voice scared him. Not in the words spoken. No. There was just something very dark about his tone. Philip sounded desperate. Distant. Depressed. And a bit edgy. But why?

Even though Scott was no expert, Philip's erratic behavior the last few days struck him as borderline suicidal. Would Philip take his own life? Scott refused to think Philip would do something so drastic. Or would he? Come to think of it, what was Philip doing way out on that deserted country road in the middle of the night?

Scott dashed into the cafeteria and scanned the mass of faces around the tables.

Off to his left, somebody called his name. "Hey, Scott, over here."

Scott turned. Krissi, Ryan, and Becka were sitting together at a table by the far wall. He waved and then worked his way through the crowded lunch room.

"What's up, Scott?" Ryan said, studying Scott's face as he approached. "You look like someone died."

Scott shot him a look. "That's not funny."

"It was a joke, Scott."

"Whatever." Scott ran his fingers through his hair. "Listen. Have you guys seen Philip?"

Krissi flushed. Ryan and Becka exchanged a look.

"What did I say?" Scott said, stealing a fry from Becka's plate.

"It's just that Krissi broke up with Philip last night," Becka said, smacking Scott's hand as he reached for another fry.

"Wow," Scott said. "That's a bummer. Still, did you guys see him today?"

Krissi, her cheeks red as roses, shook her head. "No."

"Me neither," Ryan said, then looked at Becka.

Becka frowned. "No. Is something up?"

Scott's eyes zoomed around the room to see if anybody was eavesdropping. He had learned his lesson during study hall and didn't care to cause more damage. He leaned forward as if revealing a national secret. "Last night, I wanna say around eleven-ish, I had this really strong feeling that I needed to call him. You know, one of those God-prompting things our pastor is always talking about."

"Really?" Becka said, her eyebrows raised. "I had a sense that I should pray for him too."

"Anyway, I called and he sounded—" Scott paused, unsure whether or not to say something that might make Krissi worry. "He sounded really down."

Krissi folded her arms together. "What makes you say a thing like that?"

"Call it a guy's intuition—"

"There's no such thing," Krissi said with a flick of her hair.

"Still," Scott said, unfazed by her protest, "I think he's into this tarot card craze deeper than even he realizes."

"How's that?" Becka asked, looking worried.

Scott stole another look around. "Just that he's really hung up about what's in the future—you know, like, about college, friends, stuff like that."

Ryan put an arm around Becka. "He's not the only one with those kind of questions," he said. "Take your sister and me. We're wondering what God has for us down the road too."

Scott's right eyebrow shot up. He nudged Becka with an elbow. "What's this I'm hearing, sis?"

Becka looked away. Her face turned four shades of red.

"Oh, now I get it," Scott said, as if solving a great mystery.

"Get what?" Becka said, guarded.

"Well, if things are cruising between you two," Scott said with a wink, "that explains why you were singing happy songs while washing the dishes."

Becka nailed him in the shoulder with a fist. "SCOTT! You are *so* clueless."

"The point is," Ryan said, rescuing Becka from further embarrassment, "we've been studying what the Bible says about our future, you know, next year with college and all of that."

"And?" Scott asked, checking his sister's reaction.

"That's the interesting part," Becka said. "There's a verse in Zechariah—"

"It's chapter ten, verse two," Ryan said, nodding.

"Ooh, bonus points." Scott laughed.

"ANYWAY," Becka said, rolling her eyes, "it says, 'The idols speak deceit, diviners see visions that lie; they tell dreams that are false, they give comfort in vain.'"

"Which means?" Krissi asked.

Ryan stretched. "Well, it definitely means using stuff like tarot cards is out of the question."

Becka added, "We don't know exactly what God has in mind. What we do know is that, in Jeremiah 29:11, God says, 'For I know the plans I have for you ... Plans to prosper you and not to harm you, plans to give you hope and a future.'"

"That's why it doesn't make sense to mess around with fortune-tellers," Ryan said. "God's already promised to take good care of us."

Krissi shrugged. "I guess I see your point—"

"Hey, that reminds me," Ryan said. "Didn't Pastor Todd do something on fortune-tellers and those two dudes, Paul and Stylus?"

Scott laughed. "I think you mean Paul and *Silas*. And you're right. Pastor Todd covered that in a study on the book of Acts."

"Right."

Scott grabbed several fries from Becka's plate. He popped them in his mouth and started to talk. "Well ... those guys—"

"Paul and Silas," Ryan interjected.

"Yeah, them," Scott said with a nod. "They were on a missionary trip somewhere and this fortune-teller girl was following them around being a real pain. So one day, Paul turned around and cast the demon out of her. Which, naturally, ticked off the guys who were making big bucks with her."

Becka smiled. "Looks like you actually stayed awake at least once during youth group."

Scott's eyes narrowed. "Nice. Don't you see? Her fortune-telling was connected to demon possession."

Krissi gasped at the implication. "Are you saying that ... that Madame Theo is, like, possessed?"

Scott threw up both hands. "Hey, not necessarily. And I don't claim to know that about her for sure. I'm not even saying demon possession is always going on with tarot-card readers.

I'm just saying that Philip is getting mixed up in some dangerous stuff. Even Z said that tarot cards are lethal."

No one spoke for a long minute. A food fight broke out at the next table, and Scott tossed a fry in their direction just for fun. He turned and faced Ryan, Becka, and Krissi. He wanted to tell them about the whole Rita Thomas mystery too, but he had promised Philip he'd keep his mouth shut. If only Z had answered his email about Rita's identity from last night.

For no apparent reason, Becka jumped. She reached into her pocket and pulled out her phone. "Sorry! I set my cell phone on vibrate and I'm not used to it." She flipped it open and brought it to an ear. "Hello?"

Scott watched Becka's face as she listened. "It's for you, Scott," she said, handing him the phone. She eyed him suspiciously. "Is this some kind of prank?"

Scott gave her a puzzled look. "Why do you ask?"

Becka, obviously flustered as if she had eaten a piece of raw squid, blinked twice. "The guy says he's Z."

Scott had difficulty finding his voice. A thousand questions flooded into his mind. Could this really be Z? How could he know for sure? What if this was, like Becka said, just an elaborate prank? As long as they had been communicating, Z never used the phone—they only connected by email or instant message. Why would he call this time?

He raised the phone to his ear and tried to speak. "Z?"

"Good afternoon, Scott," the voice said.

Whoever was calling somehow modified his voice, of that Scott was sure. He was also fairly certain of something else. Z was a man. But who?

"I ... Z? Is that really you?"

"I got your email, Scott. From last night."

Scott swallowed. The back of his throat burned. *It must be Z*, he thought. Who else knew about the email besides himself and Philip? Could it be Philip just messing with his mind? Scott had to be sure. He had to think of something that only he and Z would know. But what? The food fight at the next table was getting out of hand, and Scott was having trouble thinking on his feet.

"Um, Z ... I ... I—"

"You're having doubts it's me, right?"

"You can say that again."

"Then ask me a question."

"Um, okay. What did you write ... in your last email?"

"I told you a friend was in danger and desperately needs your help. I sent it along with the video file of Madame Theo's TV show."

"It *is* Z!" Scott said to Becka, exchanging a quick, wide-eyed look with his sister. He got up, walked closer to the window and away from the commotion brewing behind him.

"I don't have much time. This is very important."

Scott covered his other ear with a hand. He hoped the pounding of his heart wouldn't drown out the conversation. "Go ahead. I'm listening, Z."

"You asked about Rita Thomas."

"Right."

"Your instincts were correct. Rita Thomas and Madame Theo are one and the same person."

Scott couldn't believe he was actually talking to Z. He tried to remain focused. He closed his eyes to block out all distractions. "And?"

"My sources—which I cannot reveal, so don't ask—informed me thirty years ago, Madame Theo, whose real name is Rita Thomas, lived in Los Angeles. Rita read palms and tarot cards on a local cable channel. She had a toll-free number. Business was good. Too good. The police were called in to investigate thousands of complaints to the phone company about excessive charges. Her people were running a scam on the public that ran into millions of dollars."

Scott let out a low whistle.

"A grand jury found enough evidence to believe she was guilty of violating the RICO statutes."

"RICO?"

"That's an abbreviation for Racketeering Influenced and Corrupt Organizations Act."

"Never heard of it," Scott said, feeling overwhelmed by both the fact he was talking to Z and that Z had somehow unearthed this information.

"Scott, the government uses that law to bust people who are involved with organized crime. Rita Thomas, it turns out, was in pretty deep too."

Scott felt chilled. What was Philip getting into?

"But there's more," Z said, his hollow voice echoing through the distortion device. "Rita Thomas had one of the best defense lawyers in the country, a Zack Zimmerman, who has proved to be a shady character himself."

"Should I be taking notes?" Scott asked, his heart pounding.

"No. Just listen." Z paused. "I don't have much more time. The case went to trial, and Zack and his team of crackpot lawyers lost. Everything Rita owned was confiscated. She was ordered to repay millions of dollars. She also faced serious jail time."

"I don't get it," Scott said, trying to connect the dots. "How is she still in business—right here in Crescent Bay?"

"To avoid jail, Rita faked her death in a fiery car crash. I say faked because, while it was her Mercedes they found burned at the bottom of a cliff in Malibu, the detectives could never properly identify the body as being hers. My best guess is that she moved north to Crescent Bay, changed her name, and started over."

"And since it's been so many years ago, she figures nobody will remember, right?" Scott asked.

No answer. Scott looked at the phone and saw they were still connected. "Hello? Z? You still there?"

"Scott, I'm still here, but I must go."

"What about Philip? What should I—"

"Madame Theo's a dangerous person who will stop at nothing, Scott. Don't be fooled by her looks. If Philip lets on that he noticed a connection between Rita Thomas and Madame Theo, he could be in real trouble."

Scott's heart was pounding so hard, it tested the limits of his rib cage.

Z said, "Thanks to this tip, the local police working with the FBI, who get involved in RICO cases, are headed to arrest Madame Theo later today. But you must find Philip. Warn him about the dangers. And, Scott—"

"What's that?"

"When this is over, remember ... just love him."

"Who?" Scott asked. "Who, Z?"

"Philip. Good to talk with you. Z out."

"Don't go ... Z ..."

The connection was terminated. Although disappointed, a new thought struck him like a bolt of lightning. Working quickly, Scott followed the menu prompts that led to the Incoming Call History. Maybe, just maybe, he could tell Z's number. That way, they'd be able to call him back or at least know what area code the mysterious Z had called from.

The call display read: *Unknown*.

14

For Scott, the rest of the afternoon was a complete blur. He had a million questions, not the least of which was, how did Z know Becka had a cell phone? How did he know her number? What's more, how did Z know they were together at lunch? A lucky guess? Or was Z somewhere in the building?

Sitting in last period, ignoring his biology teacher as she droned on and on about some insect body part, Scott eyed the clock mounted above the classroom door. The second hand moved slower around the face of the clock with each minute, as if it were out of breath, too tired to make another revolution.

Scott sighed. His mind drifted back to his conversation with the elusive Z. He was stunned at how Z was able to dig up so much stuff on Madame Theo so quickly. The guy must have amazing connections, Scott decided. Maybe he was in the CIA or the FBI or some top-secret branch of government that nobody knew about. If only he had had a few more minutes to talk with Z.

More than anything, Scott was worried about Philip. Where was he? Didn't he say he'd be at school? How could he warn Philip about Madame Theo if he couldn't find him? And what would happen if he was too late?

The bell sounded. Scott dashed out of his seat like a horse on a racetrack and headed for the door. At Becka's suggestion, he kept the cell phone just in case Z called again. Once outside, Scott dialed Philip's cell. He had tried several times already between classes with no success. He figured it was worth one more try.

On the second ring, Philip answered. "Hello?"

The connection was filled with static. "Philip, it's me, Scott. Where have you been, man? You okay?"

"Hey, Scott. It's a long story. My dad woke up with a mean hangover. It didn't help when I told him I had run out of gas. He really blew a gasket, you know?"

"I bet."

"Yeah, so get this. He gives me the gas can—the one we use for the lawn mower—anyway, he drops me off with it in the middle of the highway and tells me to walk the rest of the way."

Scott pictured Philip walking for miles out to the country. No wonder he was gone all day.

"Hey, my battery is about to run out," Philip said. "Guess I left the phone on in the car all night after you picked me up—"

Scott started to panic. He had to tell him about Z's warning. "Listen, Philip, whatever you do—"

"Scott, you're breaking up. I don't know if you can hear me, but there's something I have to do before—"

"Philip—wait! Whatever you do, don't go to Madame Theo's—"

More static.

"Yes, you're right, I have to go to Madame Theo's ... hello? Scott? You still there?"

"Philip ... I said, DON'T go to Madame Theo's—"

"My battery is flashing," Philip said. "I got to know if—"

"Listen to me," Scott said desperately. "I talked to Z. Madame Theo *is* Rita Thomas. She's running a scam or worse. She lived in Los Angeles and faked her death to avoid going to jail. Z said she's dangerous ... did you hear me, Philip?"

Static filled Scott's earpiece and then nothing. Scott's heart sank. He looked at the digital display. It flashed two words: *Connection lost.*

"What's wrong?" Becka asked, appearing at Scott's side.

"I was trying to warn Philip about Madame Theo, but his battery died."

Becka offered a smile. "At least he's okay, right?"

Scott put the phone away. "Yeah, but who knows for how long?"

"Why's that?"

"Philip said he was going to Madame Theo's!"

"Yes, please come in," Madame Theo said, waving Philip toward the table. "I'm glad I had an opening this afternoon for my special friend."

Philip stepped into the candlelit room and took his usual seat without saying a word.

"You're troubled, my son." Madame Theo adjusted her turban and then placed her hands palms down on the table. "What is the source of this bad karma?"

Philip tilted his head. He knew this wasn't going to be easy. He wasn't sure why he was even bothering. After all, it wasn't like he cared anymore. Even before he had heard the last part of Scott's message, he had decided to confront Madame Theo with a few things—like her real identity.

Although he couldn't respond because his battery had run out, he was amazed to know Z had said she was running a scam. What kind of scam? From what he could tell, Madame Theo appeared genuine. She seemed somehow connected to the messages in the cards. Could she fake that too?

"I ... I have so many questions," Philip began.

"Yes, Philip. That's understandable. That's why the tarot is such a gift."

Philip studied her face. She seemed so sincere. No way could she be mixed up in something illegal. Could she?

"Tell me, Philip, what is weighing on your heart?" She closed her eyes in anticipation of his response as she had done in the past.

Philip cleared his throat. "Actually, I'm wondering if you could clear something up — something that's been bothering me ever since, well, since you got that package yesterday."

Madame Theo's eyes blinked open. "What package?"

"Remember the one that came from FedEx? It was delivered in the middle of our session."

"That is no concern of yours." Her stiff tone surprised him.

"Well, in a way it is," Philip stammered, aware that she was growing defensive. He felt a bead of sweat form on his forehead. "I mean, you know everything about me. I figure it's only fair if I know the truth about you."

Madame Theo's stare intensified. She remained as frozen in place as a statue.

Philip was finding it difficult to breath. "I … I couldn't help but notice it was addressed to Rita Thomas, but it also said a.k.a. Madame Theo. So which is it?"

"What do you think you know, son?" Madame Theo said, her voice deepening. Gone was the warm, grandmotherly tone.

Maybe it was the incense. Maybe it was the fact that he had walked more miles than he could count that morning to get to his car. Maybe it was the lack of lunch. Maybe it was the anger he detected behind her eyes. Whatever the reason, Philip was growing dizzy.

Light-headed, Philip felt as though the room tilted one direction, and then, just as quickly, it tilted to the opposite angle. Philip fought with his senses to gain some level of control.

"I just need to know if you're, you know, the real thing," he managed to say, forcing a smile.

"What are you talking about?"

"Please just tell me this. Did you live in Los Angeles?"

No answer. But her nose flared as if she were a provoked bull ready to stampede.

Philip figured he might as well go for broke. He had no idea what he was walking into. He didn't even have all the facts because he wasn't the one who had talked with Z. His curiosity got the better of him. He blurted, "Just tell me that you're not the same Rita Thomas who faked her death. Are you?"

"How dare you accuse me of such things," she bellowed in a voice that was no longer her own. Her face twisted and snarled into a knot of rage. She rose to her feet and raised both arms as if calling upon unseen forces.

Behind him, Philip heard a noise. His neck snapped around to see what was happening. The curtains that had covered the windows began to flap as if caught in a violent storm. He turned back to face Madame Theo.

"Who are you to question my powers?" The card table between them suddenly defied gravity. It hovered three feet off the ground, knocking the cards to the floor.

At first, Philip was too stunned to react. His heart pounded for all it was worth. "I ... it was just a question—"

"Silence, foolish one."

Like a pinball, the table bounced off the walls and headed directly toward him. He fell backward in his chair to avoid contact, hitting the floor with a thud instead.

"You cannot stop us!" the thing inside Madame Theo shouted.

Seconds later, Philip stumbled to his feet when, from across the room, the table swooped down on him like a bat, smashing him in the chest. He slammed against the wall with enough force to drive out the air from his lungs. He blacked out.

❦ ❦

"Can't this thing go any faster?" Scott shouted.

"Hang on!" Becka pulled their mom's car into the passing lane. "We're almost there!"

"Something's wrong with Philip. I just know it," Scott said, cracking his knuckles.

Becka turned down the street where Madame Theo's Palace was located. "There ... on the right," Scott said with a point. "That's Philip's car. Hurry!"

❦ ❦

Philip lay motionless on the floor. Where was he? How long had he been here? Why did everything hurt? A sharp pain seared his chest. A broken rib? Why was a table jammed against his chest? And why did it feel as if the table was still being driven into his body, crushing him?

His lungs burned. His head throbbed. He had no strength. His eyes cracked open and the room spun. He closed his eyes for a second before trying to open them again. It was then that he saw the flames of a fallen candle smoldering on the carpet, burning a path toward him. He tried to move and winced.

"I do not answer to you!" the unearthly voice said. Although her lips didn't move, it was Madame Theo talking as she towered over him. She held a candle dripping with hot wax over his limp body. "You will learn what happens to those who doubt."

15

Scott jumped out of the car before Becka had brought it to a complete stop. He bounded down the sidewalk as fast as his legs could carry him. If Z said Madame Theo might be dangerous, then Scott wasn't about to take any chances. As he approached the storefront, Scott felt a distinct heaviness of spirit weigh down on him. A voice in the back of his mind urged him to pray.

Becka raced to his side. "What's wrong?"

"Don't you feel it?" Scott asked.

"Now that you mention it, I do," she said. "Are you thinking what I'm thinking?"

Scott nodded. "Better pray."

"Jesus," Becka said, grabbing Scott's hand, "we've faced the evil one many times before. We know that greater is he who is in us than he who is in the world—"

"Or he who is in Madame Theo," Scott added.

"We bind the power of Satan in this place, in the name of Jesus, amen," Becka said.

Scott squeezed her hand and then pushed open the door to Madame Theo's Palace. With a whoosh the air inside seemed to fight against their entry. Once inside, they were met by a whirl-wind of drapes and a blast of pungent air. Scott's eyes burned from the acidic stench of something smoldering. He coughed and, gagging, tried to breathe.

"Over there!" Becka said, coughing. She pointed to the far corner of the darkened room.

The tall, thin figure of Madame Theo was hunched over Philip, holding a candle in her hand. She turned and faced the intruders. "Get back!" she yelled in an agonizing voice not her own. Her eyes blazed. "He's mine ... he's mine ... he's all mine. This is my domain!"

For an instant, Scott flashed back to the nightmare—the one with Madame Theo circling his bed, jabbing him with her fin-ger—but he pushed away the distraction. He stepped forward and said, "You're a liar, Madame Theo! Philip is NOT yours."

With a screech, she tossed the candle toward Philip and raised her hands like a caged animal ready to pounce. The candle ignited the carpet where it fell. The flames engulfed the floor, devouring the distance between itself and Philip.

Madame Theo clapped her hands together and the flames, like tongues of fire, started to swirl through the room, slowly at first and then faster and faster, creating a fiery wind tunnel that kindled fires throughout the room. The drapes on the windows. The curtains hanging from the ceiling. The coverings on the walls. All became inflamed in a ghastly chorus of fire.

Scott knew if they didn't act fast, they'd be consumed by the inferno. He took a deep breath and shouted, "By the name above all names, Jesus the Christ, I rebuke you!"

Madame Theo shrieked and staggered backward.

Becka stepped forward to join Scott. "We bind you, spirit of darkness."

"I will not be silenced," the demon squealed.

Scott held out a hand and the beastly thing stuttered. "I order you, father of lies, in the name of Jesus, be gone!"

Madame Theo collapsed to the floor, screeching with a rage almost as hot as the flames around them.

"Now!" Becka commanded.

Madame Theo went silent. The wind in the room came to a rest. In the distance, Scott heard the rapid advance of sirens. He cut a path through the flames to Philip's side. "Becka, here, give me a hand ... hurry!"

Scott looked at Philip's reddened face. His eyes were closed. His breath was labored. With care, but working as fast as he could, Scott pulled the table off Philip. Philip moaned.

"Easy does it, Philip," Becka said. "Just hang on! Help is on the way."

Philip coughed up a mixture of phlegm and blood.

"We've got to get him outside," Scott said, stomping out the fire with his sneakers as the flames licked at Philip's legs. They traded positions. Working together, with Becka now at his feet and Scott at his chest, they carried Philip outside and rested him on a grassy knoll under a tall oak tree.

Scott sat at his computer, exhausted. Although Becka was already fast asleep after the events of the day, it was just nine o'clock. Scott figured he'd give Z an update, that is, if Z was online. He typed in his password and paused for the appropriate greeting.

As he waited, his thoughts drifted to Philip, who had been rushed to the hospital where he was being treated for three broken ribs, smoke inhalation, and minor cuts and burns. He thought of Madame Theo too, who had been handcuffed and arrested by two FBI agents as she tried to slip out the back door of her store.

"Welcome, you've got mail," the computer voice announced.

Scott wasn't interested. Instead, he headed for the chat room where he and Becka had first met Z. He typed a message:

Z, it's Scott. Are you online?

The cursor blinked a dozen times before an answer appeared.

Great job today, Scott. How's Philip?

Scott felt the hairs on the back of his neck tingle. How did Z already know how the day went? Scott smiled, amazed at the ever mysterious Z.

I actually got to talk with him for a few minutes. He's gonna make it okay. But you know what? Philip said he wants to give Christianity another try!

Very good. I suggest you get him *The Case for Christ*. **It's a book by Lee Strobel.**

Thanks. He's got plenty of time to read these days!

Scott scribbled the name of the book onto a scrap of paper. He'd get it for Philip after school tomorrow. Scott was about to type a question when more words appeared.

Scott, your parents are proud.

For a second, Scott was puzzled by the statement. Z knew about his family and how they had moved to Crescent Bay after his father's plane crash. They had talked about it dozens of times. Maybe Z forgot. Scott typed:

My dad's dead, remember?

Scott stretched and yawned while he waited for a reply. He cracked his knuckles. After a minute, he scratched the back of his head, wondering what was taking Z so long to respond. It was, after all, a simple question.

At long last, Z typed two words:

Is he?

Author's Note

As I developed this series, I had two equal and opposing concerns. First, I didn't want the reader to be too frightened of the devil. Compared to Jesus Christ, Satan is a wimp. The two aren't even in the same league. Although the supernatural evil in these books is based on a certain amount of fact, it's important to understand the awesome protection Jesus Christ offers to those who have committed their lives to him.

This brings me to my second and somewhat opposing concern: Although the powers of darkness are nothing compared to the power of Jesus Christ and the authority he has given his followers, spiritual warfare is not something we casually stroll into. The situations in these novels are extreme to create suspense and drama. But if you should find yourself involved in something even vaguely similar, don't confront it alone. Find an older, more mature Christian (such as a parent, pastor, or youth leader) to talk to. Let him or her check the situation out to see what's happening. Ask him or her to help you deal with it.

Yes, we have the victory through Christ. But we should never send in inexperienced soldiers to fight the battle.

Oh, and one final note. When this series was conceived, there were really no bad guys on the Internet. Unfortunately that has changed. Today there are plenty of people out there trying to draw young folks into dangerous situations through it. Although the characters in this series trust Z, if you should run into a similar situation, be smart. Anyone can *sound* kind and understanding, but their intentions may be entirely different. All that to say, don't take candy from strangers you see ... or trust those you don't.

Bill

Bill Myers

bestselling author

DARK POWER
collection

nearly 400,000 FORBIDDEN DOORS books sold

Read a portion of the first chapter
of *Dark Power Collection,*
Volume 1 in the Forbidden Doors Series.

1

Rebecca's lungs burned. They screamed for more air; they begged her to slow down. But she wouldn't. She pushed herself. She ran for all she was worth. She had to.

There was no sound. She saw a few kids standing along the track, opening their mouths and shouting encouragement. She saw them clapping their hands and cheering her on. But she couldn't hear them. All she heard was her own gasps for breath ... the faint crunch of gravel under her track shoes.

Several yards ahead ran Julie Mitchell—the team's shining hope for all-State. She had a grace and style that made Rebecca feel like, well, like a deranged platypus. Whatever that was.

But that was okay; Becka wasn't running against Julie. She was running against something else.

"It's Dad ..."

For the thousandth time, she saw her mom's red nose and puffy eyes and heard her voice echoing inside her head. "They found his plane in the jungle. He made it through the crash, but ..."

Becka bore down harder; she ran faster. Her lungs were going to explode, but she kept going.

"You've got ... to accept it," her mom's voice stammered. "He's gone, sweetheart. He was either attacked by wild animals or ... or ..."

Becka dug her cleats in deeper. She stretched her legs out farther. She knew the "or ... or ..." was a tribe of South American Indians in that region. A tribe notorious for its fierceness and for its use of black magic.

The back of Becka's throat ached. Not because of the running. It was because of the tears. And the rage. Why?! Why had God let this happen? Why had God let him die? He was such a good man, trying to do such good things.

Angrily she swiped at her eyes. Her legs were turning into rubber. Losing feeling. Losing control. And still she pushed herself. She had closed the gap with Julie and was practically beside her now. The finish line waited a dozen meters ahead.

Trying out for the track team hadn't been Becka's idea. It was her mom's. "To help you fit in," she'd said.

Fit in. What a joke. Rebecca had spent most of her life living in the villages of Brazil with her mom, her little brother, and a father who flew his plane in and out of the jungle for humanitarian and mission groups. And now, suddenly, she was expected to fit in. Here? In Crescent Bay, California? Here, where everybody had perfect skin, perfect bodies, perfect teeth? And let's not forget all the latest fashions, right out of *Vogue* or *InStyle* or whatever it was they read. Fashions that made Becka feel like she bought her clothes right out of *Popular Mechanics*.

That last thought pushed her over the edge. She tried too hard, stretched too far. Her legs, which had already lost feeling, suddenly had minds of their own. The left one twisted, then gave out all together.

It was like a slow-motion movie that part of Becka watched as she pitched forward. For a second, she almost caught her balance. Almost, but not quite. She stumbled and continued falling toward the track. There was nothing she could do—only put out her hands and raise her head so the crushed red gravel would not scrape her face. Knees and elbows, yes. But not her face.

As if it really mattered.

She hit the track and skidded forward, but she didn't feel any pain. Not yet. The pain would come a second or two later. Right now, all she felt was shame. And embarrassment. Already the humiliation was sending blood racing to her cheeks and to her ears.

Yes sir, just another day in the life of Rebecca Williams, the new kid moron.

👁 👁

As soon as Becka's little brother, Scott, walked into the bookstore, he knew something was wrong. It wasn't like he was frightened or nervous or anything. It had nothing to do with what he felt. It had everything to do with the place.

It was wrong.

But why? It certainly was cheery enough. Bright sunlight streaming through the skylights. Aqua blue carpet. Soft white shelves with rows and rows of colorful books. Then there was the background music—flutes and wind chimes.

But still ...

"You coming or what?" It was Darryl. Scott had met him a couple of days ago at lunch. Darryl wasn't the tallest or best-looking kid in school—actually, he was about the shortest and nerdiest. His voice was so high you were never sure if it was him talking or someone opening a squeaky cupboard. Oh, and one other thing. Darryl sniffed. About every thirty seconds. You could set your watch by it. Something about allergies or hay fever or something.

But at least he was friendly. And as the new kid, Scott couldn't be too picky who he hung with. New kids had to take what new kids could get.

For the past day or so, Darryl had been telling Scott all about the Society—a secret group that met in the back of the Ascension Bookshop after school. Only the coolest and most popular kids could join. (Scott wasn't sure he bought this "coolest and most popular" bit, since they'd let Darryl be a member. But he didn't want to hurt the little guy's feelings, so he let it go.)

"Hey, Priscilla," Darryl called as they walked past the counter toward the back of the bookshop.

"Hey, yourself," a handsome, middle-aged woman said. She didn't bother to look from her magazine until the two boys passed. When she glanced up and saw Scott, a scowl crossed her face. She seemed to dislike him immediately. He hadn't said a thing; he hadn't done a thing. But that didn't matter. There was something about him that troubled her—a lot.

Scott was oblivious to her reaction as he followed Darryl toward the hallway at the back of the store.

So far his first week at Crescent Bay had been pretty good. No fights. No broken noses. A minimal amount of death threats. But that's the way it was with Scott. Unlike his older sister, Scott always fit in. It probably had something to do with his sense of humor. Scott was a lot like his dad in that department; he had a mischievous grin and a snappy comeback for almost any situation.

Scott was like his dad in another way too. He had a deep faith in God. The whole family did. But it wasn't some sort of rules or regulations thing. And it definitely wasn't anything weird. It was just your basic God's-the-boss-so-go-to-church-and-try-to-make-the-world-a-better-place faith.

But sometimes that faith … well, sometimes it allowed Scott to feel things. Deep things.

Like now.

As he and Darryl entered the hallway, Scott brushed against a large hoop decorated with what looked like eagle feathers. He ducked to the side only to run smack-dab into a set of wooden wind chimes. They clanked and clanged noisily. Lately, Scott hadn't been the most graceful of persons. It probably had something to do with growing two inches in the last three months. He was still shorter than Becka—a fact she brought up to him on a regular basis—but he was gaining on her by the week.

As they continued down the hall, Scott noticed a number of trinkets and lockets hanging on the wall. He couldn't put his finger on it, but they looked strangely familiar.

Then he noticed something else. Frowning, he glanced around. Was it his imagination, or was it getting colder? There were no windows, open or otherwise, anywhere close by.

Something inside him began to whisper, *"Stop.... Turn around.... Go back...."*

But why? Nothing was wrong. It was just a hallway. Just a bookshop.

"Here we go." Darryl gave a loud sniff as he slowed in front of the last door. He smiled, pushed up his glasses, and knocked lightly.

No answer.

"Well, it doesn't look like anybody's home," Scott said, his voice cracking in gratitude. "I guess we'd better—"

"Don't be stupid," Darryl said, reaching for the knob. "They always meet on Fridays."

Cautiously, he pushed the door open.

It was pitch-black inside. Well, except for the dozen or so candles burning around a table. And the faces illuminated by the candles. Faces Scott had seen at school. They were all staring intently at something on the table. Scott squinted in the darkness, making out some kind of board game with a bunch of letters and symbols on it. Two of the kids had their hands on a little plastic pointer that was moving back and forth across the board.

"What's that?" Scott whispered.

"What do you think it is?" Darryl whispered back. "It's a Ouija board."

"A what?"

"You use it to spell out words. You know, it tells you about the future and stuff."

Scott looked at him skeptically.

"No kidding," Darryl squeaked. Scott grimaced. Even when the guy whispered his voice sounded like a rusty hinge. Darryl continued, watching the others. "The pointer moves to those letters on the board, spelling out answers to anything you ask."

"No way," Scott scorned. As far as he could tell, the pointer moved on the board because it was pushed by the two kids whose hands were on it: a big, meaty fellow in a tank top and a chubby girl dressed all in black. "Those two, they're the ones moving it."

Darryl didn't answer. He just sniffed and stepped into the room. Scott wasn't crazy about following, but he walked in after him.

And—just like that—the plastic pointer stopped. One minute the little pointer was scooting around the board, spelling out words. The next, it came to a complete stop.

"Hey," a pretty girl complained, pushing her long red hair back. "What's wrong?"

"I don't know," the meaty guy answered. He turned to his partner, the girl in black. "Are you stopping it?"

"Not me," she said. And then, slowly turning her head toward the door, she nailed Scott with an icy look. "It's him."

Every eye in the room turned to Scott.

He raised his hand. "Hi there," he croaked, trying to smile.

Nobody smiled back.

"Ask it," the redhead demanded. "Ask it if he's the reason it's not answering."

"Yeah," the meaty guy agreed.

The girl in black tilted back her head and closed her eyes. Her hair was short and jet black — an obvious dye job. "Please show us," she said more dramatically than Scott thought necessary. "Show us the reason for your silence."

Everyone turned to the plastic pointer. Waiting. Watching.

Nothing happened.

Scott tried to swallow, but at the moment, there wasn't much left in his mouth to swallow.

Suddenly the pointer started moving. Faster than before. In fact, both the girl and the meaty guy looked down in surprise as it darted from letter to letter, barely pausing at one before shooting to the next. In a matter of seconds it had spelled out:

D-E-A-T-H

Then it stopped. Abruptly.

Everyone waited in silence. Afraid to move. Afraid to break the spell.

The girl in black cleared her throat and spoke again. But this time, a little less confidently. "What do you mean? What death?"

There was no movement. No answer.

Scott shifted slightly. He felt the chill again, but this time it was more real. It had substance. Suddenly he knew that there was something there, in the room ... something cold and physical had actually brushed against him. He was sure of it.

Again the girl spoke. "What death? Is someone going to die? Whose death?"

No movement. More silence.

And then, just when Scott was about to say something really clever to break the tension and show everyone how silly this was, the plastic pointer zipped across the board and shot off the table.

"Look out!" Darryl cried.

Scott jumped aside, and the pointer hit the floor, barely missing his feet. He threw a look at the girl in black, certain she had flung it across the table at him.

But the expression on her face said she was just as surprised as him.

Or was she?

☙ ❧

"You okay?" Julie Mitchell asked as she toweled off her thick blonde hair and approached Rebecca's gym locker.

"Sure." Rebecca winced while pulling her jeans up over her skinned knees. "Nothing a brain transplant couldn't fix."

It had been nearly an hour since her little crash-and-burn routine on the track. Of course, everyone had gathered around her, making a big deal of the whole thing, and, of course, she wanted to melt into the track and disappear. But that was an hour ago. Yesterday's news. Now most of the girls had hit the showers and were heading home.

But not Julie. It was like she purposely hung back. Becka glanced at her curiously. There was something friendly about Julie, something caring. Becka had liked her immediately ... even though Julie was one of the best-looking kids in school.

"The team really needs you," Julie offered.

"As what? Their mascot?"

Julie grinned. She tossed her hair back and reached over to slip on a top-of-the-line, money's-no-object, designer T-shirt. "Seriously," she said, "I'm the only long-distance runner we've got. Royal High has three killers that bumped me out of State last year. But if you work and learn to concentrate, the two of us might give them a run for their money. You've got the endurance. And I've never seen anyone with such a great end sprint."

"Or such klutziness."

Julie shrugged. "You've got a point there," she teased.

Becka felt herself smiling back.

"Anybody can learn form and style," Julie continued. "That's what coaches are for. And if you add that to your sprint, we just might be able to knock Royal out of State." She rummaged in her gym basket, then bit her lip and frowned. "Shoot ... don't tell me I've lost it."

Becka rubbed a towel through her hair, then sighed. Her hair was mousy brown and would dry three times faster than Julie's. The reason was simple: Becka's hair was three times thinner. Yes sir, just another one of life's little jokes with Becka as the punch line.

Julie's search through her basket grew more urgent.

"What are you looking for?" Becka asked.

"My pouch ..." There was definite concern in her voice as she continued pawing through her clothes.

"Pouch?"

"My good luck charm."

Becka wasn't sure what Julie meant, but she gave a quick scan along the bench.

"I just hope nobody stole it," Julie said.

Becka spotted something under the bench. It was partially covered by towels. She reached for it and picked up a small leather bag with rocks or sand or something inside. A leather string was attached at the top so it could be worn as a necklace.

"Is this it?" Becka asked.

Julie relaxed. "Yeah. Great." She took it and slipped it around her neck.

Becka watched, fighting back a wave of uneasiness. She tried to sound casual as she asked, "So, what's in it?"

"I don't know." Julie shrugged. "Some turquoise, some powders, herbs—that sort of stuff. The Ascension Lady puts them together for us—you know, for good luck."

"'Ascension Lady'?" Becka asked.

"Yeah," Julie fingered the little pouch. "'Course I don't believe in any of that stuff. But with the district preliminaries coming up, it doesn't hurt to play the odds, right?"

Becka's mind raced. She wanted to ask lots more about the pouch and this Ascension Lady, but Julie didn't give her the chance.

"Listen, we'll see you Monday," she said grabbing her backpack. "And don't be bummed, you did fine. Besides," she threw a mischievous grin over her shoulder, "we can always use a good mascot."

Becka forced a smile.

"See ya." Julie disappeared around the row of lockers and pushed open the big double doors. They slammed shut behind her with a loud *click, boooom*.

Becka didn't move. She sat, all alone ... just her and the dripping showers.

Her smile had already faded. Not because of the pain in her knees or even because of the memories of her fall.

It was because of the pouch. She'd seen pouches like that before. In South America. But they weren't worn by pretty, rich, athletic teenagers who wanted to go to State track championships.

They were worn by witch doctors who worshiped demons.

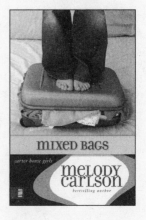
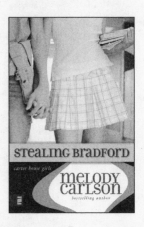

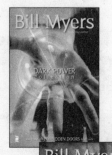

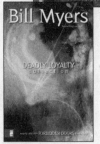

Echoes From the Edge

A New Trilogy from Bestselling Author Bryan Davis!

This fast-paced adventure fantasy trilogy starts with murder and leads teenagers Nathan and Kelly out of their once-familiar world as they struggle to find answers to the tragedy. A mysterious mirror with phantom images, a camera that takes pictures of things they can't see, and a violin that unlocks unrecognizable voices ... each enigma takes the teens further into an alternate universe where nothing is as it seems.

Beyond the Reflection's Edge
Book One

Softcover • ISBN: 978-0-310-71554-2

After sixteen-year-old Nathan Shepherd's parents are murdered during a corporate investigation, he teams up with a friend to solve the case. They discover mirrors that reflect events from the past and future, a camera that photographs people who aren't there, and a violin that echoes unseen voices.

Books 2 and 3 coming soon!

Pick up a copy today at your favorite bookstore!

Share Your Thoughts

With the Author: Your comments will be forwarded to the author when you send them to *zauthor@zondervan.com*.

With Zondervan: Submit your review of this book by writing to *zreview@zondervan.com*.

Free Online Resources at
www.zondervan.com/hello

 Zondervan AuthorTracker: Be notified whenever your favorite authors publish new books, go on tour, or post an update about what's happening in their lives.

 Daily Bible Verses and Devotions: Enrich your life with daily Bible verses or devotions that help you start every morning focused on God.

 Free Email Publications: Sign up for newsletters on fiction, Christian living, church ministry, parenting, and more.

 Zondervan Bible Search: Find and compare Bible passages in a variety of translations at www.zondervanbiblesearch.com.

 Other Benefits: Register yourself to receive online benefits like coupons and special offers, or to participate in research.